novel
women
2

Silk Scarf Publishing

Ordering Information:
For details, see www.novel-women.com

Hardcover: 978-1-7322666-5-0
Print ISBN: 978-1-7322666-3-6
eBook ISBN: 978-1-7322666-4-3

Printed in the United States of America.

First Edition

Cover Photo Credit: Denise Panyik-Dale

Praise for Novel Women 2

The book club is back in "Novel Women 2." Yet another book and story about a book club of authentic women dealing with real life issues and written by real women from their real book club, how "novel" indeed! The second book in the "Novel Women" trilogy and a perfect read for book clubs everywhere. Five Diamonds in The Pulpwood Queen READING Tiara"!"

~Kathy L. Murphy
CEO and Founder of The International Pulpwood
Queens and Timber Guys Book Club Reading Nation.

Between Friends Book Club has done it again. The ladies of the Novel Women Book Club are back in Novel Women 2 and we take a deeper dive into the lives of these fascinating characters. I especially love how the authors write like they share a brain. It makes it an even more intriguing read. Grab a glass and join the club for this wonderful book.

~Helen Little
106.7 Lite FM
The Public Library Podcast

Novel Women 2 *reminds us of the value of female friendships. At times it's laugh-out-loud entertaining and then sobering when life hands out challenges you will recognize. Readers will witness six women prove that good friendships take time, effort and intention. Friendships that started in a book club are the lifeline through the stress of a new job, getting fired, finding love, dealing with financial crisis, a sister's cancer treatments and more. And in case you didn't know, romance and intimacy are alive and well in midlife. This is more than a beach read. It's a testament to the importance of a girlfriend network for emotional support when things go wrong and to celebrate when life is good.*

~Eileen Harrison Sanchez
Freedom Lessons – A Novel

The adventures of the members of Novel Women continue in this delightful sequel as they face fresh challenges. Troubled by family and work tensions as well as new struggles in love, they rely on the strong friendships formed in their book club to gain perspective and surmount everything life throws their way.

~ Michelle Cameron, author of *Beyond the Ghetto Gates* and *The Fruit of Her Hands*

novel women 2

Kimi Sturat

• BETWEEN FRIENDS BOOK CLUB •

To Between Friends Book Club —You are and always will be my sisters, my friends.

Here's to new beginnings!

Wholly unprepared, we embark upon the second half of life.... But we cannot live the afternoon of life according to the program of life's morning; for what was great in the morning will be little at the evening, and what in the morning was true will at evening become a lie.

—C. G. Jung

Previously in Novel Women

When middle age hits – it hits hard. Marriages fall apart, children leave for college, and jobs disappear. Six women stood at that crossroad when their beloved Novel Women book club went on hiatus in the summer of 2017. And despite a summer of confusion and rediscovery, heartache and loss, these women grew closer by the ever-enduring power of love and friendship.

Brianna Lambert

Bri is the founder of Novel Women book club. She dreaded the thought of her youngest child leaving for college. Her two children had been her focus for twenty years. Now what? If an identity crisis weren't enough, a new woman entered her life and made a play for her husband. Everything comes to a head at a charity event when Bri is shocked to find her husband in an embrace with this "other woman."

Madeline Miller

Madeline is the abrasive, opinionated member of book club and has been Bri's friend since their children were in grammar school. But it's she who introduces Natasha – the "other woman" – into their lives and doesn't seem to understand that this betrays Bri on the most basic of levels.

Staci Hughes

Finally freed from a suffocating marriage, Staci traveled to Burlington, Vermont, to reinvigorate her long-stalled writing career. She meets John Marshall, a widower and falls hopelessly in love. But John still loves his deceased wife and isn't ready for a relationship.

Charlotte Egan

Carefree as a college student, Charlotte revels in her full date book and has no desire to meet Mr. Right. Her ex-husband engaged in numerous extramarital affairs, including some with her so-called close friends. She can't forgive or forget. But one day she meets a man with a velvety voice, and everything changes.

Ava Aguiar

Ava's husband Paul pressures her to sell their successful business quickly without giving her an opportunity to vet the new buyer. Ava is shocked when she discovers that she knows the buyer, Neil Bass, an ex-boyfriend who ghosted her twenty years earlier. Distrustful of both husband and ex, she doesn't know who to trust. Her husband's gambling debts are eventually laid bare and she proceeds with a divorce. At the same time, Ava's old beau professes a never-ending love for her. Surprised by the depth of her feelings for Neil despite his youthful betrayal, she decides to give their love a second chance.

Hanna Feldon

Frazzled mother of two young, over-scheduled children and the sometimes neglected wife of a jet-setting workaholic, Hanna feels resentful as she singlehandedly manages family and home. She decides to invest some time in her old hobbies. Thrilled to return to painting and running, she gains new energy and confidence – and the attention of another man. However, her husband returns just in time for them to renew their love for one another.

Prologue

1981

I SLIPPED OUT OF *Stephanie's car, calling, "Thanks for the ride." I waved until she was out of sight. The heavy tree line blocked the view of my house from the road. I prayed no one was home. Taking a deep breath, I walked along the trees dotting our long driveway, thinking what – who – might be waiting for me inside. The best thing would be for both parents to be passed out, drunk. But I was rarely that lucky.*

I rounded the bend in the driveway and noticed no cars. "Oh, thank God!" I cried aloud. No one was home. I skipped the rest of the way.

Dashing into the house, I put on my bathing suit. What luck! *I wouldn't have to invite myself to a friend's house today.*

Throwing a towel on a splintered old chair, I put my Coca-Cola on the cinder block I used as a table. Taking a sip of Coke, I noticed how wet the can was. Rubbing my finger around the rim, I thought about the dress I'd made for prom. The white satin halter fit snugly on top and its A-line skirt was perfect for swooshing around the dance floor. But I definitely needed a tan. I was so pale right now.

The crunch of stones made me look up. A car pulled down our driveway. I jumped up, wrapping my towel tightly around me as two men got out of the car. Beads of sweat dripped down my forehead as I tried to steady my breath. Who the hell were these guys?

"Are you Mrs. O'Leary?" the bald man asked.

"No, I'm her daughter, Madeline."

"How old are you?" the younger one demanded, leering.

"Sixteen," I murmured, as they moved closer. My hands started to shake.

"You're lying. There's no way you're sixteen," the bald man spat out, his face reddening. He inched closer.

Both men stood between me and the back door. I couldn't get past them into the safety of the house.

"Well, I am," I said, trying to sound tough. Something about these guys scared the shit out of me. What the hell did they want?

Baldy said, "You're sixteen, like I'm Clint Eastwood. You're eighteen and officially served."

"What?" Served? What was he talking about?

He threw a large manila envelope at me. With one hand holding the towel together, I barely managed to catch it.

As I stared at the packet, the young one said, "I don't know any sixteen-year-olds with those knockers." Both men laughed.

The doors slammed and the car backed away. Pulling the papers out, I saw fancy writing and stamps, a court's name appeared on the top. My parents' names were listed on the document with the words "Defendants" underneath. Now what?

Gotta get out of here. I left the package on the counter and called Karen, inviting myself over. Walking there, I thanked God I had a friend close by. I wouldn't come back until everyone was asleep.

*

Mrs. Casey insisted on driving me home whenever I stayed after dinner. I told her I was fine walking, but she said it was too late. I wondered if she knew what my parents were like. I hoped not. I looked at the dashboard clock. It was ten-thirty, and my parents were usually in bed by ten. I should be okay.

The smell of booze hit me the moment I entered the kitchen. Dread crept up from my gut. I kept the door at my back.

"*You stupid bitch,*" *Dad slurred, struggling to stand from the kitchen chair.*

Oh Christ. Run. Get out. *But I just stood there.*

"*You stupid bitch.*" *He walked closer and I almost gagged. He reeked of booze and sweat.* "*What the fuck is wrong with you?*" *He shook the papers in front of my face.* "*Why did you take these?*" *He threw the loose documents and envelope at me. The sheets scattered on the floor.*

"*I didn't!*" *I immediately regretted screaming and lowered my voice.* "*The bald man threw them at me like you just did.*"

He came within arm's reach and his towering six-foot-two frame trapped me between the wall and the back door.

"*Because of you they're going to take our home. You stupid bitch.*" *He slammed me into the wall.*

Ducking quickly, I cut to my left and bolted out the kitchen door. Drunk. He was slow. If my friends only knew where my skills at dodge-ball came from. I yanked the door closed.

Clunk. He locked it. "*Now you'll know what it's like to be homeless. Like you made the rest of us,*" *he screeched, slamming his fist into the doorframe, making it shudder.*

Christ! *My heart hammered as I flew down the back stairs and out into the yard. Dear God. How do I get out of here? One more year. An eternity. I tried the door of mother's wreck of a car, and thankfully it opened. Curling myself into the back seat, I swore no one would ever have control over me again.*

Chapter 1

BRIANNA

BREAST CANCER WALK—BOOK CLUB

A SOAKING WET GARBAGE bag slapped me in the face. Horrified, I peeled it away as fast as I could. Thank God it was empty. I rummaged in my pocket for a package of sanitizing wipes and rubbed my face and hands. The damn wind had picked up and the streets were scattered with rubbish. I hoped no more would hit me. I raised a hand to shield my eyes from the rain and looked for my friends, happy they hadn't noticed what just happened. I knew that if they had, they'd post it immediately on social media.

I spotted Hanna leaning on a building a few feet ahead. Hurrying forward, I asked, "Hey, are you okay?"

She shrugged. "Yes. No. I don't know."

Sniffling, she wiped her nose on an already wet sleeve. "I was thinking about that day. You know that day that changed everything." She turned away, sneezing. "God, it was awful. How she trembled and sat there, just shaking her head." Hanna rubbed her eyes. "I don't think Ashley heard anything after the doctor said the word *cancer*."

I placed my arm around her shoulder and pulled her close. I

knew how upset she was, how much she loved Ashley. "You're a wonderful sister, Hanna." I struggled searching for the right words to comfort her. "We're all here walking to help. It's all we can do now."

"I need to do more." She pulled out of my arms, striding forward. "I'm frustrated. And angry. I don't want to lose Ashley." Hanna stopped again; her sobs stronger than before.

The rest of our book club caught up with us and noticed Hanna crying. We pulled her into a group hug. No one moved for a few minutes as other Breast Cancer Walk participants swirled by us, some offering words of encouragement.

We'd signed up for this annual walk in New York City instead of holding our September book club. Tess was the only member who couldn't make it. She was living at the shore caring for a friend's dog and his home while he was away on sabbatical. But Tess wanted to help, so she sponsored Hanna's walk.

We were all here for her. Ashley recently underwent a double mastectomy and had just started chemotherapy. We could see the effect her sister's illness was having on Hanna as she stood in our circle, shaking.

I looked around and glimpsed a pizzeria a block away. "We could use a break." I pointed across the street and grabbed one of Hanna's arms.

"Yes," Charlotte agreed loudly, clutching Hanna's other arm.

"Hey!" Staci walked backward ahead of us in the middle of the street. "Great idea. My raincoat has soaked right through to my clothes. Let's pick up some of those plastic garbage bags they're giving away at the next pit stop."

Oh, that's what must have hit me in my face! Garbage bags as rain gear —clever.

"Hey, Staci. Turn around!" Madeline shouted. "You're gonna fall or walk into a car. That street isn't on the walk route and this is Manhattan, you know."

Staci pivoted abruptly and ran across the street.

"Really, Madeline. Who put you in charge? Leave her be," Ava said.

Madeline rotated sharply toward Ava. "You want to go to the hospital when she walks into a car? Fine. I don't." She huffed off.

Never fails. Madeline and Ava. One wants to be the head bitch in charge and the other isn't having any of it.

Ava joined Staci across the street, muttering something in Spanish. Her rain-streaked hair poking out of her hood had darkened to an even richer brown, heightening her olive complexion.

Just as we reached the door of the pizzeria, Charlotte pulled a gloss tube from her pocket. With one practiced hand, she uncovered it and smoothed it on her lips, popped the top back on, and dropped it into her pocket. All with perfect precision.

"You certainly have a spring in your step lately," I told her as we moved inside. "I assume it's Maxwell."

She grinned. "Hey, did I tell you I'm meeting his kids in a few weeks?"

"Are you nervous?"

"A little, maybe. I hope it goes well." She shook out her coat, hanging it on a hook, and slipped into a booth.

Ava came in the door behind me and I asked, "Hey, how is your mother?"

"She tells me everything is fine. What a load of crap! Hurricane Maria devastated Puerto Rico. As soon as they allow commercial flights, I'm going to see it for myself." She wiped the dampness from her face.

Madeline followed us inside, immediately walking to the counter. "Do you have coffee or tea?" she asked, ignoring the other people in line. She turned to us. "Hey, guys. They have hot drinks. Who wants what?"

I marveled at her appearance as she stood at the counter. Her coat might be wet, but its classic cut lay in neat contours on her body, belted in a perfect double knot. Her hat sat on her impeccably coiffed hair at a slight angle. How does she always look so put together? I glanced down at my own wrinkled rain gear and sighed.

Shouts of coffee and tea came hurtling back at Madeline as the rest of us removed our coats and gently shook off the rain, making puddles on the floor. A man behind the counter muttered something in Spanish, grabbed a mop, and headed our way.

Ava said *"Está lloviendo. No podimos evitar el charco. Lo siento."*

We chuckled at the man's raised eyebrows as she told him we were sorry for the mess.

The rain pinged angrily on the windowsill behind me. I was glad we were warm and dry inside. We still had many more miles to go and my legs ached. None of us had practiced the suggested twenty-mile weekly walk. We'd managed only a five-mile practice before attempting the 26.2 miles today, and still had another 13.1 tomorrow. I hoped we'd make it.

Madeline sipped her tea as she scrolled on her phone. "I'm checking the weather forecast."

"Jesus. Not again." Ava pointed to the window. "Just look outside!"

"Let's get a couple of hotel rooms," Madeline suggested. As usual, it sounded more like a command than a suggestion.

"I agree. I don't want to stay in a tent when it's raining this hard. What a damn mess it would be." Charlotte checked her reflection in the window, carefully taking off her hat and fluffing up her short blond hair.

I looked at Hanna to see if their talk of hotel rooms was bothering her. After all, this wasn't supposed to be a silk pillowcase kind of event. But she seemed a million miles away.

Staci cleared her throat. "Well, I don't want to stay in a hotel. I want the full experience. I'm writing about it, after all."

Madeline rolled her eyes. "Oh, please. I'll get someone tomorrow who can give you all the information you need. It's for your blog, not a national newspaper. You won't miss your chance at a Pulitzer."

"Nice! Real nice! And thanks for pointing that out, Madeline. But I'm sleeping in the pretty pink tent tonight. You all can do whatever you want." Staci stood and headed to the restroom.

"Hey, I think we're all forgetting why we're here," I declared.

Hanna looked up. "It's okay. Stay wherever you want. I'll sleep with Staci in the tent. It's the least I can do." She curled her hands around her steaming coffee. Strain was etched all over her face.

This walk was as much about making Hanna feel better as it was to support the cause. Some of these women just didn't get it. "I'll stay with you, too," I said, trying not to let my annoyance show on my face or in my voice.

Madeline rose. "We should get going. If we take too long a break, we'll be stiff. That'll make it harder to continue."

"Wait." Staci was back from the restroom and saw us reaching for our coats. "Señor, can you take a picture of us. Please?" She handed him her cell phone.

Complaints and moans all around, but we sat back in the booth, three on either side. He snapped a few shots. Staci immediately posted one of the pictures.

"I tagged all of you." She put her phone back in her inside coat pocket.

"You posted it before we looked at it?" Charlotte asked. "What if I don't like what I look like?"

Staci shrugged. "You can untag yourself if you really want to."

"Oh, please. We're soaking wet. How do you think we look?" Madeline grumbled, reaching for her coat.

Clicking on my phone, I brought up the picture. We definitely didn't look like the pulled together Novel Women Book Club now. Especially me. I looked like a middle-aged frump.

"Let's get some plastic bags at the next pit stop," Staci said as we put our coats on and ambled toward the door.

*

9

"Girls, how's my bonnet?" Ava asked, posing with one hand on her hip and the other flipped palm up. She'd placed a grocery store bag on her head and tied the loops together under her chin. An infectious giggle ran through the group as we all modeled our garbage bag couture.

We started across the Williamsburg Bridge back into Manhattan from Brooklyn. The bridge was a sea of pink. Madeline and Charlotte kept grumbling about hotel rooms, so I grabbed both of their arms and started skipping.

Charlotte sang, "'We're off to see the wizard . . .'"

At four p.m. the rain turned vicious, stinging our faces, driving down hard and icy cold. We sought shelter in a nearby library, barreling through the door and banging it shut behind us.

"Whoa!" Staci slipped on the wet marble floor, slamming into a metal detector.

Heads snapped toward us as the librarian rushed forward, shushing us. We stood like statues at the entrance, as still and quiet as we could.

Madeline trained a steely gaze on the librarian. "Shushing us? Really? You should be happy our friend didn't break her neck. There should be mats when you enter. Or do you have a lawyer on speed dial?" She walked toward the wall of windows by the entrance. "Will you look at the weather? I'm not staying outside in this." She snorted pointing out the window.

"Enough. Stay wherever you want. Just stop complaining." I turned to Staci, asking if she were okay.

She nodded.

"This is for Hanna, not us," I chided. I glanced at Hanna now backed into a hallway, shoulders slumped, head downcast, looking overwhelmed by everything.

I walked over to her. "My legs hurt. How do you feel?"

Hanna looked up. "Great. I'm glad I started running last summer. Legs feel fine."

Normally, she'd crush this walk. Physically at least.

She rubbed her temples. "My head hurts a little. I guess it's the weather."

Tension and worry were more like it. Our perky, athletic, girl next-door friend was going through the motions robotically, but her mind was with her sister.

The pelting rain finally slowed to a misty spray, so we ventured back outside and continued the walk. As we passed the United Nations on our way to Randall's Island the clouds brightened. According to the forecast, the reprieve was temporary, but it would let us finish the walk torrent-free.

My pace slowed after the twenty-mile marker. I felt every rotation in my hip. At times I thought it might lock in place. This walk was my bright idea. I had to finish. Despite being bone tired.

Staci strode beside me and we chatted about John. She smiled broadly. "A part of me wants to be free of men, but whenever I think of him, I get so excited."

Charlotte came up behind us. "Excited? About what?" Her lips were perpetually shiny, smeared with whatever pink sensation was popular in gloss.

We both turned. Before Staci could answer, Charlotte interrupted her. "We're going out for a girl's night." Charlotte pointed her finger directly at her. "Staci, you promised me last spring and we still haven't done it! We'll go next Friday, no more damn excuses."

Staci threw her arms up in a gesture of surrender. "All right. Fine."

Charlotte grinned, victorious. "Finally. We'll have such a good time."

Staci rolled her eyes. "I'm sure we will." She took her hat off and released her locks from the ponytail. How the hell she still had perfect beach waves in her hair in this weather astonished me. Even with mascara streaked down her face, she was still beautiful.

A few blocks later my hip screamed. *How much longer was this damn walk?* Shit, I have a job interview on Monday. I hope I'll be able to walk. I started counting steps.

Finally, I heard Charlotte shout. "Oh, thank you Lord." She pointed past the bridge.

We turned to see. From this angle, the scene looked like the tulip fields in Holland, a vast sea of pink gently blowing in the wind. I was moved by the sight of so many people working together to help eradicate breast cancer.

I caught sight of Hanna. I could tell from her expression that she was blown away, too.

A tear escaped my eye and I wiped it away.

"Wow!" Staci exclaimed. "Will you look at that?"

We all marveled at the pink canvas of tents, balloons, banners, jackets, hats, and scarves that had taken over Randall's Island.

"Bri!" Madeline shouted.

I jumped. "What?" I jabbed a finger at her. "You're not going to say anything more about hotels, are you?" Her intense need to be heard above everything and everyone else was getting to me.

"Hmm . . . You seem touchy. Never mind." She walked away.

Had I offended her? Did I care? I decided I didn't. Maybe I was just tired.

The thousands of people below made me think of an undulating wave. We limped down the hill to the huge field and collapsed onto picnic benches, resting before looking for food and a place to wash up.

We were numb from exertion.

Hanna's phone rang. "Hi, Mom," we all heard her say. Her body froze, eyes widening. "I'll be there as soon as possible." She clicked off. She had turned pale, eyes moistened.

"Hanna. What's wrong?" I put an arm around her shoulders.

"Ashley . . . she had a . . . ah . . . life-threatening reaction. To the chemo." Hanna jumped up, looking left then right. "Sorry, I have to go home. I have to go now!"

We rose in unison and scurried behind her, Ava, Madeline and I ordering cars.

Hanna didn't speak until we reached the road. "You don't have to go with me." She paced anxiously waiting for our rides.

"Of course, we do," I said.

A car arrived within two minutes and Hanna and I jumped in.

It was the longest hour I've ever spent in a car.

Chapter 2

HANNA

IN A HEARTBEAT

I PRAYED THE WHOLE way to the hospital, begging and bartering with God. I barely heard anything Bri said.

I don't think the car came to a complete stop before I thrust the door open and attempted to jump out.

Bri's hand grabbed my arm. "Hanna. Hanna! Wait! Let him stop first!" she screeched.

I tried to calm myself by breathing deeply. But my legs felt like Jell-O as I exited the car. I willed myself through the hospital's outer doors and stopped at the main desk to ask for my sister.

Hospitals are mazes to me. I've learned to always ask for directions. With their constant additions and alterations, it's never the same as your last visit. I'm not sure I understood a word the woman said. Thank God Bri was there to guide me along those endless corridors.

I heard her voice, but not what she was saying until she said, "We're almost there."

My heart rate picked up, my mind unfocused, and my breathing started catching. I could only breathe in short, shallow breaths.

I wanted to stop short, to turn around. After all, if I don't see it, it can't be true. But I forced myself to keep going.

Bri held my arm tightly as we wound through the twisting hallways. I was grateful for her. She helped keep me strong.

I saw my mother standing outside Ashley's room.

Bri stopped. "I'll be in the waiting room. Call me if you need anything."

We hugged.

I approached my mother. "How is she?"

"Brace yourself," she told me. "Ashley's been sedated and intubated because of her reaction to the chemo. But the doctor believes she'll be okay. Don't get emotional. She might be able to hear you. I don't want you scaring her." She took my arm and led me to a curtained off area in the emergency room.

Light blinded me as my mother pulled back the curtain. My eyes teared as they struggled to adjust. There in the middle of the fluorescent glow lay my older sister. She didn't look like the headstrong, vibrant woman who had always told me what to do. Instead, she was a pale imitation, tubes and intravenous lines crisscrossing her body, looking twenty years older. Her hair was matted on her head and bruises climbed up and down her arm. A hospital gown hung loosely on her. She'd be horrified to realize she was being seen looking like this. Oh, my beautiful sister.

The air rushed out of me like I'd been sucker punched. The beeping of various sensors monitored her vitals. I moved next to her bed as my legs wobbled. Turning, I walked toward a chair in the corner to steady myself and watched the nurse checking her blood pressure, temperature, heartbeat. I wanted to ask a million questions but couldn't form the words. But all my other senses were on high alert. The bleeping of the heart monitor assaulted my ears like a heavy hauler on the freeway and the clicking and sucking noise of the ventilator sounded like a factory's exhaust fan. I wanted to shield my eyes from the harsh light and cover my ears to block out the sound.

No, no, this can't be happening. The room smelled of heavy disinfectant with an underlying putrid odor. I felt nauseated.

I jumped up. "Where's the bathroom?" I asked the nurse and she pointed.

I barely made it. I patted cold water on my face and stared at the mirror above the sink. I looked so much like Ashley. Tears poured from me as I collapsed onto the toilet seat and cried quietly.

Someone knocked on the door.

"Hanna, are you okay?" Mom asked.

"I'm okay. I'll be right out." I held on to the sink to help myself rise. My tears had exhausted me. Or maybe I was just tired from the walk. I splashed water on my face again, determined to handle this like an adult and not a scared child.

Mom and I walked the few feet back to Ashley's bed. The doctor and nurses were removing the tube and injecting an intravenous solution to help wake her up.

Some color had returned to her cheeks. That gave me hope. I sat in the corner out of the way and said a silent prayer.

After about an hour, I told my mom and Ashley's husband, Josh, that I was going to call Mark who had texted and called me a dozen times. I just hadn't been up to the conversation.

"Hey." I stepped outside the room and whispered into the phone.

"Honey, what's happening? How is Ashley?" Mark paused, waiting for me to answer.

I couldn't find the words. I thought if I uttered a single word the tears would follow. And I might not be able to stop them.

"Hanna, honey—talk to me," Mark said adding, "Never mind, I'll be there in a few minutes."

"What . . . about . . . kids?" I mumbled.

"I've got that covered. I'll be right there."

I stared through her open hospital door and saw Ashley

breathing on her own. Wrapped snugly in a blanket, only her hand and the intravenous drip peeked out. Josh sat next to her gently stroking her fingers and hand. "Mom, I'm going to tell my friends in the waiting room to go home. I'll be right back."

"Hi, everyone," I said walking into the room. All my friends jumped up and came over to me. "Ashley's breathing on her own and the doctor believes she'll be okay. Thank so much for coming and for participating in the breast cancer walk. I couldn't ask for better friends." I hugged each one tightly. "Mark will be here soon. We walked twenty-six miles today. You must be exhausted. Go home. I'll keep you posted."

"Are you sure you don't want me to stay?" Bri asked. "Can I get you anything before I leave?"

We needed nothing—only Ashley. "No thanks. Go home."

By the time Mark got to the hospital I could barely keep my eyes open. After a while, the doctor returned and told everyone to go home and get some rest.

I held on to Mark's arm. As we drove home, he tried repeatedly to start a conversation. I just stared out the window. It dawned on me that if Ashley died, nothing would ever be the same again.

*

I woke the next morning when Mark came into our bedroom. My mom called on our home phone.

"Ashley's sitting up and feeling great," Mom said. "Demanding to go home! The doctor believes the treatment worked and she'll be released shortly."

"Oh, thank God!" Relief flooded me. "I can be there in thirty minutes."

"No need. She may be gone by the time you get here."

"Okay. Tell her I'll bring dinner over tonight for everyone." I got out of bed and searched my night table for a pen and scrap of paper. I knew nothing I suggested would be good enough for my mother, and I wasn't in the mood to argue with her. "What do you think I should bring, Mom?"

"Get the recipes from my suitcase at Ashley's. Pick a simple chicken dish and don't use preservatives," Mom ordered.

She always brought recipes with her no matter where she went. She never used anything but what she called *pure food*. Any recipe I picked from her collection would take me most of the day to find the "right" ingredients and then prepare it. But I didn't care today. All I cared about was my sister. "Mom, will this happen again? Are the chemo treatments really that dangerous?"

"The doctor told Ashley that they'll change the therapy to prevent this type of severe reaction. She'll stay in the hospital after the next infusion to be on the safe side."

Wiping a tear from my eye, I looked at Mark. "Ashley's better. She can go home." I dropped the phone on the bed and covered my face, crying happy tears. But deep inside, I was still scared. I'd come so close to losing my sister. What if the new treatment did something worse to her? How could the doctors be sure it was safe? How could anyone?

Chapter 3

BRIANNA

REENTRY

BEEP. *BEEP. BEEP.* Jolted from my thoughts, I pushed the car's accelerator. Jesus, buddy. Have a coronary, why don't you? Christ, how long did I make him wait? Thirty seconds at the light. I could hear Madeline in my head. *What an idiot! So much more important than everybody else—aren't you? It's your own damn fault you're late. Leave earlier, you jerk!* I smiled. Sometimes I just love her.

I've been thinking about Hanna's sister and it was keeping me up at night. How one minute everything is fine and the next second—bam! Really makes you assess your own life.

My cell phone rang. I jumped in my seat. *Jesus! I better start focusing on the road!* "Hi, Ava!"

"Hola," Ava said. "How's the new job going at Elevated Events?"

"Well, I haven't been fired yet!" I choked out. "Seriously, I'm really enjoying it and learning a lot."

"That's great. I knew you'd love doing event planning." I could almost see the grin on Ava's face.

I thought about the energy at the office. It was like Grand

Central Station—a structured but chaotic mess. The company had ten event planners and various staff members across their three office locations. Shelly Cross, who owned Elevated Events, was perpetually on the phone. The only time I hadn't seen her with an earpiece was during my interview a week ago. Just yesterday, though, Shelly transferred me after my first week to work with her senior planner, Nicole Crestfield, in a branch office in Chester. It was closer to home – much more convenient.

I thought about how much I liked Shelly and was a little sad to be leaving the main office. I hadn't met Nicole yet. The idea of a transfer made me a bit anxious. But . . . well . . . how bad could it be?

*

By the end of the following week, I knew just how bad it could be. I left work every day with a pounding headache. I didn't have a clue what was expected of me, so I tried to stay quiet and absorb everything. No one bothered to train me. I learned everything through missteps.

Ava called on my way home that Friday. She was thinking of going to Puerto Rico soon to check on her mom. It had been a month since Hurricane Maria slammed into the island and some commercial flights now flew into San Juan. The sporadic cell service had made it extremely hard to reach her.

"My mother says she's fine." Ava said. "But I'm betting she's putting on a brave face because she doesn't want us to worry. The devastation on the news is horrific. I need to see for myself and try to bring my mother here if it's as bad as I suspect."

"Let me know if I can do anything," I said. "And, Ava, thank you again for helping me get this job." *I think.*

*

That night, around eight-thirty, I crawled into my home.

"Hi, honey," Eric said as I walked through the door.

"Hey," was all I could muster. I sat down at my kitchen counter with my coat still on.

"I have some Hunan chicken in the warming tray." Eric went to the refrigerator and pulled out a beer. "Would you like a glass of wine to go with it?"

"Make it a double."

Eric laughed as he grabbed a bottle of white and a glass.

"My brain is on fire." I shook my head.

"Honey—" Eric started.

I interrupted. "I'm serious."

He placed the wine in front of me.

I tried to reach my hand out but decided I didn't have the energy. "Jesus, this is overwhelming."

"Hey, it's okay. You've been working twelve to fourteen hours a day. It's a lot, Bri." Eric kissed the top of my head. "Let's relax in the family room."

"I don't know if I can get up. Give me a few more minutes."

He let me be, but I could see the skepticism on his face as he left the kitchen.

I finally meandered into the family room and plopped down on the couch across from Eric. His face twisted in amusement.

"Don't you dare laugh at me," I demanded.

"Now would I . . .?" He exploded in laughter.

"I know you've been doing this for decades. Blah, blah, blah . . ." My neck ached. I wasn't sure how to make him understand. "This is all new for me. Not something I've done for years." I yawned. "There are so many moving parts. Nobody explains anything." I yawned again. "I'm sorry, but I'm going to bed."

"Wait. I wanted to spend some time with you. I haven't seen you all week."

"Hey, now you know how I felt all those years you collapsed after a long day at work and all I wanted was a little attention." I shrugged and wandered upstairs, barely getting my clothes off and my teeth brushed.

Eric came up a few minutes later. He nestled into me and whispered into my ear, "I'm proud of you, sweetie."

The last thing I remembered was him kissing the side of my head.

*

My first unsupervised assignment was supposed to be easy. I had to transport a few hundred people from their hotel to a seminar at the local civic center and return them after the event was over. I made the arrangements with the busing company and checked the week before the event, the day before the event, and the morning of the event. Everything was on schedule. Nicole handled the rest of the seminar planning.

The busing company picked up the attendees on time and delivered them to the Garden State Civic Center as instructed.

The leadership seminar, hosted by Fine Line Information, was only a day in length, but half of the attendees came from out of state and planned to return to their hotel for the night. As the event wrapped up, I went to the venue lobby expecting the buses to be waiting at the curb.

They weren't there. *OMG, where are the damn buses? Shit. What do I do now?*

Nicole briskly walked by me to the revolving doors, checking her watch.

"Bri, where are the buses?"

"Ummm," I started. "I spoke with the bus company's rep this morning and confirmed the pickup time."

"It's four-fifteen. I don't see any buses. Do you?" Nicole's steely voice vibrated, low and menacing. "Why aren't you on the phone calling them?"

I grabbed my purse off my shoulder to reach for my phone, but dropped it, spilling the contents on the floor.

Nicole turned with a groan, shaking her head.

My face burned. I scooped up the items, dumping them randomly in my purse, and called the bus company. It took several rings for them to pick up, while Nicole, clearly exasperated, tapped her foot on the marble floor. Each ring made my heart beat faster. Finally, on the fifth ring someone picked up.

"There was an accident, and the buses should be here in ten minutes." I told Nicole. I thought that seemed reasonable. "Would you like me to inform everyone?"

She looked around at the people waiting. Most were talking among themselves. No one seemed impatient or upset – except for my boss.

"You should have prepared for this kind of delay and had a soft drink and snack cart to keep these people occupied," she snapped. She swiveled on her heel, walking toward the revolving doors again, then threw a command over her shoulder. "Get the venue management here now."

Scurrying away, I wanted to cry. How could I possibly have foreseen this? Was I supposed to spend the client's money on a snack cart just in case the buses were delayed? Was that reasonable? But Nicole was pissed, clearly thinking I should have planned better. Hanging my head, I refused to make eye contact with her.

By the time I had found the manager and returned to the lobby, the participants were loading onto the buses. Relieved, I blurted out a quick apology before darting into a seat on the last bus.

As I walked by, Nicole turned away and stared out the window.

I had liked Shelly in the main office, but Nicole was another matter entirely. Thirtysomething, single, driven, condescending, she was like a teenage mean girl with total authority. Clients liked the job she did, so she didn't lack for repeat customers. But the staff cringed every time they were assigned to her.

The seminar officially ended when we delivered everyone back to the hotel. Our day had started at seven a.m. and I hoped to be home around six p.m. The staff, exhausted, had loaded into a bus that brought us to the office. No one spoke on the way back.

"Brianna!" Nicole shouted across the room as soon as I walked through the door.

I entered her office, dreading a reprimand, but before I could sit down, she said, "Do the exit report for the function right away." Nicole's face was flushed, and she almost spat out the words. "Speak with the seminar heads and get their take on it. Both good and bad. I want it on my desk first thing tomorrow morning. Do you understand?"

I wanted to throw her Baccarat paperweight in her face. That type of report took at least a week, with everyone contributing. How the hell could I get all that done tonight, by myself? "Not sure I can have an actual report done by then. What if I can't reach everyone?"

She glared. "Just do it." Picking up her bag, she pushed past me and left.

I hollered after her, "But I need your input. Where are you going?"

She pivoted abruptly. "I'll put my own sections in tomorrow."

The staff stared from me to her, watching her storm out the door. One of the other planners, Mia, came over to me. "I'll write up my piece and e-mail it to you now." She turned, raising her voice so everyone could hear. "Sandy, Jane, and Corrine, can you also do your exit write-up and forward it to Bri?"

"Really, now?" Jane lashed out. "Let the new girl do it."

Corrine shouted at her. "What the hell, Jane? Help her out. We all know what Nicole is like."

Jane shrugged, nodding.

Shouts of "sure" floated through the office and everyone returned to their desks. I thought for a second of quitting, but the support from my coworkers buoyed me and I dashed to my cubicle, pulled up an old report as a reference, and got to work.

I didn't arrive home until 1:30 a.m. Eric was fast asleep, snoring.

Madeline and Ava had convinced me that I'd be great at event planning. The charity functions I ran involved planning, but . . . How could anyone compare those amateur events to what an experienced professional does?

As I got undressed, I told myself that worrying about this job was trivial compared with what Hanna's family was going through. I understood the fear and the loss all too well. Death had visited me early, taking my mother in a car accident. My father couldn't cope and disappeared. I lost both of my parents, my home, and my childhood in one fell swoop. Scars permanently etched my soul from that tragic accident. I thought that catastrophe had prepared me to cope with whatever life threw at me. It had not.

I tried to slip into bed quietly, but Eric woke.

He rolled on his side to face me. "Bri, what the hell time is it? Are you just getting home now?"

"It's one-thirtyish. Go back to sleep."

"What? This is too much. We're going to talk about this in the morning."

Just what I wanted. Another argument.

I rolled on my side and pulled the blanket over my head. Exhaustion quickly overcame me as I compared last summer's spouse snatcher Natasha to bitchy boss Nicole. My last thought as I drifted off was that I should avoid women whose names began with an *N*.

Chapter 4

MADELINE

A Breath Before

"IT'S TEN-TEN, MRS. Landin. I've got appointments all day with only a few minutes between each one. This will set me back." I watched the mother yank her three children into the room. Her son, Micky, had speech therapy sessions with me twice a week.

"I understand, Mrs. Miller. But some mornings are more difficult than others." She grabbed the youngest child, still in his pajamas, and simultaneously pushed Micky into a seat. Micky pulled out a book and buried his nose in it. The middle child plopped down next to his big brother. "No, Conor. Come on. We'll wait outside for Micky. Let's go."

Looking at Micky as the door clicked shut, I noticed his shirt was inside out. I shook my head. "I will never understand tardiness."

Micky looked up from his book. "Huh . . . ?"

*

The next morning, I called Bri while I was doing my bills. "Darling, how is Hanna's sister? And how was your first week working for Ava?" I cleared my throat to prevent myself from saying anything further. Ava and I could never work together. We'd argue about everything, all day long.

"Ashley is home and doing better. But I'm not working for Ava. Remember? You talked me into this event planning job," Bri said.

"Right, I forgot. But it's with Ava's friend?" I asked as I looked over our statements. A figure caught my eye on the American Express. Jeez, how many bottles of wine did Stan buy? That line item put us over our monthly budget.

"Yes, and I hate to cut this short, but I'm already at my desk working and I don't want the boss to see me on the phone. Can I call you over the weekend?"

"Of course. Let's go somewhere fun for next month's book club. How about that quaint restaurant in Bedminster? I believe it's called River's Edge. I'll make the reservation." I folded the American Express bill and returned it to the envelope. How unlike Stan to go over our budget. I placed the envelope on top of the pile to speak to him about it later.

*

I looked around the kitchen for anything I might have missed. I'd cleaned the pots and put them away. Dinner was in the warming tray. I opened the 2009 La Prohibición from Spain we'd saved for a special occasion and poured it into a decanter.

Looking out our kitchen window, I saw Stan cleaning the deck furniture. Feeling a surging tide of warmth, I smiled. It was a lovely autumn day, unseasonably warm and perfect for drinks outside before dinner. I grabbed some sprigs of mint leaves, separating them for mojitos while I kept an eye on Stan. It was our turn to host David and Vivian. David and Stan had been partners in a management company that rented space for their separate CPA firms for more than twenty years. Both firms saved on overhead by sharing space and other expenses. Stan and I had become close friends with David and his wife, Vivian. We even vacationed together.

"I can't wait to show this to David," Stan said as he walked through the sliding glass doors with some sort of gizmo in his hand.

I laughed. "You know you can't out gadget him."

Stan shrugged. "How does he always manage to get the latest techno devices before the rest of us even hear about them?"

In a rare moment of affection, I wrapped my arms around him and kissed him passionately. *What had come over me?*

Stan stood motionless. "Uh . . ."

"Thanks for cleaning the deck furniture." I couldn't think of anything else to say, so I pulled back and patted the corner of my mouth, checking for excess moisture.

"I can clean the deck furniture everyday if you'd like." A smirk covered his face as he stepped closer.

I squirmed away. "I need to make sure the powder room is presentable."

"It's always presentable, just like everything else around here," Stan hollered after me. He sounded annoyed. I couldn't blame him.

What's wrong with me? Where did that passionate kiss come from? I looked in the bathroom mirror. My face was flushed. Maybe a hot flash was coming on. Though I hadn't had one in a long time.

Looking at the faucet, I wiped it with a paper towel to bring up its shine. I was amazed at how quickly I'd recovered from the cancer walk. I was happy that Hanna's sister was home. I'd always wanted a sister, but I couldn't imagine loving someone that much and watching this happen to them. I decided to call my younger brother tomorrow. He's all the family I have left.

Our guests arrived. We sipped Stan's famous mojitos on the deck, bantering back and forth. It was comforting to have such long-time friends. I never found it easy to make them – and when I did, it all went wrong somehow. Like with Natasha this past summer. Sometimes I wished I were more like Bri. Everyone liked her. I think most of book club simply tolerated me for her sake.

Vivian tapped my arm. "Madeline, the centerpiece is stunning.

You didn't have to go through all this trouble for us." She smoothed her Ted Baker skirt with its matching top.

I also noticed an incredible pair of Stuart Weitzman shoes that picked up just the right hint of turquoise in her skirt. "Of course, I do. Look at the care you take when we come to visit you. I feel like a queen in your home. You spoil us lavishly."

Vivian flushed but seemed to appreciate the compliment. We moved into the house for dinner. David's phone rang nonstop, vibrating relentlessly. I was about to tell him to turn off his phone when he excused himself, making a joke about some pesky client who insisted he take his calls, no matter what time it was.

Vivian threw a stern look at David, so I left it alone. When he returned to the table, neither his expression nor his demeanor seemed troubled.

Two hours passed in a blur of laughter and harmony as we moved from subject to subject, sometimes agreeing with one another and sometimes arguing just for the fun of it. We were like choir members singing in perfect tone, balance, and blend, just like always. But David's phone continued to vibrate. He didn't answer it, but a shadow crept over his face and he grew quiet, looking preoccupied. A shiver ran down my spine. Life had made me a suspicious person. Something wasn't right.

*

"Sarah, it's quite simple." I rolled my eyes. "Go back on the portal and copy your schedule for next semester and send it to me. Or better yet, take a picture and text it to me."

"Mom, really," Sarah barked. "I'm working on a paper due tomorrow and you want me to drop everything and send you a copy of my schedule? I'm a sophomore in college. I can handle my own classes."

"As long as we are paying for that college, we have every right to see what your schedule is, and don't you forget that." I couldn't stand back talk, especially from my kids. "If you disagree, we can always forward you the student loan forms. And the next time you have a paper due, don't wait until the day before to finish it."

"Ugh!" Sarah screeched. "I went over my schedule with my guidance counselor. You think you know better than she does?"

I could hear her say "you don't" under her breath.

"Don't you remember how poorly she advised you the last time you registered for classes? Why on earth are you giving me a hard time?"

"It's not that. It's everything. You're like that bird parent. No, not bird . . . You're . . . a . . . helicopter parent." Sarah let out a noisy breath. "I gotta go. I'll send you my schedule when I can." She hung up.

I slammed the home phone down. Neither of my children had ever talked to me like that before. I felt like driving to her college and yanking her out of school. But the image I conjured made me stop—me screaming at my daughter in her apartment on school grounds. Campus police showing up to escort me from the premises. Sarah refusing to talk to me ever again.

*

After my Saturday morning speech therapy session with Micky, I met Bri for lunch. We had spent so much time together last summer planning the Build-A-Home event. Now that she was working, I missed being able to see her whenever I wanted to.

"I'll have the beet salad and an iced tea, unsweetened," I told the waiter.

"I'll have a cheeseburger and fries," Bri said. "And what the hell—give me a Coke, too."

"Is there something you want to talk about, Bri? You're eating like a teenager."

Bri laughed. "I am, aren't I?"

"You know it's hard to burn off those two thousand calories you're about to ingest."

"Well, we all can't be you! And thanks for making me feel guiltier than I already do." Bri patted my hand. "You're right, of course, but this new job has me spinning like a top. I'm just not sure I'm any good at it. So, I eat to comfort myself."

"Of course, you're good at it. You've got what it takes to be a terrific event planner. Heavens, you sound like my children." I noticed David entering the restaurant with a man I didn't know. Must be a new client.

Our lunch came and I watched as Bri stuffed herself.

"Are you pregnant?" I didn't mean to say that out loud.

"Good God, no." Bri roared with laughter. "Not possible anymore. What are you thinking?"

I shrugged and looked at David's table—a good excuse to change the subject. "Bri, do you know who the man David is with? They're to my left."

Bri glanced over. "I believe his name is Ben Kroy. He's an attorney with a firm in Morristown. I've met him a few times at bar association functions that I attended with Eric."

"Must be a client of David's." I stood. "I'll be right back."

As I turned to walk to their table, I noticed that David and his associate were reviewing documents so intensely that they didn't hear me approach.

"David, I don't want to disturb your lunch. You look busy. Just a quick hello."

Startled when he heard his name, he flipped over the documents he had been reading. I put my hand on his shoulder to prevent him from rising and kissed his cheek, then turned to his colleague, introducing myself. Was he a business associate, client, or something else? David simply introduced him as Ben Kroy, then waited in silence for me to leave.

"I hope you enjoy your lunch," I told them, then went back and sat at my table.

Bri asked me a question, but my mind was miles away, and I didn't respond. Shadows slithered in the corners of my thoughts, but I couldn't figure out what they meant.

"Madeline, helloooo . . ." Bri bellowed.

Blinking, I returned to earth. I noticed her phone was lit from a text with a lovely picture of her children, Julianna and Logan, both now in college. "That's a nice picture." I pointed at her phone. "I think Logan looks like his father and Julianna is a combination of you both."

Bri looked down at the picture. I could tell she missed them. "Next time you come over, remind me to show you a picture of my grandfather at Logan's age. He looks just like him, except for the hair color."

She smiled and turned her phone over. "Both your children look like you. I imagine they must be like your parents. Although . . ." Bri drank some water. "I don't remember seeing any pictures of your parents hanging on your walls. You'll have to show me some pictures of them next time I'm over."

"They look nothing like my parents!" I said, more forcefully than I meant. I motioned for our waiter to get our check.

Bri raised an eyebrow.

"I'm sorry. I'm tired today. A little off." I folded my napkin placing it on the table. "Did you ever read the book *The Gift of Fear* by Gavin de Becker?"

She shook her head.

"It's about that nagging feeling you get when something's off. I can't seem to put my finger on it. But…."

"I get that sometimes, but I just ignore it," Bri said.

"Don't. Read that book. I'm telling you; you won't ignore it ever again."

As I got into my car and drove off, a wave of fatigue overcame me. *How strange. Maybe I'm coming down with something.* No way was I cooking tonight. I stopped at West Side Market and picked up a prepared meal of chicken parmesan for dinner. A relaxing night would do me good.

I told Stan at dinner about seeing David that day. "He was with an attorney named Ben Kroy. Is he a friend of David's? Or a business associate?"

Stan told me he didn't know Ben Kroy. He knew nothing about the lunch.

I persisted. "Have you seen him in the office before? He's got short brown hair, he's about your height and age."

"Are you crazy? That description fits most of the men in town," he snapped. "Madeline, why does it matter who David has lunch with? I don't know why you always have your nose in everything." Stan stood and put his plate in the dishwasher. "I have work to finish."

I heard the study door close as the hairs on my neck twitched.

*

The following week I forgot all about David's lunch date as we boarded a plane in Newark to visit our daughter. A violent storm centered around the Raleigh-Durham airport, causing our plane to circle through turbulence for a while before landing safely. Some of the passengers looked green as they departed the plane. Our poor daughter, Olivia, had waited for hours to pick us up.

"Not sure that could have been avoided," Stan said, pulling his suitcase off the luggage carrier.

"I don't know about that," I said, but didn't press the issue. Stan always made excuses for everything instead of calling it what it was: a weak-ass pilot who couldn't navigate around a storm. But it wasn't worth wasting my breath to set my husband straight.

Olivia was graduating a year early from UNC at Chapel Hill and enrolled in the master's program to begin in the fall. She liked

North Carolina and planned to stay in the area after she graduated. I was excited to see her. I especially wanted to see how her new apartment was shaping up after helping her move in a few months ago.

"Mom, Dad!" Olivia waved us over.

"Olivia, sweetheart. Sorry you had to wait so long for us. We had an incompetent crew who couldn't seem to navigate a little thunderstorm."

"Mom, that was no small thunderstorm. I've been watching the weather channel in the airport's lounge. The wind gusted at 40 miles an hour and there was so much thunder and lightning. I was terrified for you."

"Liv, you must know by now your mother believes she can do anything better than anyone else," Stan said, piling the luggage into Olivia's car.

"Stanford, really." I plopped into the front seat. "For that, you can sit in the back."

Olivia took her time adjusting her seat belt and the mirror. She was clearly losing the tristate hustle. She moved deliberately, almost too cautiously. If I'd been driving, I'd already be at her apartment.

The rain had turned to a fine mist and the roads were empty. I stared out the window, thinking about a time when my parents took my brother and me home after Christmas dinner with our grandparents. Drunk, screaming at one other, they swerved into traffic and off the road, slapping one another while cigarette embers and ash flew around the car. I was seven or eight. My younger brother slid over the back seat and curled into me, holding on tightly, eyes clutched shut. Maybe he thought I could protect him. I never let him think otherwise. I felt my heartbeat pick up and closed my eyes.

Stan coughed, bringing me back to my daughter's car and the peace I'd fought so hard to achieve. I took a deep breath and opened my eyes. We arrived at our daughter's apartment a few minutes later.

Olivia pointed at the living room as we entered. "Mom, look, I painted the living room a neutral color. I couldn't take that red paint anymore."

We had rented a nice apartment for her senior year. She had saved us a year's tuition by graduating early and while she was continuing her education at UNC, she didn't want to live in the campus apartments. I didn't blame her.

"It's lovely, dear," I said, looking around at the clean and tidy place. It looked like a staged home for sale with its trendy, colorless palette, but was void of personality. "Your home only needs a touch of you, honey, otherwise you've done an amazing job."

"Well, Mom, the idea of transitional style means it's simple with clean lines without the fuss," she replied.

What magazine had she picked up that nonsense? But I didn't want to fight her. "Sure, but a photo of your family isn't fuss."

Olivia laughed. "Okay, you're right. One picture of the fam coming up."

Our daughter fed us some cheese and crackers and we had a glass of wine before heading to bed. After I turned out the light, I heard the soft tapping of rain against the windows. The sound often soothed and lulled me to sleep, but tonight it was magnified like a ticking cuckoo clock. *Tap, tap, tap* . . . It unsettled me. I flipped on my side and looked at my husband. He snored softly. I brushed my fingers gently on his face.

I'd do anything for him. Yawning, I teetered on the edge of sleep drifting in this warm, pleasant haven as I heard the rumble of distant thunder. The storm wasn't over, but I wasn't worried. I'd learned how to survive storms a long time ago.

*

A loud crash . . . maybe a plate smashing onto the floor. Loud voices from somewhere close. I looked around. I was back in my childhood bedroom. Danny, my brother, ran into my room and threw himself under the blanket on my bed.

"Make it stop," he cried.

"It's okay. Stay here." I left my room and tiptoed to where my parents were fighting. I crouched down and peeked around the corner of the living room into the kitchen. My father's arms were loaded with grocery bags and he was screaming at my mother.

"What the hell have you been doing all day?" he raged. "Sleeping?" He tried to push some of the dishes to the corner of the counter to put down the heavy bags. "This place is a shithole! What the hell is the matter with you?"

My mother whimpered, "I wasn't feeling well. I'll take care of it. Just put the grocery bags on the floor."

He continued pushing the pile of dishes to make room for the bags when another plate crashed to the floor.

I cringed. My father's face turned bloodshot red. He took the bags and swiped the entire counter.

Crash! Plates, a glass bottle of milk, glasses, cereal boxes, and remnants of food slid off the counter and shattered on the floor.

"There! Clean that up." He stormed out of the house.

A car started. I knew he'd head down the street to the local bar and drink till he couldn't walk. Then he'd drive home.

My mother began to weep. I rose from my hiding space, thinking I might comfort her.

She turned on me abruptly, her face beet red. "Oh, so now you show up? Fine. You clean up this mess, Madeline." She grabbed a bottle half full of vodka, the sole survivor from the countertop massacre, and stormed past me, slamming her bedroom door shut.

I looked at the chaos. Milk dripped off the counter. Cereal mixed with broken glass and plates. I had to clean it up so Danny wouldn't get hurt.

*

Thunder and lightning exploded outside, startling me out of my drowsy state. A tear traveled across my cheek and landed on my pillow. Damn, that seemed so real. I had forgotten so much. I must have blocked it out. Jesus, I was only six years old then.

I slipped out of bed and peeked through the curtains watching the storm. My unease had brought on this waking flashback. Something was wrong. I just don't know what yet. Suddenly, an image of David at the restaurant floated into my consciousness. What was my gut telling me? I sure as hell am going to find out.

Chapter 5
STACI

"COME ON, STACI, we'll have a great time," Charlotte pleaded. Her boyfriend, Maxwell, was away and she'd been trying to get me to go out with her since my divorce was finalized eight months ago. I'd finally agreed to go with her during the breast cancer walk but then backed out. But she was – in polite terms persistent. In plain language, she was a freaking dog with a bone.

"Okay," I agreed halfheartedly. I thought it might distract me from dwelling on John night and day.

*

The revolving mirrored ball blinded me as I walked into the after-hours event. "Jesus, is this some kind of disco party?" I slammed into a chair, almost falling over it, my eyes struggling to adjust to the dark. "Charlotte, what have you gotten me into?"

She laughed. "Beats the hell out of me." Charlotte looped her arm in mine as we made our way to the bar.

The place was packed—two, sometimes three, people deep.

It looked like an abandoned bar that had been resurrected for the night with strobe lighting and cheap eighties paraphernalia. I bet the owners kept it dim deliberately. I shuddered to think what I might be walking on underneath my new Brian Atwood heels.

God, I needed a drink. I grew dizzy at the odor—a mixture of mold and decades-old cigarette smell. "Let's just go home, Charlotte." I pulled at her arm. This singles' crap scared the hell out of me.

"Leave now? We just got here! Come on, loosen up." She squeezed between two people at the bar and ordered drinks.

I sipped my cocktail through a small red straw and looked around, wondering why I'd agreed to come. All I wanted was to be with the man I'd met this past summer.

Charlotte, however, had other ideas. She signed me up on a few online dating sites the moment my divorce papers were official and told me she'd help navigate this new chapter of my life. But after the call from John, I was happy waiting for him to arrange our next meeting. I prayed it would be the beginning of a relationship.

"Are you crazy?" Charlotte had screeched when I told her I didn't want to go tonight. "Staci, it's a numbers game. You can't put all your eggs in one basket."

While I didn't understand her dating philosophy, I was tired of dodging her texts and calls. Maxwell, Charlotte's new man, was away on a business trip and she seized the opportunity to badger me.

"Tonight's the night," she told me when I tried to refuse. "This is the night that'll officially launch you back into the singles' scene."

Launch, really?

"Come on, let's walk around." Charlotte woke me out of my reverie, gesturing left. We circled the bar. Divorced years ago, my friend was a pro at this now.

Her mouth moved . . . .

"What? Can't hear you!" I screamed. The band's speakers were blasting. I should have brought earplugs. We found a small round table in the back and sat.

"How did you find out about this?" I shouted.

She shifted closer. "I get these party notices from Chapter II. You know, the online dating service that caters to the over-forty-five crowd." Charlotte showed me the app on her phone. "This is an eighties party. Guess we should have dressed for it. Looks like everyone else did."

The band took a break and the high-decibel level dropped dramatically, replaced by a soundtrack. I rubbed both ears. I wanted to convince Charlotte to leave before the band returned. My nice comfy couch was calling me.

The event posting should have come with a few alerts—like, the fact women outnumbered men three to one. Most of the middle-aged men certainly took the eighties theme seriously, with tight shirts and too much product leaving their few remaining hairs standing at attention. Not to be outdone, the women wore their clothes even tighter, with garish makeup that would frighten a child in the daylight.

"Don't let this scare you." Charlotte held up one hand pointing it around the room. "I told you about the first time I went out after my divorce, didn't I? Remember? Our dear friend, Bri, took me to some wine-tasting charity dinner that her husband's law firm had sponsored. You should have seen all those guys eyeing me. I felt like a minnow in a sea of sharks. Ha!" A smile crossed her lips. "Now who's the shark?" Charlotte stopped talking. "Well . . . was a shark." She blushed and her eyes darted over the room.

"I don't want to be a shark," I protested. "I'm just looking for a nice man. And newsflash—I found one, just like you did. I don't need to put myself through this."

She jabbed my arm. "Come on. I'm being facetious. I'm not a shark. I just feel comfortable with men now. Besides, you don't know what this thing is with John. He's already walked away once."

Charlotte leaned forward. "Dating a few people helps you to compare what you like and don't like. But most importantly, you learn to depend on yourself. Hell, at least let yourself have some fun before tying yourself down to another guy."

Charlotte finished her drink and reapplied her Chanel lip gloss in a fiery red that accentuated her short blond hair. "I remembered how Bri and some of my single girlfriends pushed me out the door. I kicked and screamed about it, but it really was the best thing I could have done. Otherwise . . . ." Charlotte stood and shrugged her shoulders. "I'm getting us another drink." She sashayed off in her four-inch heels.

I thought back to the days right after Charlotte's divorce. She'd been so different then - sulky and lethargic. The first time she'd told book club about that charity wine tasting, she admitted that she'd cried all the way home, broken, lost, wanting her old life back. Now, I thought, watching her ordering the next round of drinks, she's transformed herself into a lioness, her prowess deft, confident in who she is. But I'd seen her with her new man. Maxwell soothed her fiery nature like aloe on a burn.

As I watched from my seat, a tall, dark-haired man approached Charlotte, tapping her on the shoulder. She turned and smiled, looking him up and down. Dressed in jeans with a well-tailored sports jacket and button-down shirt, he stood out in this crowd of older, balding men. I was surprised the women didn't swarm him.

Charlotte leaned back on the bar, giving him her full attention. She playfully slapped his arm, talking, smiling, whispering in his ear. *God, she's flirting with him. Shit. I don't remember how to flirt.* She took something from him, got our drinks and swayed her way back to the table.

"What did he give you?" I asked as she sat down.

"Just his card. I've got Maxwell, so I'm not interested. But I thought maybe you'd be. He was really handsome." She placed a bright green drink in front of me along with the man's business card.

"What? The last thing I'm gonna do is call somebody who just hit on you. What in the name of God would I even say? 'Hi, you don't know me, but my friend gave me your business card after she decided she wasn't interested?'" I picked the card up and threw it toward her.

"Yeah . . . ." Charlotte shook her head. "That could be awkward. I didn't think it through." She nodded toward the glass. "Drink that. It'll make the men here look better."

"Great! Order me another." I laughed as we clinked glasses. Being around her always lightened my mood. I looked down at the neon green drink with its orange-and-cherry wedge. Knowing Charlotte, I knew it would be strong, so I only took a sip. *Whoa! Lots of vodka.* I coughed a bit. "What is this concoction?"

"A Green Flash. Just some vodka and other stuff. Tasty, right?"

"So, explain to me why I have to have multiple eggs in my basket, and you get to have just one?" I asked, knowing the answer. "Why can't I have John if you have Maxwell?"

"Staci, dear. Maxwell didn't sleep with me and then break it off. He's committed to me." Charlotte licked her lips. "Besides, I dated for five years before he came along. I know I can survive just fine without a man. Don't you think all women should be able to do that before plunging back into a relationship?"

Why'd I ask? The second sip went down easier. Maybe she was right. If I could spend all those years with that narcissistic asshole of an ex-husband, tonight shouldn't scare me this much.

But no matter how many deep breaths I took, I felt uncomfortable. *Do I just want John because I don't want to endure this scene?* I closed my eyes and remembered our first kiss. No. He was the real thing.

"I'm ready to go. This isn't working for me." I thought I'd jump out of my skin if we didn't leave soon. All I wanted were my pj's.

Charlotte dropped her arm from around the chair. "Give it a few more minutes. Okay?"

I looked down at my left hand. Why hadn't I put my wedding ring back on before leaving? That way, I could wave it and tell everyone I wasn't available.

"Listen, Staci. You think there's no one here for you." Charlotte said, her face serious for once. "You're probably right. Forget the whole meeting a nice man thing. You need to get accustomed to being out without that awful ex-husband of yours. If you don't want to talk to anyone, just don't." She nodded along as she spoke. "Sit back, relax. Don't take this so seriously. Have fun with it. Imagine the stories we'll bring back to book club."

She might be right, but . . . .

Charlotte had caught her husband having sex with a friend when she came home early one day. Blindsided, she'd crumpled. She thought they had a great marriage, but after that first rude discovery, she learned he'd had one affair after another. My divorce, on the other hand, had been mutual. We'd grown apart. I couldn't wait to get away. I felt like the Road Runner—*beep, beep,* and I'm gone. But being single scared me. I didn't know how to act, what to say, what to wear. I didn't have a clue.

The band shuffled back onstage. I slumped in my chair. The worst rendition ever of Madonna's "Material Girl" blasted out of the speakers. Excusing myself to find the bathroom, I pushed through the crowd. Where did all these middle-aged single people come from? Were they all trying to find love again? Or just looking for a one-night stand? Did anyone else feel as desperate as I did? I finally made it to the ladies' room and waited in line. Of course.

The other women chattered eagerly to one other, comparing notes, admiring each other's '80s outfits. No one seemed as out of place as I did. I would have preferred the wine tasting that Bri had taken Charlotte to for her "launch." This was awful.

When I returned to our small table, Charlotte was holding court with two well-dressed women. She grabbed my arm, bringing me close, and pointed, shouting, "Staci, this is Anna and Barbara."

Hi, I mouthed. The blaring music made any real conversation impossible.

The ladies nodded. They looked like they had just come from work, one wearing an attractive tailored dress and the other in a creamy linen suit with a white blouse. Both sported sexy, pointed pumps.

I leaned over the table and screamed, "What brings you ladies here tonight?"

"We're here to meet our dream man, what else?" one of them offered. "You know, Mr. tall, dark, handsome, rich, dependable, kind, and trustworthy." She placed both hands over her heart and cackled with her friend.

"They must be at another bar," Charlotte bellowed. "'Cause they're sure as hell not here."

We all laughed. All giggling like schoolgirls, having a damn good time. I started to relax.

Maybe too much. Sitting back in my chair, I knocked my drink over. Never fails, my clumsy-ass self. At least the damn glass was empty.

"Staci, it's your turn to buy a round of drinks," Charlotte shouted.

"Fine, but after this we leave." I trotted off to the bar—or at least tried to. It was packed. The only place slightly open was over by the band. Squeezing my way around the bar was difficult. As I approached, an arm wrapped around mine and pulled me like a rag doll up a large step and onto the stage.

"'Lady when you're with me . . .'" a gray, long-haired man sang. He pushed his face close to mine, so we were only separated by the microphone. I squirmed. He grasped my arm so tightly that I couldn't move. His wet, sweaty hand made my skin crawl. He belted out notes, his breath spewing a toxic mixture of whiskey and cigarettes. I turned my face away, looking back at the bar as the singer broke into the chorus. "'You're my lady . . .'"

No, no, no. I'm nobody's lady. Get me out of here! I looked out over the packed dance floor and noticed most people had stopped dancing. Instead, they were grinning, watching this Willie Nelson wannabe croon at me. I cringed. Too damn polite to push him away, I inched my way off the stage.

Then I spotted Charlotte with her phone at the edge of the dance floor. *Jesus, she is filming this? I'm gonna kill her!*

I wiggled away from the singer just as the song ended and the band took a break. My arm still wet from his touch; I desperately needed a shower to rid myself of the stench of this place. And of him.

"Charlotte, give me your phone now!" I roared.

She cackled like crazy. "I uploaded it! Wait till you see your face." Charlotte was almost doubled over with laughter. "I mean, this could be a YouTube moneymaker. This was some launch into the dating scene."

I spun around and headed for the door. "I'm leaving."

She ran after me, pulling my arm to stop me as we left the bar. "Staci. It's all right. I didn't upload it. Wait. Just watch the video. Don't take yourself so seriously. Come on. You need to laugh at the situation, at yourself. Otherwise, being single is gonna be a hard adjustment."

The video started playing. Charlotte stood next to me, chuckling and pointing. I winced at first, but slowly Charlotte's words took hold and allayed my embarrassment. I realized that had it been one of our other friends, I'd be convulsing on the floor. Why not laugh at myself? Charlotte was right. I needed to lighten up. I relaxed and looked at her, realizing I'd be okay, really okay. My friends would help me through this next chapter of my life.

"I promise I won't upload it to Facebook, but I'm sure as hell going to show it at book club. I can't wait to tell them all about our little adventure." Charlotte practically oozed with delight.

I knew the video would never make it to next week's book club. She'd send it to our friends tonight. As we walked to the car, Charlotte wrapped herself around my still moist arm.

She released her hug and we continued to the car. "Boy, Staci, I didn't realize you were such a sweaty person."

"That's not my sweat."

Charlotte flinched, realizing where the sweat came from. Grabbing my dry arm, she tried to wipe the sweat back on me. "Yuck! Thanks for sharing."

I broke away from her, a huge smile spreading across my face. "Hey, don't mention it. Isn't that what friends are for?"

Chapter 6

CHARLOTTE

"**B**RI, I HATE everything!" I threw the dress I'd just taken off onto the bed. I grabbed my robe and sat on my bedroom chair, staring at the chaos strewn everywhere.

Bri laughed. "I thought you weren't nervous about meeting Maxwell's children." She started folding some of my discarded sweaters.

"Well, maybe I am . . . a little." I went over to the closet.

"It'll be okay." Bri yawned. "His children will see that he adores you."

"I don't know if that means anything." I shrugged and walked into the bowels of my walk-in closet, noticing a bright blue silk blouse. "Maybe, just maybe," I muttered.

"What?" Bri asked. "Can't hear you. How deep is that closet?"

"Nothing," I yelled.

As I reentered the bedroom, I saw Bri stifling another yawn. She looked so tired. "It was nice of you to stop by after work," I told her. "That job's really getting to you, huh?"

Bri stood, stretching. "Yes. I feel like an idiot most of the time."

She reached for the blouse I was holding. "That's a great color for you." She handed it back. "You'll be fine tomorrow. Don't worry so much. Those kids are gonna love you."

"Go home, Bri. You need to get some sleep." I held up the blue blouse. "I'll wear this."

Bri kissed my cheek as I ushered her to the door. "By the way, I loved the video with Staci. It was so damn funny. The look on her face was priceless. It gave me a much-needed laugh." She left.

I returned to my bedroom and straightened the mess. I looked at the blue blouse critically. It looked nice and not like I was trying too hard. I matched it with a pair of black slacks and low-heeled boots I'd thrown beneath the chair. Why was I making such a big deal of this?

Maxwell's children were flying in for a weekend to visit their dad. His daughter, Emily, was a senior in college and his son, Kevin, a freshman. Eight years ago, Maxwell's wife, Kara, had told him to leave. She'd been having an affair. It devastated him.

Meeting him at a friend's party over the summer, I thought he was sexy and couldn't wait to jump into bed with him. At that point, all I wanted was a bit of fun. But Maxwell had other plans. I almost lost him with my careless nonchalance toward real love. Why waste your time? I'd thought. They might claim they love only you, but the next thing you know, they're lying and cheating. Like my ex-husband. But Maxwell helped me trust again and to see beyond my pain.

"Shit." I threw the blouse on the bed. It does matter what his kids think of me. I needed this to go well.

*

I pulled into Maxwell's driveway. Before getting out of the car, I swiped my glossed-up lips with a little extra and finger combed my hair. I thought back to the summer and how I'd nearly lost him. I didn't want to chance anything else going wrong. By the time I pushed the doorbell, my heart was fluttering.

A young woman in ratty sweatpants and a stained college T-shirt opened the door. She held one arm on the doorknob, slouching toward me, effectively blocking my entrance. She slowly looked me up and down.

Charming. "Hi, you must be Emily," I said cheerfully.

"Yes, that's me." She turned and walked toward the kitchen.

Her hair was matted at the back of her head and messy tendrils had escaped the ponytail. Her bedhead was in desperate need of a washing.

Not the warm welcome I was hoping for. I took a deep breath and walked in.

"Hi, Maxwell." I smiled broadly. He was staring out the window with a glass of wine in his hand. The kitchen, usually a spotless mixture of gleaming countertops and pristine stainless steel, was streaked and messy.

"Hi, Charlie." He stayed rooted in his spot and didn't kiss me like he did when we were alone. "Kids, this is Charlie." He looked at his daughter. "Emily greeted you at the door, and this big guy is Kevin." He patted his son on his back.

Not sure I'd call that a greeting. I gestured to both kids. "Hi."

An awkward pause followed. Maxwell, normally so attuned to me, faltered, looking from me to his children. Finally, he asked, "Charlie, glass of wine?"

His naturally sexy voice sounded constricted, abrupt.

"Sure."

He turned, grabbed the bottle of wine, and poured me a generous amount. I hiccupped. *Shit, no. This only happens when I get nervous.*

Maxwell topped up his own glass, then stepped back, not making eye contact.

I held my breath to stop the hiccups from gaining momentum. After taking in every detail of the messy room and the uncomfortable faces, I gulped some of my wine. Exposed, standing alone in the middle of the kitchen, I scanned it. All I wanted was to hide from their stares. I walked to the breakfast table and sat down.

"Dad, I met her. Now can I get back to my stuff? Please?" Emily barely finished speaking before she turned and left the room.

"Emily," Maxwell began in a deeper tone.

"What?" She turned and snapped her hands on her hips.

Maxwell dropped his chin.

Emily huffed back around, shuffled down the hallway and slammed a door somewhere in the house.

Maxwell followed her, leaving me and Kevin in the kitchen. He looked like he wanted to escape but knew that would be impolite. We both just stared at the floor.

Finally, I broke the silence. I was the grownup here, wasn't I? "How were your first few months of college?"

"Fine." His glance never moved from the floor.

"So, you're at the University of Colorado at Boulder?" I asked, straining to keep the conversation going.

"Yes," he replied, now looking toward the hallway.

"Your father told me you're an engineering student. What discipline?"

"Civil."

He made me feel so uncomfortable that I gave up. "I'm going outside on the deck. Would you like to join me?" I already knew what he'd say.

He fidgeted. "I'm good." He started to leave but turned back. "It was nice meeting you." Politeness satisfied, he ambled away.

It was a bright sunny day and seemed warmer outside than in the house even though it was autumn. I wasn't sure Maxwell's children had accepted that their parents had separated. But it had been eight years. You'd think they'd have gotten over their parents' divorce by now.

Maxwell found me on the deck, staring at the lake.

"Sorry, Charlie. This isn't how I thought this would go." He sat next to me, still guarded.

"Why is Emily so angry?"

He stood and motioned for me to follow. We walked down the steps, through his backyard, to the deck chairs on his dock where we had watched the sunset so many times before.

After a few minutes staring out at the water, he spoke. "The kids, especially Emily, have never given up on the idea of us getting back together." He set his glass down and pivoted toward me. "Kara was living with the man she left me for, but they broke up about a month ago. Emily wants us to try again."

What? A chill shivered down my spine. My hand shook as I placed my wineglass on the table. I wrapped my arms around myself. Cold. It had become cold. *This can't be happening.*

"Charlie? Don't look like that. Emily is always trying to get Kara and me back together. It's her main mission in life."

I'm sure my face betrayed me. I didn't want to say anything. I tried to smile. I lay my head back in the chair and closed my eyes. I tried to hide the bedlam I felt swirling around inside me. So many mixed emotions.

"Charlie?"

I opened my eyes. I focused on a dinghy rocking back and forth at his neighbor's dock. "How do you feel about getting back with Kara?"

I froze and counted the seconds. *One . . . two . . . three . . . four . . . .* My breath caught. Four beats without an answer.

Maxwell looked out over the lake before replying. "Nothing . . . not after all these years." He shrugged off the comment. "I really hoped the kids would've accepted you more." When he turned back, his face was scrunched, tense. He let out a heavy sigh.

I didn't think I could move. Those few beats belied what he'd said. I heard screaming in my head. *Get up. Get up. Run, leave, never look back.*

"Maxwell, your kids are visiting, and you should enjoy them. Call me next week after they're gone." I couldn't believe that came out so easily. Now all I had to do was get up. I hoisted myself out of the chair.

He stood also, looking confused. "Are you leaving?"

"I think your children want to be alone with you. You don't get to see them that often." I turned and walked around the outside of the house to my car, so I didn't have to go back inside.

I drove in a daze, confused, my mind wandering in the quiet of the car. Then, with a moment's epiphany, I understood. All my ex-husband's lying and cheating had started with a pause, at least four beats before he'd answer my questions.

*

Opening the kitchen door, I saw Grant and my neighbor and friend Mia talking in our kitchen.

"What's happening?" I asked, unaccustomed to seeing my husband home from work at two o'clock in the afternoon or Mia in our kitchen at all. "Why are you here at this hour?" I put my carry-on bag down and looked from Grant to Mia.

One . . . two . . . three . . . four . . . "Charlotte, you're home a day early." My husband wrapped me in his arms and kissed my forehead. "I just stopped by to pick up some files I forgot this morning." Grant tilted his head and smiled.

"I had to bring my son to the doctor, you know, for that follow-up from his broken arm. I saw Grant's car pulling into your driveway and came over to give him your mail. The courier delivered it to us by mistake." Mia pointed to the mail on the kitchen table. "I better get going. I have a ton of errands to do before the kids get out of school."

"I have to go, too, honey. See you tonight." He opened the door.

"Grant. Where are the files you came home for?" I asked.

He turned slowly and looked me in the eyes. One . . . two . . . three . . . four . . .

"I put them in the car already, sweetie." He pecked my cheek and was out the door so fast I couldn't say another word.

*

The next morning, the damn sun baked me. I'd drunk a few glasses of wine after coming home from Maxwell's and had forgotten to draw the blinds and close the bedroom curtains. My head pounded as I sat up. I needed water and sunglasses. *Crap. How much wine did I drink?* I'm acting like Ava, drinking alone and seething.

After a long shower and many glasses of water, I called Bri.

"Charlotte, don't you think you're overreacting?" she asked after I told her the sad story.

"No! You had to be there." Why didn't she just take my word for it? "There was a four second pause . . . "I'm telling you; I know these things." I paced back and forth in my kitchen.

"Then why call me? Come on. You're not sure either." Bri paused. "I've seen the way he looks at you. And now, really? You think he wants to go back to his ex-wife after all these years?"

"That's the problem. They didn't break up because they fell out of love. Maxwell really loved her. She just dumped him out of the blue." I stopped pacing. He was as naïve as I was. What if she really did want him back? Would she use the kids to get her way? I didn't know anything about her.

"I think you need to speak with him. When do his children leave?" Bri asked.

"Sunday afternoon."

"Call him after they leave," Bri said. "I hate to do this to you, but I have to go to work now. I'm in the parking lot. I'll meet you for drinks tonight. Eric and I don't have any plans, but I don't know when I'll get out and it will probably be late. This new job is killing me."

"Jeez, Bri. Working on a Saturday night. What does Eric say about it?"

She laughed. "You don't want to know."

I smiled in spite of myself. Don't we all have something? "You're right. I'll call Maxwell after his kids are gone."

I felt so alone after my call to Bri. The weekend dragged. My friends and family could have kept me company, but I wasn't in the mood to explain myself, so I stayed on my own. I hoped Bri would manage to get out of work early and meet for drinks like she'd promised. But as the hours passed, I realized she'd been held up.

Close to midnight, my younger son, Chad, called. I hadn't seen him for almost a year. He was due to be transferred soon from Kaneohe Bay in Hawaii to Stateside, and I couldn't wait to see him again.

"Mama Bear! How are you?"

I could just see that lopsided grin of his. "Much happier now, hearing from my favorite number two son." Elated to hear his voice, I sat up in bed and took a sip of water from the nightstand.

"Hey, I got a favor to ask."

"Anything, honey."

"Remember you said that. What did you think of the pictures of Tucker I messaged you?"

"Oh, he's just adorable. He's a Newfoundland, right? How old is he?"

"Well, Mama Bear, yes he's a Newfoundland and he's six months old. I need someone to take care of him while I'm overseas."

"What? Where overseas?" I stuttered.

"Kuwait."

I took a deep breath.

"I'll be at your house in a few days with Tucker. If you can't take him, I'll have to make other arrangements. But you'll love him, and he'll keep you company."

Jesus, the things a mother will do to see her son.

*

Sunday was overcast, which matched my mood. The thrill of speaking with Chad had subsided, replaced by a growing anxiety. I hadn't heard from Maxwell yet. The man who always calls—hadn't. Around eleven a.m., I put on my running shoes and gear and went out for a brisk run. I left my cell phone home. *I'll show him.*

By noon, my sour mood worsened when I returned to the house and saw Maxwell hadn't called. Antsy, I showered and left to run some errands. My phone never rang.

That's it! I called him. No answer. Maybe they're still at the airport.

I left him a message. "Hi, Maxwell. Surprised I haven't heard from you. I hope all is going well with your children. Maybe we can get together tonight after they leave? Give me a call."

By five p.m. I was hyper-cleaning my home to relieve my stress. I even cleaned out the garage. *Damn it.* He'd made me love him.

At eleven that night my cell phone finally buzzed.

"Did I wake you?" Maxwell began. "Kids had a late flight. Sorry to be calling at this hour."

"How was the rest of your visit?" My calm tone belied the frustration screaming at the back of my mind.

"Tough," he replied. "The divorce is still hard on them."

"It's been eight years," I replied, a little too tersely. My sons gave up their quest of getting my ex and I back together after the first year. Why in the world were Maxwell's kids still pressuring them?

"I know. It's just that . . . the divorce really rocked their world."

"Maxwell, it rocks everyone's world. And throwing hissy fits because they aren't getting what they want after eight years is simply ridiculous." I paused to calm myself down.

"Well," he said, his voice booming. "I don't see my kids throwing hissy fits. I realize your sons were able to accept the divorce, but that doesn't mean all children can." He softened his voice. "It's complicated."

I squeezed my phone. "What does that mean?"

"Nothing. Everything. Let's talk when we're both not so tired. Let's grab dinner this week."

What the hell? "When? What's so complicated?"

"Good night, Charlotte."

I clicked off. How long would I have to wait to find out what "complicated" meant?

Chapter 7

AVA

CALIENTE

I STARED OUT THE airplane window as we descended. The closer we got, the more pronounced the devastation appeared. It was six weeks after Hurricane Maria, but it looked like it had swept through yesterday. As we landed, I saw debris everywhere. How was my eighty-three-year-old mother dealing with this?

I had received a message from nurse Juanita Capo that my mother was okay just two days after the storm. Juanita explained that she could call because she could tap into a weak cell signal from the hospital roof. She said a lot of people had taken refuge there. She had written down all their names and contact numbers and was trying to reach as many families as possible. We felt lucky knowing our mother was alive and uninjured, especially compared to families who had no communication at all those first few weeks.

As I drove from the airport to my mother's home, it was obvious that not much had been cleared off the roads since the hurricane weeks ago. Some streets were littered with trees and wreckage, while others were impassable. It took the cabdriver nearly two and a half hours to reach my mother's home, normally a half-hour drive. I had waited a few more weeks after commercial flights began again to ensure that I could actually reach her home. I can only imagine what it looked like right after the storm. Why was the cleanup taking so long? My stomach started roiling and I gripped the door's armrest tightly. I should have come sooner, not listened to my mother. But I'd spoken to her every day after cell service resumed and she never complained. She sounded as if the hurricane had never hit.

We finally arrived. I jumped out of the cab, yelling. *"Mami, mami . . ."*

Mami whipped around the side of the house in a dirty apron with her hair pinned up and a bucket of chicken feed in her hand. "Ava, shush, you are scaring the chickens. What's all the commotion for?"

I threw my arms around her, almost knocking us both over in the process.

"Ava, *por favor, me vas a romper.* Stop."

"Sorry. I can't believe how long it took to get here from San Juan. Those roads! What is going on here? Do you have electricity, running water?" Words rushed out of my mouth so fast that I barely registered what I was saying. I walked to the porch and flicked on a light. Nothing. "Why didn't you tell me you have no electricity? That's it. Pack a bag. You're coming with me home to New Jersey."

"No. *Basta.*" She shook her head, turned, and walked to the back of the house, singing to the chickens. "Go home, Ava."

I looked at the ground and inhaled a few deep breaths. I should have known better. You can't tell my mother anything. She must decide for herself. But the shock of seeing the island firsthand had made me forget how to handle her. I put my bag in the house and surveyed the damage. The house itself, constructed of concrete cinder blocks, was in good shape. A few of the terra cotta roof tiles had flown off, but the roof looked like it had held and I didn't see any water damage. The property, however, was a mess. Trees down and debris strewn everywhere. I changed into a pair of shorts and a tank top and found my mother in the backyard.

"Were you scared when the hurricane hit, *Mami*?" I asked, picking up a few branches by the back door.

"Of course, but Gabriel brought us to the hospital to ride out the storm. He's such a fine man. Can't wait for you to see him again."

Mothers. I must remind myself not to do this to my daughter. "When did you come back home?"

"Gabriel checked out both places first and brought us back home two days later. He comes to his mother's every night. He rides a scooter and knows where all the detours are and usually gets here in about half an hour." *Mami* continued to spread the feed and murmured to the chickens. "I don't have electricity, but Gabriel brought a gas generator for his parents' home a few years ago. He brings gas when he can and food from the hospital. Don't worry, lots of people are helping out."

Don't worry, she says. "*Mami*, this is uninhabitable. Please come home with me until the worst of this is over. Please?" I begged.

"I'm fine. I don't want to leave. I miss my novellas shows and the news, but otherwise it hasn't been so bad."

Ugh. "I'm gonna start clearing those branches away in the front. Where should I put them?"

"Ava, it's okay. It will get done. Why don't we go see Lola next door and have a cold drink?"

My tank top was soaked through already from the humidity and I had only moved a single tree branch. I'd forgotten how humid it was here. "Okay, let's go."

Lola lived next door. Each house sat on about two acres, half of which was wooded, giving the homes some privacy. Rolling hills fell away from the front and back of each property, providing beautiful views of the sunrise and sunset. You could see the ocean in the distance from the front yard.

The generator at Lola's was noisy, but it kept the refrigerator running and we had *Mavi*. It tasted like heaven—it had been a long time since I'd had some.

*

I woke up several times covered in sweat, unaccustomed to sleeping without air conditioning. Around three a.m. I left my bed to look out the small window. The moon shone like a huge, illuminated globe. A slight breeze drifted up from the ocean, gently rustling the curtains. Breathing in the air sweetened by the sea gave me a sense of peace. It also helped cool me down.

As I watched the trees swaying gently in the breeze, I thought back to the first time I'd talked to Mami after the hurricane. I remembered the moment she uttered my name.

"¡Mami! ¿Estás bien?" I'd panted, tears welling in my eyes. Hearing her voice released the fear that had built up since the hurricane hit the island. It had been torture, not being able to speak directly to her. Of course, she was cheery, happy to hear from me, asking about the kids, never mentioning the devastating storm she'd just lived through.

"Si," Mami answered when I asked her directly how things were there. "La casa está bien." There's no electric or water. Lola's son takes care of us. He's a doctor.

I was terrified she didn't have enough food or water. And instead of focusing on what was important, she wasted time telling me that her best friend's son is a doctor. "¡Mami!" I interrupted her. "Do you have enough to eat and drink?"

"Si," Mami switched to English. "Gabriel comes every night from the hospital. He's a good son. And so handsome. Aye, ya, yai!"

"That's great, Mami. I'm glad you have someone that can help. But you didn't answer me: Do you have enough to eat and drink?"

"Si." Mami said. I could almost see her shrugging as she continued to praise Lola's son, the doctor.

Mami weathered the storm as she did most things with brave determination. She was still a force to be reckoned with. Leaving the window to return to bed, I heard a rooster crowing. I knew those blasted roosters would crow intermittently all night long. *Mami* was used to their racket, but I wasn't and reached for a pair of ear plugs, grateful I had brought them. Finally sleep took hold and I slipped into its peaceful embrace.

*

Commotion woke me. The ear plugs had fallen out during the night and I heard my mother singing, probably to those damn chickens. I turned over, covering my head with the pillow. The noise of the generator filtered through, and sporadic pounding noise made any further sleep impossible.

Grabbing a towel, I headed into the bathroom. I turned on the faucet and—nothing. Shit, I forgot. No running water. I looked in the mirror. My hair was at grease level 1, so I could hold off for another day or so. But damn, I'd better find some way to clean up soon. I threw on shorts and a top.

My mother's kitchen was small with a beautiful blue and yellow patterned tile on the floor, cool on my bare feet. I could smell the coffee from my bedroom. *Mami* must have brought a pot of coffee over from Lola's. Her coffee was always the best. *Mami* even left some steamed milk out for me. I heard my mom's singsong voice coming from the backyard. I went out and saw Lola, my mother, and a man I assumed was Gabriel. Mom had been right. I didn't mind admitting it. This was not the gangly teen I'd known thirty plus years ago.

Black curly hair with a sheen on his athletic bare chest, he raised an ax high over his head and brought it down with ferocity. *Ah, that's the pounding.* He looked more like an ad for *Muscle & Fitness* magazine than he did a doctor as he split the wood from the fallen branches and trees in his mother's backyard.

Mami grabbed my arm and pulled me over to Lola's. "Gabriel! Gabriel!" she yelled.

Her enthusiasm embarrassed me, and I felt a flush rise to my cheeks.

He looked up, put down the ax and walked toward us.

"Gabriel, this is my daughter, Ava. You know, the one I've told you about." *Mami* beamed.

I wanted to run back into the house and hide in my room. "*Mami*, please." I spoke directly to her, giving her my most disapproving look, the one my kids call the *stink eye*. I turned to face Gabriel. I noticed his soft bronze eyes and full lips. I stretched my hand out. "It's good to see you again. What's it been? Thirty years?" Both sets of maternal eyes were watching us. I ignored them. "Thank you for taking such good care of *Mami*."

Gabriel wiped his hand on a cloth he grabbed from a back pocket and shook mine. "It's nice to see you again. It's been a long time, but your mom has told me all about you."

I cringed. Jesus, she's been trying to set me up since high school. "Sorry—mothers. What can I say?"

He chuckled.

"Can I help with something? My mother insists everything is just fine." I glanced over my shoulder at her. "But from what I've seen, Puerto Rico is a disaster."

He nodded. "You're right. Cleanup is at a snail's pace. Basic needs aren't being met. It's unbelievable in this day and age." He crossed his arms over his chest.

Mami and Lola laughed behind us. Was it at us? Or the situation?

"I brought food from the hospital," Gabriel added. "Please go get something to eat from our house. I'll be done in a few minutes."

I thanked him and headed to Lola's house. My mother and her friend grinned at me like two Cheshire cats.

Lola was the main reason *Mami* hadn't come back to New Jersey after *Papi* died. They were best of friends growing up together on the island. My dad became good friends with her husband, Peter Ruiz.

When an adjoining lot with a small house went up for sale ten years earlier, the Ruizs convinced my parents to buy it. My parents moved there after *Papi* retired.

The couples only had four wonderful years together as friends and next-door neighbors before Lola's husband died. My father passed shortly thereafter.

After *Papi's* funeral, my brother and sisters tried to get *Mami* to move back to New Jersey. But she loved her life on the island and wanted to stay with her dearest friend, who suffered from arthritis. The two of them shared the heartache of losing their husbands. Consoling one another, they gardened together, fed their chickens, and gossiped about some island trifle.

Both women kept grinning at me as I consumed my breakfast. At first, I was embarrassed by their obvious amusement, then angry, then I found it hilarious and started laughing. That made *Mami* and Lola howl.

"What's so funny?" Gabriel asked as he entered the house.

That made us laugh even harder.

Mami heated up the rest of the breakfast Gabriel had brought home. She ushered him into a chair, piling an enormous mound of scrambled eggs and ham on his plate with a side of cooked tostones. "We are being silly women. Don't mind us," she said, sliding a cup of coffee toward him.

I settled down, asking how injured people were coping with no basic services.

"The volunteers are getting supplies out to people. The worst injuries remain in the hospital. But plenty of people are suffering from the lack of mobility and all the shortages."

"How long have you been a doctor here?" I asked.

"I'm a trauma surgeon working in Manhattan, but every year I spend a few weeks with Doctors Without Borders and then rotate back to my normal schedule at New York–Presbyterian."

His mother interrupted, glowing with pride. "Yes, he's such a fine doctor that he travels everywhere, healing the sick!"

Gabriel patted his mother's hand. "I just happened to be visiting Mom when we heard the news that a big hurricane had formed in the Atlantic and was headed our way. I was set to fly back the day the storm hit. I called my supervisor in New York and told her that no flights were leaving, and I'd come home when I could."

"But how are you still here?"

He wiped his mouth and sipped his coffee. "I'm on a leave of absence from the hospital right now. They're used to me taking a few weeks each year, usually vacation time, and volunteering with Doctors Without Borders." He paused, looking up from his scrambled eggs. "There are a few of us that assist in other countries and the hospital has been incredibly supportive. I'll be going back in a week or so."

"My Ava volunteers with Sister Mary Joseph and Aiding the Children." Mami grasped my hand, her face beaming. "They bring children from all over the world who need lifesaving surgeries."

Gabriel put his fork down, sitting back in his seat, studying me with a hint of a smile pulling at his lips. My eyes caught in his gaze.

Unnerved, I could feel warmth blossom in my cheeks and hoped he didn't notice it.

I looked away and cleared my throat, shifting into business mode. "Forget that *Mami*, did you hear what Gabriel said? He is going back to New York. You need to come home with me. Lola, you can come with us, too, until the electric, water and gas are back."

Both women exploded in Spanish. Gabriel stood up and laughed. Heading out the kitchen door he said, "Good luck with that."

Didn't he understand? I couldn't leave my mother here like this. How could he leave his mom? I had to get back home. My business was being handled temporarily by a friend who is a broker for her own small independent company. She had agreed to do it as a huge favor. I couldn't ask her to keep doing it indefinitely.

Lola and my mother were still exchanging rapid-fire Spanish, so I went outside to talk with Gabriel. "How can you leave her here with no power or water?"

"I'm told power should be restored in this area soon." He picked up the ax. "I'll be here for another week or so. Of course, I'm worried, but I must get back to work in New York. I'll have family members look in on her and ask them to check on your mother also."

"But . . ."

"Unless I bodily pick her up kicking and screaming, my mother won't come to New York with me."

Ugh. I knew this fight all too well from my own mother. Now what? I turned back to the house, hearing the first *thud* as the ax hit.

*

Two days later, the moms, Gabriel, and I went to town. I had gone in earlier with him and purchased another scooter so we could take both mothers with us. While Gabriel checked in at the hospital, I called my office. I told them cell service was still spotty but was improving in the San Juan area and beyond.

I hoped the scooters would help our mothers travel until the roads were repaired and the gas shortages resolved. The bikes didn't need a lot of gas, which was in shorter supply than a few weeks before. Whoever was handling the recovery was doing a poor job. What a damn mess the island was!

My mother caught on faster to driving the scooter than I did. Settled in behind her, I let her continue driving the last mile into town.

Chef José Andrés had come to Puerto Rico to feed the masses. God bless him. He set up food stations in many of the towns so people could have a hot meal. His vast pots of paella were astonishing.

After enjoying that hearty meal, local musicians played merengue, salsa, and bachata on the opposite side of the square and many people began dancing. One thing was for sure, Puerto Ricans can make merry no matter what!

Our mothers saw neighbors they hadn't seen in a while and ran to hug and kiss them.

I spied Gabriel changing a young boy's bandage while answering questions from his parents. He caught me looking and winked.

As ravaged as the place was, the spirit and beauty that poured out of the people in the square that night totally convinced me that Puerto Rico will be okay. It might take time, but Puerto Ricans have the basic qualities needed to rebuild, ingrained in their character and their essence. Lola and *Mami* grabbed me and we danced around the square until the moon rose, bright and full.

Chapter 8

BRIANNA

I ARRIVED EARLY AT Oscar's. No one had volunteered to host book club and I just couldn't face it this month. The hostess informed me our table wouldn't be ready for another fifteen minutes.

I strolled up to the bar humming a tune, my spirits soaring after working a day without Nicole in the office. I ordered a pinot grigio and waited for the book club members to arrive.

What a pleasant day it had been. I had finished all my work by lunch for the first time since I'd started working. I kicked back and absorbed the energetic vibe of the place. Without Nicole scowling, everyone at the office was happy all day, talking and laughing. I even heard music coming from the lunchroom.

Madeline arrived right on time.

My good mood persisted, and I beamed at her. "Our table isn't ready. Sit and have a drink."

Madeline looked around the bar, scowling. "Of course. They're all late." She motioned to the bartender. "I'll have what she's having." She looked at me. "Pinot grigio?"

I nodded.

"How's that job going?" she asked, settling herself on a stool.

"Not so good. I just don't seem to do anything right. Ever!" I said, exasperated. "Let's not talk about it. I actually had a good day for once and want to hang on to my happy mood."

Madeline smiled. "Fair enough."

"What's happening with you?"

Madeline glanced around the bar and the restaurant before answering. "Did you ever get a feeling that something isn't right?"

"Of course. Every day now."

Madeline grinned, then turned serious. "My parents were alcoholics."

My eyes widened and I put my glass down.

"When you're the child of alcoholics you learn things that most people never do." Madeline sipped her wine, looking straight ahead at the glasses behind the bar. "You learn patterns." She paused, her voice emotionless, even clinical.

"I'm so sorry, Madeline. I never knew." I turned toward her. "All this time you never said anything."

Madeline waved her hand dismissively. "It was a lifetime ago and I didn't see the need to talk about it. But I learned how to watch my parents and judge every gesture, every word, every reaction. And I figured out different predictable patterns. So, when my father came home, I'd watch from my bedroom window to see how he got out of the car, which he parked in the backyard. If he stumbled and wobbled, he'd fall asleep within a half hour. If his face was tight and his fists were clenched, I'd take my brother out the front door and we'd stay in the woods for hours until we knew he'd stop screaming. We knew it was safe when the lights in the kitchen were out."

"Oh my God, Madeline! Clenched fists? Did he beat you?" I couldn't believe what she was telling me. "Where was your mother? Your other family members?" I was having trouble staying in my seat. I wanted to get up and throw my arms around her.

"Please don't!" Madeline raised her hand in a stop sign.

I had so many questions I wanted to ask, but I tightened my lips on them.

"I don't need a therapy session. I'm telling you this for a reason. Just listen." She took a deep breath. "When I get to know a person, I naturally zone in on their patterns. It's like an emotional radar. Take you, Bri, I could tell within the first few seconds of being here that you were in a happy mood. Your shoulders are up and back, your eyes are wide open, you were bouncing to the music coming through the speakers. I could go on, but . . ."

"Like mind reading," I said.

"No. Nothing like that. We all behave in certain ways at certain times. I call them patterns." Madeline's brows furrowed. "Please don't tell the other women. I don't want any pity. I'm fine. It was a long time ago." She looked at me. "I only mentioned it, so you'd understand why I feel something is off."

"Okay. You mean with me? I'm not happy with my boss, so maybe I'm not acting how I usually do."

"No, no, no. It's not you. It's Stan's friend, David. I'm seeing subtle nuances in his behavior that he's never exhibited before. Something is different and it's unnerving."

"Wow. I don't know where to begin." I touched her arm. "Have you gone through therapy?"

"Bri, please stop asking me inane questions. Don't make me regret telling you." Madeline drank her wine. "I don't want to revisit that time in my life. Forget I said anything."

"I'm sorry. I won't push. If you ever want to talk about it, I'm here." I never in a million years would have suspected Madeline had anything other than a charmed life. "My childhood was also messed up. Not as bad as yours, probably, but I'm here if you ever want to talk." Speaking about childhood brought thoughts of my father into my mind. He left me with my mother's parents when I was so young. Told me I'd be better off. Madeline's not the only one who felt abandoned.

Stupid as I am, I still hoped he'd track me down one day. But he never had.

I shook the thoughts out of my mind and returned my attention to Madeline who was talking to the bartender. Impulsively, I reached over and hugged her deeply, not caring if she pushed me away.

Patting my leg, she pulled away from my embrace.

"Well, it feels good to say something out loud anyway. My honed-in radar is pinging, but there's nothing I can do about it. This feeling . . . Stan thinks I'm crazy, but mark my words . . ."

"Ladies, your table is ready." A young girl motioned for us to follow.

"Where is the rest of book club?" Madeline asked.

Clearly, any further discussion about her childhood was over. "I don't know."

We looked at the menu. Our waitress brought water and asked when the others would be joining us.

"Soon, I hope." I texted all of them.

Madeline drummed her fingers on the table. "This is soooo rude!"

"Let it go. We'll have a lovely dinner together. It doesn't matter."

Madeline started to say something but stopped. "Well, I'm hungry and I'm ordering."

"Me, too," I said. We both relaxed and asked our waiter for another wine.

Halfway through our dinner Staci showed up.

"I'm so sorry I'm late," she said, sliding onto the chair next to me. "I loved the book and just had to get here to talk about it."

"You're an hour late. I can't wait to hear your excuse." Madeline put her fork down and stared at Staci.

Staci shrugged. "Jeez, take it easy. Everybody's a little late now and then."

Madeline grunted. "You're always late."

"Look, I'm sorry. I was talking with John. I haven't spoken with him all week and he's coming here in a few days and . . . well . . . ."

I nodded. "It's okay. Are you excited?"

"Yes. No. I'm a nervous wreck." Staci motioned for the waitress and ordered a glass of wine and a salad. "Did Charlotte tell you about us going out together? Wasn't that . . . ?"

Madeline interrupted her, holding up her phone. "We all got the video."

I laughed.

"I have no idea how Charlotte dealt with the single scene as long as she did. It was horrible." Staci leaned forward and almost knocked over my wineglass. "I mean, we had a good time together, but as far as meeting Mr. Right, it was all wrong."

"Oh, come on, you can't judge by one night out." I held on to the stem of my glass.

"Yuck," she uttered. "In any event, John is coming down from Vermont to visit me. It will be the first time we've seen one another since June."

"That's great. Maybe we can meet him." I turned to look at Madeline, who was staring out the window. I tapped her on the shoulder.

"What?" Madeline jerked her head toward us.

"Did you like the book?" I asked, trying to keep things calm.

"Oh good. Let's talk about the book. I loooved it," Staci sang.

Madeline looked at Staci, then back at me. "Where the hell is everyone else?"

"Oh, hold on." I grabbed my phone and looked through the text messages.

"Okay. Ava is still in Puerto Rico." I scrolled further down. "Charlotte wasn't up for it tonight. And Hanna's getting her home ready for her parents to move to and dealing with Ashley." I could almost hear the wheels turning in Madeline's head.

"All understandable reasons except that they didn't let you know. You had to track them down." Madeline stood and threw her napkin on the chair. "I'm going to the ladies' room."

"Yikes, what's up her butt?" Staci grimaced.

I sighed, shrugging. "I'm not sure."

When Madeline returned, she seemed more relaxed. "Bri, I agree with Staci. *Little Fires Everywhere* was exceptionally good. Beautiful prose and a deeply felt story. It's just too bad we don't have all of the book club here to discuss it."

Excitedly, Staci turned toward her but knocked her glass against her plate causing a loud clink. "Oops. Sorry. Wasn't it sad that the daughter left like that?"

"Why don't we hold this book over till our next meeting so we can all talk about it?" I cajoled. "I'll assign another anyway, but this book is worth a discussion."

"What are you going to do if they don't show up next time? Keep holding it over?" Madeline hissed.

"I'll let the girls know you missed them tonight," I said, appealing to her with a look.

"Fine." Madeline subsided.

"I've been thinking of inviting someone else into our book club now that Tess has decided to stay at the shore for the next few months. Maybe even more than one person. What do you think?" I asked.

Madeline held up a hand. "I'll screen them. I'll make sure they show up."

I started laughing first, followed by Staci.

Even Madeline smirked as she grabbed her coat. "I've got an early appointment tomorrow. Sorry to run out on you both."

I stayed, waiting for Staci to finish her last bites.

"Madeline's right, of course, but her delivery is so severe," Staci offered.

"She tries to control everything and sometimes you can't."

My phone vibrated as I waited for my car. *Damn! It could only be one person. Yup. Nicole. It's 9:45 p.m., for God's sake.* I didn't answer. I needed the last few minutes of this wonderful night before I was ready to deal with her. I decided to call on my way home. When her contempt of me might be offset by the two glasses of wine I had earlier. *Maybe I should bring a bottle into the office.*

Chapter 9

MADELINE

INDEED

S TAN WAS WATCHING TV in our bedroom when I got home from book club. "How was your evening?" he asked.

"These women are so rude. I just can't take it anymore. I don't care what Bri thinks. I'll be right back. I'm going to send out an e-mail tonight," I growled, heading down the hall into my office.

"Maybe you should calm down before you send an e-mail out?" Stan shouted after me.

"No!"

Hanna, Ava, and Charlotte:
You're a sorry-ass bunch of women. Bri works hard to keep this little book club going. Why is it so hard for you to do what is expected when an invitation is sent out? Just respond!

I've heard all of you complain about people not RSVPing to your events. Why is this different? Because it's every month? The least you could do is let Bri know whether you are coming or not! We had a table for six tonight and Bri and I and eventually

Staci who was late as usual, sat there waiting for you to show up. Finally, we went ahead and ordered. The waitress wanted to know "if the others were coming" and Bri had to text you to find out. Really!!!

You all know book club happens every month on the second Thursday. Mark it on your calendars! And Bri even sends out two e-mails to remind you. Stop waiting to see if you get a better invite.

Bri asked the two of us who showed up if we wanted to add new members to book club. I'm a definite on adding new members. But first I'm giving them a quiz to check their manners. You all failed!

Chapter 10

HANNA

FISH AND HOUSEGUESTS

M Y STOMACH CHURNED as I paced in the waiting room, waiting for Ashley's treatment to be over. When I'd arrived at her home this morning, Mom and Dad had looked exhausted. I told them I would take Ashley for her treatment so they could get some rest. Surprisingly, my mother didn't argue.

Our parents had flown to New Jersey as soon as they'd heard about my sister's diagnosis. They'd been staying at Ashley's for about a month. Mark and I had offered to host them, as we had more space and weren't far from Ashley and Josh's. With Ashley's improved condition my parents agreed to move to us this weekend. Mark and I were now converting the newly-renovated-hobby room into a bedroom for them.

It was a shame they'd barely had a chance to enjoy California after having moved there from Illinois when Dad retired. But there was no way our parents could stay away if one of us was sick. They'll go back to the sunny west coast as soon as my sister goes into remission. *God, I hope she goes into remission.*

"Hanna," Ashley called from the chemo treatment room. "I'm done."

"Oh." I ran into the room and gently placed my hand on her shoulder. "Are you feeling okay? I'll get the car and drive you home right away."

Ashley smiled. "Relax. I won't feel the effects until later today or tomorrow."

If these weekly treatments were this draining on me, I couldn't imagine what my sister was going through. We're lucky that Dad is a retired doctor. He answered the thousand questions we all had every day. While Dad's calming manner always made us feel better, mom's nervous energy had the opposite effect.

I'd been working to organize my home for their arrival. I knew it had better be in tip-top shape.

*

"Honey, can we fit a queen-size bed in here?" I called to Mark as he walked by the room.

"Let's measure to be sure."

I rummaged around and found a small retractable tape measure. I handed one end to Mark.

"Yes, it will fit." He released the tape. "I guess we have to buy them a bed."

"I don't think two seventy-year-olds want to retire each night in a sleeping bag. So yes, we have to buy them a bed."

Mark laughed. "When are they moving here again?"

I collected the last of the remaining canvases and paints to store in the basement. There went my studio. "Saturday. We need to get a bed today while you're around. I hope they can deliver it by the weekend."

"Any idea how long they will be staying with us?"

I turned to him, surprised. "Well, I imagine until Ashley's stable and feeling like she doesn't need so much extra help. Why? Are you having second thoughts?"

Mark paused and seemed to be carefully considering his words before speaking. "No, not at all. These are special circumstances. It's just, you know, the rule."

"Yes, I know I've heard it our entire marriage. 'Fish and company begin to stink after three days.' Any longer than that and you are encroaching on one another's space." I punched him in the arm. "Funny, the rule doesn't seem to apply when we are staying with *your* friends and family."

He smiled, rubbing his arm. "Like I said, these are special circumstances. Better call your parents first and ask what type of mattress they prefer. Hard? Soft? There are so many different choices. And you know your mother."

Boy, do I ever. Heading to the basement with my hands full, I wondered what it would be like to live with my parents again, especially my mother. They would be at Ashley's a lot, but still . . . .

*

Slogging through my e-mails the next morning, I found one from Bri reminding everyone about last night's book club. *Shit!* I felt bad that I had forgotten all about it until Bri texted me last night. A message from Madeline caught my eye. I read it with my mouth open.

I couldn't believe it. What a bitch! Right or not, was that any way to address your friends? I know I shouldn't do this but the hell with it . . .

Reply
Madeline: You must be kidding! I'm helping my critically ill sister and rearranging my home for my parents to move in and you send me this nasty e-mail? Really???
You should take your own advice and learn some manners.

*

My parents arrived bright and early Saturday morning. The kids were at sleepovers and Mark got called in to work, so I was the only one home to greet them. Their room was ready, and the bed had been delivered yesterday for a hefty fee, but it was worth it. I had cleared out half of the hallway bathroom cabinets and one shelf in the linen closet for them. Thankfully, since they only had two large bags each, there was plenty of room.

Mother insisted we go to the grocery store and pick up their essentials. She liked everything to be in order.

"Of course, Mom. Let me get my purse."

Mom looked in the pantry. "I'll need some space here also," she yelled after me. "What a mess. No matter. I'll organize it."

Ugh. And so it begins—back living with Mom!

After we returned from the store and found room for my parents' provisions, I drove them to Ashley's. She was on the couch under a blanket, reading. Her color was good, and she was thrilled to see us.

I took a deep breath and my body relaxed. This is what our family needed, to be together—to care for one another.

While they talked, I went into the kitchen and emptied onto the counter the large paper bag I had brought. It contained the killer lasagna and a Caesar salad I'd picked up from Scarlatti the night before. It was one of our special Italian restaurants.

Mom, entering the kitchen, shrieked, "What is that?" Her gaze was frosty. "Your sister is deathly ill." She lowered her voice. "And you feed her processed food? Throw it out now!" She took the aluminum container and opened the cabinet where the garbage bins were.

"Whoa. Stop right there." I touched her shoulder. "That is a freshly made meal from our favorite restaurant." I took the tray from her. "There are no preservatives in it. I wanted to surprise Ashley with her favorite meal. Jeez, chill out, Mom!"

Thwarted, she lingered by the bins. "Well, how do you know what's really in that?" She pointed to the lasagna.

"Mom, it's fresh, not frozen. And it's actually better than yours." I turned on the oven, wondering why I had made that last remark. After all, I knew better.

Mom opened her mouth, then just huffed out of the kitchen.

After caring for Ashley and feeding her family dinner, I went home. I brought the leftover lasagna, fed Mark and the kids, and made sure homework got done. Later that night, Mom insisted we watch a family-friendly show together. It was too much for one day. Exhausted, I wanted nothing more than to read in bed and pass out. But I sat down with the family in the living room.

Brandon grabbed the remote and clicked on *Supernatural*.

"Mom, Brandon put a show on he knows he's not allowed to watch!" Katie yelled. She seized the remote from her brother and clicked through the channels. She stopped on *Sofia the First*, a sweet Disney princess movie. "There, that's better."

"Yuk." Brandon sank into the couch, putting one of the throw pillows over his face.

I stood to take the control from Katie when my mother grabbed it out of her hands, shaking her head. "What was that dreadful show Brandon put on? Did you see those skimpy outfits on those girls? Hanna, you let them watch this trash?"

Mark coughed, probably to stifle a laugh.

"Mom, just pick a show you like." I strode into the kitchen to make popcorn and escape the line of fire.

The kids kept bickering, their voices louder than the microwave.

"Children!" Mom shouted. "Stop that squabbling right now. I'll pick something."

I could feel the kids' eyes rolling.

When I returned with a bowl of overflowing popcorn, I noticed Mom had switched to that channel that shows rerun programming from the 1960s with *Gunsmoke*, *The Virginian*, and *Perry Mason*. The look on the kids' faces was priceless as we all settled in to watch an episode of *The Big Valley*. I had to stifle my own laugh.

A couple of minutes of blessed peace was followed by: "What's this dark yellow gob on the popcorn?"

"I believe it's called butter." I shifted in my seat, jabbing Mark in the side.

Mom examined the kernel in her hand. "This isn't butter. It's an additive. Hanna, what have I taught you all these years?"

Wow. And it's only Day 1.

*

A few days later Mark left on a business trip. The lucky bastard.

Even though I had to endure daily lectures on my many faults as my mother, father, and I prepared fresh meals, cleaned both homes, and helped with kids' homework, I also now had two built-in, free babysitters. I took advantage and signed up for a five-night community college art course held once a week. I also continued the weekday morning walk I took with some mothers in my neighborhood after our kids caught the morning bus for school.

Amanda and Laura, my walking-buddy neighbors, had watched me struggle walking both of my huge dogs and asked me to join them. One condition, though—no dogs. Laura was highly allergic. I agreed, despite the fact that meant taking the dogs out later in the day.

I looked forward to our walk every weekday morning. The exercise and conversation were just what I needed and of course it was also an hour free of my mother's nagging.

"Hanna, you look like you lost some weight," Amanda commented one morning soon after Mark had left on his trip.

I looked at my stomach. I don't know why I do that. Every time someone mentions weight loss, I immediately look at my stomach. "Thanks. It's due to my mother and her obsessive meal planning. The time and effort she puts into every meal is unbelievable." I was

starting to feel winded. My stamina had faded since I'd been helping Ashley and had stopped running. Hell, I'd run five miles every
other day this past summer. You'd think I'd be in better shape. *Age
is creeping up on me.*

Taking a deep breath, I said, "My mom is a food fanatic. Did I
ever tell you? She's never eaten a potato chip!"

"What? No way!" Amanda shook her head. "She must have had
a few as a child. She just doesn't remember. There's no way that she
never had a potato chip."

Laura agreed. "Let's hook her up to a lie detector."

We all laughed.

"Seriously. Mom is neurotically fixated about what she puts into
her mouth. Come over for lunch one day. You'll see."

They said in unison, "No thanks."

We laughed again and turned back. It felt good to blow off
steam with them.

"I've noticed your dad walking those massive beasts of yours,"
Laura said. "That must be a nice break."

"It is. He's just amazing." I turned to face her. "He could stay
with us forever. It's Mom that's the problem."

"'Problem'?" Amanda whipped around. "Speaking of problems, did you hear Jim Snyder's wife is suing him for custody of
Gracie?" She looked like the cat that caught the mouse. Amanda
lived for gossip.

Hearing Jim's name made me stumble, but I quickly regained my
pace. I didn't think they noticed. I've tried hard not to think about
Jim, especially with everything going on with Ashley. "I thought she
left with some guy she had the affair with. Went to Florida?" I was
stunned by the news. Poor Jim.

"I guess she wants her daughter to move to Florida. It makes
sense, doesn't it? I couldn't live in another state away from my children, could you?" Laura said.

"But she was the one who left. Not Jim. I don't understand. If she wants custody, she should be forced to come back here." My anger sizzled at how unfair it was. Unfair to Jim.

Amanda tilted her head. "Why do you care?"

Shit! I tried to mask my irritation. I didn't want either of them to know I felt this way. "Jim's just a really nice guy. He was Katie's soccer coach and my running coach." I panted, winded.

"Oh, I didn't know you knew him. Tell us what he's like," Amanda probed.

"He's really nice. He told me that Marci left with the contractor who was working on their house—and never looked back." I took a deep, replenishing breath. "He was great coaching the kids and the small running team he put together in town. He really encouraged us."

"So, you'd take his side over his wife's? Seriously?" Amanda started to walk faster.

"Hey, don't make this a sister thing! I'm just saying what he told me." I picked up speed, finally feeling warmed up and getting my second wind.

Laura pointed to a small hill up ahead. "Let's go there and circle around and head home."

I thought back to the summer and Jim. How we had become good friends. And how everything had changed that day on the beach when he kissed me. How close we'd come to giving in to our feelings. "Great." My stomach ached and I was tired of hiding how upset I was for Jim.

*

My walking buddies spent the entire week talking nonstop about Jim and Marci's marital problems. By Friday, I'd had enough. I feigned a pulled muscle and limped home after the bus left. I waited a few minutes in the garage and then got into my car and drove. No destination—just away. Away from the gossip and my mother both.

I drove around and thought of Jim. Before I realized it, I was in the parking lot of the fitness center where he worked. I turned the car off and sat there. All these conversations about him and Marci had shifted Jim to the front of my mind again. I didn't pine for him, but I did want to tell him how sorry I was about the custody case. I knew how much he loved his daughter and how great a dad he was. He didn't deserve this. I stared at the large two-story windows of the center, trying to decide if I had the guts to enter. But I did nothing. Just stayed stuck there as if in a fog. Finally, it dawned on me I'd been sitting there for an hour. *What the hell am I thinking?* I shook myself out of my stupor and drove to Ashley's.

I met my parents at my sister's house and assisted with the daily routine of cleaning, cooking and helping the kids. Mark would be home this afternoon from his business trip. I wondered if I should tell him about that kiss with Jim. I felt such guilt over it. I wondered what my book club buddies would say. Maybe I should ask Bri what she thinks. *Ugh!* Then I'd have to tell her the whole damn story. No, I don't want to venture into that hornet's nest. Maybe I'll look for a book about an affair and suggest we read it in book club. By talking about the plotline, I'd find out how everyone feels without anyone suspecting me.

*

That night, Mark and I were getting ready to go out to dinner alone. Mark showered and opened his drawer for fresh underwear.

"Why are my underpants folded like this?" He pulled them out to show me. "Don't tell me your mother's doing the laundry now?"

I grabbed the briefs from him. "I'm sorry. She got to it before I did. I'll keep our laundry in here until I have time to wash it."

Mark grumbled but looked at the well-organized drawer. "You know, your mom really knows how to keep everything perfect. There's a military precision about the whole shebang. The house is in tip-top shape."

"Are you trying to annoy me?" I threw the underpants at him. "Because it's working."

We'd both forgotten about the laundry by the time we arrived at the restaurant. The first sip of my martini hit the spot and all my built-up tension of the past week started to melt away.

"How long are your parents staying?" Mark asked out of the blue.

"I don't know." I sighed. "Until Ashley is better, I guess."

"It's a tough time for everyone." He touched my cheek. "We'll get through it."

I knew that eventually my parents, especially my mother, would irritate Mark and he'd blow up at her. I couldn't believe I wished he'd go on more business trips after all the grief I gave him last summer. I had felt like Clare in Audrey Niffenegger's, *A Time Traveler's Wife,* never knowing when my husband would disappear or reappear and when I could count on him. But if Mark were away now, I wouldn't have to run interference between him and my parents.

Mark was driving, so I had another martini and a glass of wine. By the time we arrived home, I was drunk. I walked into the house and turned right, walking straight into our bedroom. Mark walked down the hall to the family room and said good night to my parents, who were watching TV. At least in the morning I wouldn't have to hear her lecture on the immorality of getting drunk, along with her listing the damage I've inflicted on my organs. But I was sure she'd find something else to whine about.

"How were they?" I asked Mark when he entered our room.

"Good." He grabbed me around my waist and kissed me deeply.

My inebriated self giggled and fell onto the bed.

Sitting next to me, he shushed me, putting his hand gently over my mouth, which only made me laugh harder.

After I quieted, he went into the bathroom and got me a glass of water.

I drank it dutifully. "Okay, I'm better now.

Mark sat on the bed next to me. "Christ, we don't just have the kids, now we have your parents. Kinda of kills the mood—you know."

"Oh, poor boy. Pretend you're a teenager again." I stood up and straddled him as he sat on the edge of the bed. Whispering in his ear, I said, "I can pull out my old cheerleading outfit and we can really be teenagers for a night."

Kissing his neck, I felt my husband stirring. "Yeah, go get that outfit." His voice was deep and throaty.

Yes, there was one good thing about Mom staying with us. I've lost enough weight to squeeze into my old clothes.

*

The next morning Mom made omelets that actually tasted like they had cheese in them. I didn't ask. I wouldn't know what organic substitute she'd used, so what was the point?

Both kids had basketball games and Katie had ballet class on Saturdays. Mark and I went our separate ways, one with each child, planning to rendezvous at dinner. My parents would meet us at home after helping at Ashley's.

I felt bad for my parents. They took care of Ashley seven days a week. I loved them for their unstinting commitment to her recovery. For everyone's sake, I hoped Ashley would go into remission soon. I suggested we hire help, but my mother wouldn't hear of it. I recognize what a good heart she has, but at the same time, it's hard to listen to how much criticism she dishes out especially involving food. Mom is nothing but positive and heartwarming to my sister, saving up all of her anxiety and taking it out on me. But of course, I wasn't the sick one.

I arrived home with groceries around four-thirty. Mark was already there and came out to help me.

"Are Mom and Dad home?" I asked as we carried the food into the house.

"The car is here, but I haven't seen them."

We put all the bags on the kitchen counter. The house was so quiet. Usually when my parents are here, Dad watches a sport show with the TV blaring while Mom curls up, reading a book. I don't know how she stands the noise.

I noticed that the dogs were in the house rather than running around in the backyard where my mother sequesters them whenever she's in the house.

"I call the treehouse," Katie screamed.

"What? No way! You had it yesterday," Brandon countered.

Oh God! I am sick of all the fighting over that damn treehouse. I decided Mark could handle it and nudged him, pointing at the kids.

As both kids tried to fit through the sliding glass door at the same time, racing to the treehouse, I noticed something moving high up. I followed the kids outside.

There, coming down the rickety rope and pole ladder, were my parents. Mark came up beside me.

"You don't think?" I murmured to him.

"Nah," Mark said.

I remembered the steamy night Mark and I spent up there, the night he'd come home from his business trip, the night I'd almost given in to Jim. Stopped in the nick of time.

As they descended, I noticed Dad's shirt buttons weren't lined up.

It couldn't be. I headed back into the house. *I just don't want to know.*

Chapter 11

STACI

YEARNING

NAUSEA ROSE AS I stepped out of the shower. I grabbed two towels, wrapping one around me. I flipped my head over and covered my wet hair with the other. Had I eaten today? I couldn't remember. I sat on the toilet for a few minutes breathing slowly. *Oh God, he'll be here soon.*

I switched my thoughts to Madeline. I was still pissed at that ridiculous e-mail. "Rude"? Ha! She's the rude one. Who died and left her in charge anyway?

But no matter how I tried to divert my thoughts—it wasn't working. *John . . . I'm not ready for this.* What do I say to you? Where do I put your stuff? My bedroom? The guest room? Will you have stuff? It's a seven-hour drive. You must be staying over.

He had left me crying in Vermont last June. Now he'll be here in a few hours. What do I say when I open the door and find him standing there?

Do I run into his arms?

No, too much. A casual hello? Maybe too subdued. Even though we'd spoken on the phone, I felt awkward. My stomach churned. *Dating sucks.*

I stared at my reflection in the mirror. Look at all those wrinkles. Smoothing cream over my face all these years hadn't helped. These damn LED bulbs were just too harsh. *Ugh! Everything's wrong.* I turned and walked into my bedroom, plopping onto the bed.

Over the last month I had hoped and dreamed and even prayed a little about John. I'd made him perfect. Have my expectations exceeded the actual man? How will either of us live up to my imaginings? Two hours to go. . . . *Oh God!*

*

The doorbell rang. I stopped, frozen, heart pounding in my chest.

It rang again.

"Coming!" I shouted, instinctively running to the front hallway.

I halted. A thousand different scenes ran through my mind. I took a deep breath. My hands trembled as I opened the door.

"Hi," I squeaked, trying hard to smile confidently. But only the right side of my mouth lifted. The rest of my face froze when I saw him.

"Hey," he said, looking down at me with that devastating smile.

I stared for a moment before taking a step forward to kiss him on the cheek, forgetting about the step down. I fell into his arms.

"Easy there," he said, holding me.

Straightening immediately, my face burned. "I'm so sorry," I muttered. "Please, come in." My stomach clenched tight. I'd wanted that moment to be perfect. *What a fool I just made of myself!*

"This is quite a place you have," John said, hovering near the door. He seemed a little unsure of himself. *That was a first.*

"Please." I motioned for him to come into the family room. "I'm selling this house in a few months after some work is completed." I sat in a wingback chair near the fireplace. "The family room and kitchen renovations are complete. But the rest of the work is taking so much longer than expected. And the dust just won't go away!"

As he strolled down the hallway, I wondered where his overnight bag was. A duffel? Anything? Maybe he'd left it in his car, intending on staying in a hotel.

Interrupting my thoughts, John asked, "Is that what you want?"

"Ah . . . .?"

"To sell the house?"

"Oh . . . yes. I want nothing more to do with this house." I folded my arms across my chest. "Honestly, I never wanted anything to do with it." I wanted to tell him how miffed I was at this ridiculous situation, with workmen tromping through here whenever, doing renovations to George's exact specifications, trying to make it perfect before it goes up for sale. Part of me still suspects George just wants to keep it.

John sat on the couch facing me. "Where will you go?"

His deep voice made me forget how angry I was with my ex. "Town house, I think. Somewhere around here."

Calmer, I studied him for the first time since he'd arrived. Long legs dressed in regular jeans, not skinny or boot cut or relaxed, and a plaid Ralph Lauren flannel shirt that accentuated his vibrant green eyes. His dark hair tumbled, curling at his shirt collar. His smile warmed his face and my heart.

"Staci," he said.

His rugged good looks seemed out of place in my prissy house. "Huh . . ." I realized I was staring and snapped myself out of it. "Would you like a drink? Beer, water, soda?" I jumped up.

He grabbed my hand. "No, thanks."

His touch sent goose bumps up my arm. "Ah, would you like a tour of the house?" I pulled gently away, afraid of being too close to him. I walked to the doorway.

He came up behind me. I didn't turn. I couldn't.

"Staci, we should talk," he said softly.

I moved through the door and into the hallway. *No, not yet. You didn't come all the way here just to dump me again. Did you?*

"I need some water," I confessed.

He followed me into the kitchen. I asked him to sit at the island so I could stay on the other side. Away from his warmth, his scent. His touch.

He must have realized how anxious I was and quietly sat down.

I placed a glass of water in front of him.

After a minute or two of silence, he asked when I thought the house would go up for sale.

"Never, probably." I didn't tell him this was my husband's baby—that it stroked his ego. This cold, monstrous house gave him a sense of entitlement. He'd arrived. Unfortunately, he had left the rest of us behind.

Realizing how cryptic I sounded, I added, "My ex really loves this house. I've told him I'd be glad to move out. Instead, he calls daily for updates and instructions on the renovations. It's exhausting. I can't wait to move." I finished my water and placed the glass in the sink, hoping I was ready for whatever he had to say. "You wanted to talk?" I stood, grasping the countertop.

He rose from his seat and walked toward me.

My heart leapt.

He stood next to me, his hands on my arms.

Oh, how I've craved his touch! His scent was the same as I remember: a mixture of musk and evergreen. So clean. My mind whirled. I looked into his eyes.

"I'm sorry about what happened. I never meant to hurt you." He raised his fingers to my shoulder and caressed my arm.

My knees buckled. I gently pushed away from him, needing some air.

"I'd like to try again." He held out his hands in apology. "But slowly. I'd like to get to know you better. It was so fast before. I just wasn't ready." He looked down, his arms relaxed, his cheeks rosy.

It's what I wanted. I should be happy. But slow? "What do you mean by slow?" I asked, my gaze burning into him.

He studied me for a moment. "I guess I need some time still, but I don't want to lose you. That's all." He shrugged.

"Okay," I whispered.

"Okay," he repeated, smiling.

He wrapped me in his arms and tenderly kissed me.

That kiss! That's exactly what I remember, what I dream about. Heavenly, soft, warm, healing my wounded soul. We stayed in the embrace until my phone vibrated. It was George. I pushed decline.

"Hey, how about you show me around town? We could get a coffee or a drink?" He pushed a section of my hair off my face.

"Sounds wonderful." I turned to get my stuff. "Hey, I want to hear all about those calves we fed that day, too." I put my phone in my pocket. "Let me get my purse and coat. I'll be right back."

In my room I checked my phone. There were five texts from George and one voicemail. I turned it off, brushed my hair, applied some lipstick and headed back to the kitchen. I felt like skipping, but knowing me, I'd fall or bang into something. So instead, I strode down the hallway as gracefully as I could, sliding into John's arms.

*

Late afternoon delivered a picture-perfect fall day. A mosaic of riotous colored trees sprawled before us, framing an endless blue sky. *Such a glorious day to be alive*, I thought as we drove into town.

"Way back when, this town was called Black River because of the river's black bottom. The townspeople renamed it Chester after their home in England," I said, glancing at him. "Of course, the Black River is a puddle compared with Lake Champlain, but . . . ." I shrugged.

John laughed. "I've only been on Interstate 95 before. I had no idea how beautiful this part of New Jersey was." He turned to his left. "Is that the remnant of a cornfield?"

"Yup. And after the harvest they have a huge corn maze that draws lots of out-of-towners." I pointed to the opposite side of the road. "Here we are. Do you like pie? They have the best in the area."

"Yes, I do."

I pulled into Addison's parking lot.

"This is quite a production," John said, looking from the petting zoo to the fragments of corn and produce fields.

He seemed pleased that I had brought him there. We're not from such different places, not really. "It's late in the season so we can actually get a parking spot. You wouldn't believe how many people cram in here in early fall." I pointed to a small building with brightly painted barn doors. "They even teamed up with a winery so you can schedule a wine tasting there."

"Clever." John walked to the back of the parking lot to get a better view of the fields beyond.

Watching him brought back pleasant memories of my father and his affection for the outdoors. My dad would have loved John. Would have loved being on his farm helping however he could. And feeding those calves would be the highlight of his week. My mother—never. But what did she know? She loved George. Ugh! My mother didn't even know I was dating anyone. She'd never approve of John. Not that I care. I don't listen to her.

We meandered into the farmer's store and I grabbed a basket. "What kind of pie do you like? Come here and look at these beauties." We had to walk sideways through the aisles packed with farm produce, specialty items, and an assortment of store-baked goods.

We decided on an apple walnut after a lot of discussion. John wanted some of their homemade ice cream, too.

"I already have some at home," I said. Walking to the checkout I spun back around, smashing headfirst into a sign mounted to a Thanksgiving display. *Oh dear God. When am I ever going to pay attention?* My nose hurt and I touched it to make sure I wasn't bleeding. I prayed John hadn't noticed. The boy behind the register looked away when I put my box on the counter. Yup, he saw it and was probably trying not to laugh. I fumbled for my wallet and paid.

I found John by the spreads and dressings looking at the variety of salsas. "It's a lot of work to produce all of this plus the farm." He replaced the mango salsa and looked at me. "Are you all right? Your face is red on one side." He grabbed the pie bag.

Thank goodness he didn't see me head butt Mr. Turkey! "I had an itch and over-scratched it." My face warmed and I averted my gaze. "You know, I used to take my sons on hayrides here when they were young." I pointed outside at a wagon, trying to steer his focus away from me and back to the farm.

In the car I continued to point out landmarks as we traveled through lush farmland and up to the top of Schooley's Mountain. I always talk too much when I'm nervous. *I'm panicking. I don't know what to say or do. What does all this mean really—his coming here?*

We stopped at a local pub and sat at a beautifully renovated wooden bar from the mid-1700s. I had picked this pub for its quaintness and tavern lore. After all, not many pubs in Vermont can claim that George Washington ate there during the war.

"How about I cook you dinner tonight?" I gushed, twirling my hair between my fingers. *Why am I babbling and cooing?* I guzzled a large mouthful of hard cider. The bubbles went up my nose and made me cough. At least I didn't spit cider all over the bar.

John patted my back and asked if I were all right. I've never understood why someone pats your back when you're coughing, but everybody does it. Embarrassed, I excused myself and went to the restroom.

Looking in the mirror, I was relieved to see that the redness from Mr. Turkey had vanished. I tried to calm down. My hammering heart was having none of it. I chanted to myself in between deep breaths. *Whatever happens—happens.* He wants us to try again. Slowly? What if I step out of his *slow* parameters?

Sitting down as casually as possible at the bar, I asked John if he liked Italian food.

"Yes, very much." He put his beer down and turned toward me.

"Have you eaten today?" It was almost five p.m. "We can order appetizers to keep you going until dinner."

"And spoil what I'm sure is an amazing dinner you're making me?" he teased. "I'm fine, I had lunch on the way down."

The pub was relatively empty. I turned in my seat to look out the huge bay window into the valley below.

John looked up from his beer, following my gaze. "Nice view."

I smiled and decided to be brave. "It's really good to see you, John." I fixed my eyes on his handsome face.

His green gaze settled on me and my lips tingled, waiting patiently.

John tilted his head and murmured, "It's great to see you, too!"

I believed he meant it. A peaceful silence lingered between us as we finished our drinks. I didn't feel that I had to fill it. A few leaves fell from a large oak tree next to the window. Caught in some spirals of breeze, they pirouetted and swirled to the ground.

*

Dinner turned into a semi-collaborative venture. I asked John to spoon some bruschetta on the toasted bread I placed on the island. After watching him for a few minutes, I turned my attention back to dinner. I wiped some moisture from my face, realizing I might be over my head with this amazing recipe that I'd downloaded and was attempting to make for the first time—*cacio e pepe*, a minimalist Italian version of mac and cheese. I paired it with roast pork loin with rosemary and garlic. Both recipes had been sitting on my iPad from some online gourmet magazine for months. *What the hell was I thinking?* I'd asked the butcher to butterfly the pork loin to avoid the hardest part of the dish. But cooking is like dating. Even when you have all the right ingredients, sometimes the recipe just doesn't work.

I prepared the pork loin and put it in the oven. I laid out the *tagliolini* and the rest of the pasta recipe. *Here goes nothing.*

As the pork cooked, I ran around lighting candles to bring some romantic ambiance to this cold space. My kitchen lacked any intimacy with its overly large-scale, ultramodern fixtures with ultrabright overhead lighting. I was embarrassed by it. John's home was warm, real. This was all show.

"There's a bit of an echo in here," John said.

"There's a bit of an echo in the whole house." I shrugged. "It isn't what I wanted. My ex worked exclusively with an architect and designer. I had no say."

"Really?" John stopped chopping. "No input at all?"

I hate talking about George. I shouldn't have mentioned it. "Let's finish the prep and I'll explain over dinner." I hoped he would forget.

I uncorked a bottle of Sangiovese and took a bottle of Sauvignon Blanc from the refrigerator in case he wanted white. I held both up. "Which do you want with dinner?" I asked, thinking he'd prefer the Sangiovese.

"I'll have the red." He placed the bruschetta on the table and picked up a piece. "Staci."

I turned.

"Open up." He tipped the bruschetta into my mouth.

He was so close that his smell overwhelmed me. "Let's sit," I said, quietly backing away, afraid I might overstep the *slow* boundary by wrapping him in my arms and covering him with kisses.

I fussed at the sink for a minute or two, regrouping. I filled a pitcher with water and brought it to the table.

Sitting, I raised my wineglass and boldly said, "To us."

We clicked glasses.

"Dinner is really good," John uttered after a few bites. "Excellent."

Smiling, I whispered a prayer of thanks that it turned out as well as it had.

His gaze warmed me from across the table, teasing and tantalizing in the soft glow of the room.

"Tell me about the construction around the house. Why so many renovations when you just plan to sell?"

"It's mostly been updating the kitchen and bathrooms. Plus, a fresh coat of paint." My shoulders sagged at the thought of my daily dealings with George and the contractors. "It's been going on for almost a year. But the end is in sight."

John ate quietly.

Now what? What did I say to make him so quiet? It was driving me crazy trying to figure him out. I started talking quickly, telling John that George had changed during our marriage, growing coarse and angry. I told him that I shouldn't have stayed for as long as I did, but that I wanted my sons to be old enough to cope with the divorce. "I really don't have any regrets because my sons are my treasures," I confessed. "The last ten years George controlled every aspect of my life." I spun the *cacio* around my fork. "Maybe I should have pushed back. I just . . . well . . . didn't care anymore about *us*, so I vanished into a world I created without him."

Jesus, how must that sound to someone who adored his wife? How does that make me look? I surveyed his face carefully, looking for any hint of disapproval.

"Marriages are difficult. A few of my friends who I thought would be perfect together grew to detest one another. You never know how time and experiences play out," John remarked.

I put my fork down and started playing with my napkin in my lap. He must have noticed my unease because he changed the subject. He talked about the calves we'd bottle-fed in Vermont last June and about his daughters.

After we cleaned the dishes, I brought him into the family room and made a fire. I noticed the shock on his face and laughed. "Yes, I can make a fire with real wood."

We sipped wine and watched the logs crackle.

Looking at his face in the firelight, I noticed a faint smile edging his lips and wondered what he was thinking.

John put his wineglass down on the table and turned to me. His hand brushed my hair off my face again, leaving it tingling.

I braced myself, my lips trembling for his kiss. All my fantasies lingered before me. My pulse throbbed as my body longed for his touch. A craving so pressing and absorbing.

Slowly his lips met mine. The velvet warmth of this mouth sent a surge of anticipation throughout my body. Our mouths became needy, demanding more.

We never made it into my bedroom. We made love right there, half clothed.

Sated with one another, we fell asleep on the floor in front of the fireplace.

*

Slow? This is slow?

Sunlight streamed in from the two-story windows, waking us at dawn. We lingered in each other's arms. I tore myself away for a quick shower. The water tickled then soothed my sensitive skin. I started mouthing the words to "Walking on Sunshine" and bobbled to its imaginary rhythm. The song's words sobered me when I got to, ". . . don't want you back for the weekend . . ." By the time I got to the verse about "waiting forever," I realized I should have picked a different song.

Reality set in. I didn't doubt my feelings for John, but I knew I'd have to wait for a more definite relationship until he was ready. I dried my hair without any musical accompaniment, threw on some workout tights and an oversize shirt, and applied a touch of makeup.

John had straightened up the family room and was wearing his jeans and shirt from yesterday, though his feet were still bare. *Ah . . . he's got sexy feet.*

I watched him from the hall as he stared out the French doors into the backyard. I wanted to burn this beautiful moment into my mind forever.

As he started to turn around, I said, "John, I've brought you a new toothbrush and some towels. Follow me. I only have one bathroom not under construction." Walking down the hallway, I sidestepped scaffolding left up by the painters. Tempting as it was to join him, I decided not to and headed to the kitchen.

I started humming that song again as I made us breakfast, then stopped. I didn't need any more reminders of my tentative situation.

When John returned, I handed him a cup of coffee. How easy it is for a man. A shower, a comb through the hair, even when wearing yesterday's clothes, they manage to look fantastic. At least John did.

We were laughing and giggling together when all of a sudden, I heard a voice: "Just what the hell is going on here! You're shacking up with the help?"

What? Looking toward the noise . . . *Christ, it's George.* I threw up both arms in surprise and my tea spilled everywhere.

My ex rushed from the hallway into the family room.

This can't be happening. "George! What are you doing here?" I moved around the counter, heading toward the family room. I noticed John stand out of my peripheral vision, squaring his shoulders. As I passed by, I put out my arm, signaling him to stay back and said, "I can handle this."

"Why you— get the fuck out of here. You're fired!" George spat the words, pointing at John.

"Who the hell are you?" John yelled back angrily.

"You idiot! He doesn't work for you. Why would you think that? And even if he did, so what?" I hollered. "You have no right to barge in here!"

Stepping into the family room, I stood in front of George, blocking his way into the kitchen.

"The truck in the driveway . . . contractor," George spluttered, trying to push by me.

"Get out! But first, give me back the house keys," I demanded, pulling my cell out of my shirt pocket.

George's face turned beet red. I could only imagine what John was thinking. I had to de-escalate this situation before it became any worse. I could sense John was standing right behind me.

"Staci," he said. "Let me by."

"I've got this," I declared again, extending my arm. "George, leave now or I'm calling my attorney." I flipped the phone around so he could see the contact page with my extended arm. "We're divorced! Remember?" I wanted John to know that I didn't need anyone's help to deal with this.

"This is still my house!" George bellowed, but he did step back into the family room.

I came closer to George and put my hand out. "I told you that I'd be happy to move out of here. You wanted me to stay here and keep an eye on the workers! Give me those keys right now."

George looked like he was going to throw the keys to me, but after a moment of thought, thrust them back in his shirt pocket. "You're not the only one with an attorney on speed dial. You'll be hearing from mine today!" He stormed out.

I wanted to collapse into a ball on the sofa. I didn't want to face John. How in the name of God could I explain being married to a man like George? *He'll think I sold my soul for a life of luxury.*

I took a deep breath and turned to face him. "I'm so sorry." Tears formed in my eyes and I forced myself not to break down and cry. John's rigid posture relaxed. I looked down, embarrassed.

He wrapped his arms around me and kissed the top of my head. I felt the tension in his muscles.

Breathing slowly, I couldn't think of what else to say. Eventually, I backed away from his embrace. "I don't know what just happened. I've never seen . . . ." I wiped away a tear.

John guided me to a chair and I sat. He went into the kitchen and brought back a glass of water. "I think your ex-husband still loves you. I've only seen men act like that when their hearts were being strangled."

He sat in the opposite chair.

My hands shook as I sipped the water. "He really was a decent man once. I was a fool to stay with him so long. It's just . . ."

"You did what you thought was right." John grabbed my free hand, caressing it. "It's part of who you are." He kept his eyes on my face, speaking softly. "Are you sure you're over him?"

My head sprang up in surprise. "Oh God, yes! For many years, yes!"

John relaxed into the chair. "You might want to get the locks changed."

How embarrassing George's ridiculous outburst was. Would John decide I wasn't worth the trouble, now that he saw how awful my ex was? It only added to the mountain of insecurities I had with this fledgling relationship.

John must have sensed my thoughts. "Staci, I'm not judging you or even him for that matter. I'm just trying to make sure that the marriage . . . the relationship is truly over." John stood, grabbing my arm and pulling me up with him.

I threw my arms around him and squeezed him with all my might. We started kissing and within minutes our clothes were off, and we were stumbling into the hallway. I pulled him toward the closest bedroom.

At two p.m. John stood at my front door. He was having dinner with his daughter in Connecticut on his way home. "Would you like to come with me to a wedding? My friend's kid is getting married in a few weeks."

"Yes, of course." I blushed, excitedly, pulling him back for one more kiss before he left.

Oh, thank God! Another date. I would see him again. I felt so alive as I watched his truck pull out of the driveway. These last few hours had been my least lonely in years. As his truck faded into the distance, I started singing, bobbing to "Walking on Sunshine." *That damn song! But now if felt right.*

Chapter 12

MADELINE

DEBACLE

"MADELINE, DAN'S ON the phone," Stan hollered.

I ran to the bedroom to pick up the phone, wondering why my brother had called the house and not my cell. "Hi, Danny."

"Hey, sis," he gushed.

"Why are you calling me on this number?"

"Your cell is off or not working," he said. "I wanted to know: are you coming to the family gathering at Aunt Alice's next weekend?"

I walked to the dresser where I'd plugged in my phone to charge it last night and it was off. Stan must have unplugged it and turned it off before he went to bed. He hates phones ringing in the middle of the night and always turns off my phone if I leave it plugged into the charger. It annoys the crap out of me. Our children don't live at home and I want them to be able to reach me if they need to. Usually, I leave the phone on vibrate on my night table.

"Sorry, what?" I asked, distracted by how annoyed I felt.

"Are you coming to Aunt Alice's gathering?"

"No. Sarah and Olivia aren't going, and I only ever went for them." I turned my cell on.

"Come on, Maddy. My kids will be there, and they miss you."

I cringed. Dan's the only one allowed to call me Maddy, but I still hate it. "I have a better idea. Why don't you guys come here instead and spend the weekend with us?"

"You know I'll come to your home anytime, Maddy, but not during the annual family gathering."

I heard commotion in the background. "Where are you?"

"At Sally's soccer match. Come on, Sis!" he begged.

"Why? What did these people ever do for us growing up? Absolutely nothing!"

"Mads, it was a different time. You need to forgive and move on."

I shut my eyes. For years I'd endured these so-called family gatherings while my girls grew up. I thought it was important for them to have an extended family. But I didn't owe these people anything. Anger coiled in my stomach.

"You know, every time we go to one of these gatherings at least one of my dear cousins or uncles asks Stan for a loan or to invest in something they've cooked up."

"Please, please come. Come for me."

"Fine, but we're not staying over and we're only going to make an appearance. Just for you, Danny."

"Love ya, Sis. I'll call Aunt Alice and let her know."

*

I enjoyed the gathering after all, even without my daughters. Sometimes my anger gets displaced and I take it out on people who don't deserve it. And sometimes I hold on to the injustice of something longer than I should. It's not like I complained to my aunts and uncles and they did nothing about the situation at home.

Inevitably someone brings up the past. Usually Uncle Kent or Aunt Jayne, our family's official *O'Leary* storytellers. They begin every time capsule by saying, *Well . . . it was a different time, you know . . . and . . .* " Without these precious hand-me-down memories, my father would forever be nothing but a monster to me. But Aunt Jayne and Uncle Kent's stories transform him into someone I wished I'd known. The Navy pilot, the football quarterback, the ladies' man. So many of their stories centered around him, rather than his cousins or siblings. He was the chosen one, handsome, bright, and strong. That is, until alcohol sapped his life-force.

*

"Stan, honey, I'm here," I said into my cell phone. We loved meeting at this restaurant for lunch. It was around 11:30, early enough that I had my pick of tables. I chose one by the large picture window and watched Stan walk out the door of his office building and cross the street to the restaurant.

"Hey," he said and kissed my cheek before sitting down. "It's a beautiful day."

I glanced outside again and nodded. "Sorry we had to meet so early. I have appointments all day starting at one o'clock and need to be in my office by twelve-twenty-five."

He laughed. "I'm always hungry. You know that."

"Yes, dear, I know." I smiled back at him. "You have the metabolism of a twenty-year-old. You're very lucky."

Cars screeched to a stop outside of Stan's office building. We turned to watch the commotion across the street. Three black sedans parked illegally on the road right in front of the lobby's large glass doors. Four men and two women exited the cars. Two of the men opened the trunks and pulled out flat boxes like the ones you use for moving, then headed into the building.

"That looks ominous," I said, opening my menu.

"It does. Wonder what business they're headed to?"

"I'm sure you'll find out." I decided on a Caesar salad with grilled chicken.

Stan's cell rang, and I gave him my you-know-better look. He looked down at the caller ID. "It's the office. I'm gonna pick this up."

As I watched him listen, his face flushed. "What, what do you mean? I'll be right there."

"What's going on?"

He pointed at the black sedans. "Those people are in my office." He threw a few dollars on the table even though we hadn't ordered anything.

I followed him across the street and up to his office. Total chaos! As we stood in the doorway, mouths agape, we watched a woman direct the employees to go to the reception desk, where another agent jotted down their name, address, and what they did at the firm.

"Go sit in the conference room," he told them. "We'll be in to talk to you soon."

"What the hell is going on here? Who are you people? I'm calling the police!" Stan roared.

A man from the corner office emerged. "Sir, who are you?"

Stan stood in his best power pose: bent elbows and hands-on hips like Superman. "Who the hell are you?"

The man reached into his front jacket pocket, pulling out a black wallet with an ID card from the state attorney general's office, following that with a search warrant. Another man from a back office came out lugging a heavy box.

"We've done nothing wrong! Why are you here? This is some kind of stupid mistake, for God's sake." Stan wheeled around, looking for David, but he was nowhere to be seen.

The agent approached him and repeated, "Who are you, sir?"

"I'm Stan Miller. The owner of Miller Accounting Solutions, LLC. Where is David Shepard?"

The agent handed him a paper. "Let's go into your office," he said. "Which one is yours?"

Stan pointed and then turned to me. "Go home, Madeline. This is some sort of idiotic mistake. No need for you to be here."

"No damn way am I leaving. I'm calling Arthur right now. Don't say anything until he gets here." I swiped my phone, my hands shaking a little, searching for our attorney's phone number.

Finding the number, I pushed call and his secretary answered on the second ring. My heart couldn't have stood more than that. "Finally, I'm Madeline Miller. Arthur is our attorney. My husband Stan has attorney general agents in his office. I need Arthur immediately."

"I'm sorry, Mrs. Miller. He's in a client meeting," the young woman softly said. "I'll have him call as soon as he's done."

"No, you won't. Interrupt that meeting this minute and tell him I need him immediately or he'll have a malpractice suit on his desk by tomorrow morning."

"I'll try, Mrs. Miller. Please hold."

"Hold my ass!" I spun around. The room had gone quiet and everyone was staring at me. I turned and faced the window overlooking the courtyard below. Bile rose in my throat. I walked over to the water fountain and took a drink. It made the burning sensation worse.

"Mrs. Miller, what is going on? I'm in an important meeting." Arthur Goldstein said.

"I don't give a damn about your meeting. There are attorney general agents or whatever you call them all over my husband's office, talking to his staff and removing documents. You need to be here right now."

"Mrs. Miller, ask the agents for the search warrant and read it to me, please," he said, spacing out every word like I was a child or some kind of idiot.

"Hey, you, with the ponytail. Do you have a search warrant? Give it to me this instant!" I screamed.

"One more word and I'll handcuff you for obstruction. Go sit down and shut up." The agent pointed to a chair in the conference room.

Instead, I moved within inches of her, our noses nearly touching.

Arthur must have intuited what I was doing. He said, "Madeline, stop. Don't provoke them. You'll just make it worse. Tell Stan to say nothing. I'm coming right now. Madeline, do you hear me?"

"Fine!" I ended the call and pushed past the agent, bursting into Stan's office. "Don't say anything, Stan! Arthur is coming right now."

Turning to the agent, I said, "Arthur Goldstein is our attorney and he'll be here shortly. He's advised us not to say anything without him present."

"Madeline, there's no reason you need to be here, honey. This is all a mistake." Stan looked at the agent, probably hoping he'd agree.

But this didn't feel like a mistake to me. They were looking for something. What the hell was going on? "No. I'm going to sit right next to you and make sure you follow Arthur's instructions." We sat on the client side of Stan's desk and watched as the agent rifled through it. I knew my husband. If I didn't stay and keep him quiet, he'd feel compelled to say something. I wondered what he'd said before I'd stopped him.

The agent unplugged Stan's hard drive from his computer. I bit down hard to keep my mouth shut. He wrapped the cord around it.

No, I couldn't stand it. I jumped up. "Where do you think you're taking that? How is my husband supposed to work without his computer?"

"Mrs. Miller, we are confiscating all the computers and files in the office. It's all in the search warrant."

Hearing drawers slam shut outside the office; I sank back down into my chair. I closed my eyes, massaging my aching temples. Where the hell was Goldstein? This was justice? Ha! Exactly like taking a home away from a family.

Air rushed out of my lungs like I'd been hit with a bat. Stunned, my mind whirled. *Shit. Where did that come from?* I forced my eyes closed. *Stay calm—breathe.*

Suddenly, I was standing in my childhood backyard with those two goons serving me with foreclosure papers. All those years ago. My heart was pounding, and I could hardly breathe. *What the hell is happening?*

"Mads. Madeline?"

Stan grabbed my hand. "Are you okay, honey? You're so pale!" Giving my hand a tight squeeze, he said, "Don't worry. I told you this is all a mistake."

Hearing his voice and feeling his warm hand brought my focus back to him, pushing my memories back into their crypt. "I'm fine, dear. Just fine," I said quietly. Looking at Stan, his shoulders slumped, his hands shaking, I was determined to endure whatever this turned out to be. For me, for him, for our family.

Steeling myself as I rose from the chair, I thought: *No, Mr. Attorney General. You don't scare me. I'd been through worse and overcome it all.* "Come on, Stan, let's wait in the conference room for Arthur."

Chapter 13

AVA

BAILANDO

"AVA, THANK GOD! I was ready to get on a plane and fly down there." Neil paused, his voice coming through loud and clear on my phone. "It's been a week since I heard a word from you. I can't stand it—it's making me nuts. I'm booking a flight tomorrow!" He took a deep breath. "I'm not leaving you and your mother to cope on your own."

Whoa! "I'm sorry about not getting to you sooner . . . cell service is spotty . . . I have to go into town to make calls." Humidity closed around me as I stood outside the hospital, and a bead of sweat rolled down my back. "Listen, there's no need to come. Really. We're fine and we're not alone. There's family and my mother's neighbors, one of whom is a doctor. He's taking care of his mother and mine." My stomach churned. I didn't want him to fly down with the island in turmoil. "My mother's place is tiny, and the hotels aren't open yet."

"Ava, I should be there with you." Neil argued. "I don't care if I sleep on a couch."

"Neil, relax. It's okay. I've got this. It's like camping and we both know how you feel about that."

"What does that matter? I can curl up in a sleeping bag as long as you're with me."

Yeah, right. I held in my laughter. Neil would never tolerate the conditions here. He'd drive my mother and me crazy until we returned with him to the mainland.

"That's so kind of you." I was trawling my mind for something to say, anything to keep him from getting on a plane. "You can't stay at my mother's home; there's only two bedrooms and we're not married. She'd be in church saying the rosary every day if she knew we were sleeping together." *Utter nonsense, but would he believe it? — the stereotype of a Latino Catholic mother and her beliefs.*

"Come on, Ava. In this day and age—really?"

Maybe not. He sounded exasperated. I wasn't even sure why I didn't want him to come. I thought back to our conversation at the airport when Neil dropped me off. How I'd told him: "I need some time. I'm recently divorced. What's the rush?" He'd looked disappointed, but I'd learned to trust my gut. We'd been moving too fast and my instincts told me to chill.

Thinking about it now, I knew I'd made the right decision. Neil had been trying to insert himself into every aspect of my life. I don't want that. Not now. I want space. I care deeply for him, but was this love? I wasn't sure.

"Neil, I'll be home in a week or so. I'm tending to my mother. I'll see you when I get back," I declared. "I have to go now. Bye." While I felt bad, I clearly had to be firm with him.

The last few months with Neil—my first love, the man who had reappeared just when my marriage was collapsing—certainly helped me recover from the pain of divorce. But I wasn't sure we could rekindle that old *first love* magic. Maybe it felt like we could at first, but now . . . he had become controlling. Having just left one controlling person, I certainly didn't want to trade one in for another.

I'd procrastinated a full week since coming to Puerto Rico before calling Neil, but I was quite happy to speak with my kids.

I had scootered into town earlier to take a shower at the hospital, thanks to Gabriel. I also made a few work-related phone calls and bought some supplies. By the time I finished, my basket was stuffed, and I could barely buckle the straps in place. I'd never been good at judging spaces and distance.

Rain from the night before made the trip difficult. Branches had fallen and there were puddles everywhere. Water covered the streets in many places and hid the potholes created by the hurricane weeks ago.

I'd managed to dodge the puddles and other debris going into town that morning, so I wasn't worried about the return trip. Happily, I sang "Good Vibrations" as I steered toward home.

At one spot, water splayed across the entire road. Slowing down, I climbed off the bike and carefully walked it along the water's edge. As soon as I cleared the puddle, I got back on, singing and swerving around various obstacles on my way home.

During a chorus of "Can't Stop the Feeling," I swirled around a sharp bend in the road and slammed into a runoff—water pouring from the hilltop on my right. I pulled the handles sharply toward the grass on the far-left side of the streaming flood. But I didn't quite make it.

"*Damn!*" I landed on my ass in mud on the bank by the water's side. I jumped out of the muck. The scooter's front tire was in a hole at the edge of the water, the back tire wedged on the bank. Miraculously, the supplies had stayed in plastic sacks and were still dry.

My wrist throbbed with a sharp pain as I tried to lift the front tire out of the hole. *Ouch!* I turned the scooter off and examined my wrist. It was red, but I didn't see any cuts and I could move it. Probably just bruised. Moving gingerly, I pulled the scooter back on the road and started it up again.

Steering was uncomfortable, but I was able to bring in the supplies and put them away. Convinced my wrist was only strained at most, I picked up a rake to clear the light debris that had fallen from last night's storm. Mud caked my shorts and top, but I decided to clean up later so I wouldn't dirty another outfit. *So much for that shower!*

The pulling motion of the rake made my wrist throb. I studied it, moved it around. I hadn't fallen on it that hard. Why did it hurt so much? I went over to Lola's to see if she had any ice. Luckily, she did. That small generator was a godsend.

My mother, of course, refused to let me do anything until Gabriel checked out my wrist. I hoped he'd come home to his mother's that night. Sometimes he stayed over at the hospital.

Mami wrapped a plastic bag of ice around my sore wrist. Grabbing my good arm, she ushered me out of the house, planting me in a chaise lounge facing the front. I sank back, relaxing, enjoying the ocean breeze that slid up the mountain. Nothing was missing except an icy cocktail and maybe . . . I never finished the thought as I heard a scooter coming up the hill.

Mami called for Gabriel before the scooter even stopped.

"Jesus, *Mami*, you'd think I had a heart attack."

Gabriel unwrapped the ice. He prodded and probed, twisting and touching all around my wrist. "The bone isn't out of place, but I think you may have a fracture. I won't know for sure until you get an X-ray. I'll bring you in with me in the morning."

"But it wasn't a big fall. How in the world could I have fractured my wrist?"

"It was probably harder than you thought, or you twisted it in an odd manner. So many things can go wrong." He looked at me as if he were deciding whether to ask a question, but instead walked to his house. "I'll be right back."

I looked at my wrist. His touch had been light. I noticed the hair on my arms was raised and wondered why I had goose bumps. I wasn't cold. Maybe the shock of the injury?

Gabriel returned with a makeshift sling and rewrapped my wrist with ice, draping my arm in the sling. He smelled slightly of anti-septic and citrus from his day at the hospital. His wildly screwy hair has its own set of rules and I was suddenly struck with an impulse to twist my fingers through it.

Realizing I was staring, I turned my head. *Mami* and Lola were watching us.

Gabriel stood. "Keep the ice on as long as you can stand it. It will keep the swelling down."

"How is she?" *Mami* asked.

He smiled reassuringly. "I don't think it's bad. Maybe a small fracture between her thumb and wrist."

"Shouldn't she go to the hospital now?" *Mami* paced around the room.

"It's dangerous to try to navigate in the dark with so much water on the roads. Better to wait until sunrise. The bones aren't separated. Don't worry. She'll be okay."

Surprised at how easily he soothed my mother, I wondered if he could show me his technique. Was it just his great bedside manner?

"We're so lucky to have you here. Aren't we, Ava?" my mother asked.

I wondered what she was up to. "Yes, *Mami*. Very lucky."

I glanced at my shorts and realized I hadn't changed. *Damn it.* It felt like ages ago, that morning's refreshing shower at the hospital. My hair hadn't been that greasy since I was a kid. I'd tried to wash it the day before in the sink, using bottles of water, but I couldn't get the shampoo out without wasting a lot of precious water. The shower today had felt wonderful and made me crave the modern conveniences I had always taken for granted. Luckily, I hadn't dunked my hair in the mud.

"*Mami*, can you help me wash this off?" I asked, pointing at my muddy outfit.

A huge smile crept across her face. "*Si.*"

*

The next morning exhaustion overcame me. Whether the pain in my wrist was taking a toll or the lack of any modern amenities, I dragged myself out of bed hankering for coffee, lots of coffee.

I watched Gabriel outside talking with his mother as I downed two cups of strong coffee in ten minutes flat. What was his story? Maybe I could find out on our way to the hospital.

My arms wrapped loosely around him as we made our way into town on the scooter. It hurt too much to keep the sling on, pressed into his back. It felt better in front, even if I couldn't clasp my hands together. Gabriel took it slow, probably realizing I was balanced less than securely.

His curly locks tickled my nose. He piqued my curiosity. Did he have children? A wife? Maybe a girlfriend? If so, where were they?

It was hard to talk to him at home without one or both of the mothers smiling and watching. I wondered if he'd noticed their antics.

Gabriel pulled into the doctor's lot and I shimmied off the scooter.

"Okay, let's see if there's a fracture. Follow me." He guided me to the X-ray room.

My wrist had swollen overnight and maneuvering it for the X-ray hurt. I hoped I could take another shower, but that seemed doubtful if it needed a cast.

"Doctor, do you need help?" A young woman asked from the doorway, her eyes remaining on him.

"No, not yet Carmela. Thanks," he replied.

She hovered in the hall. Gabriel started to say something to me and must have felt her standing there. He called over his shoulder, "I'll call you when I need you, Nurse. Thanks."

She swiveled and left, her rubber-soled shoes squeaking on the tile floor.

Did the nurse have ulterior motives for lingering? She was certainly eager to help Gabriel. Was she trying to impress him? And was it professional or personal?

He stepped closer to me and lowered his voice. "I have good and bad news. Which do you want first?"

"The bad, of course."

"You have a fractured scaphoid bone. That's the bad." He held up the X-ray to the diagnostic imaging device. "The good is that you don't need surgery. The bone is in place and it's a small break. Just a soft cast." He took the X-ray down, placing it in a folder with my name on it. "No lifting of anything with this arm for six weeks."

Ugh. "Thanks. Hey, is there any way I can take another shower after the cast is on? I can put a plastic bag over it. Please?" I gave him my best pleading look.

He smiled. "Okay. I'll tape the bag so no water will get in. Then I'll get someone to bring you to the showers."

Gabriel strode to the door and called for a nurse. By the time he took a half step back into the room, Carmela rushed in.

He popped back, surprised at her quickness. "What . . . Where did you come from?"

"I was just in the next room, Doctor, helping a patient." A slight blush rose to her cheeks.

She stood only a finger's width apart from him. *Hmmm . . . not sure about Nurse Carmela. She's all up into Gabriel's space. And the way she looks at him!*

"Please take Ava to one of the back rooms down the hall. I'll be there to put a cast on as soon as I can. Maybe give her something to read. It could be a while."

Off I went out through the waiting room and back into the bowels of the ER. It was buzzing—people, noise, clamoring. Though I barely had a chance to notice. Nurse Carmela speed-walked me through the room. I had to quicken my pace and lengthen my stride to keep up.

"In there," she said, opening a door.

No magazine, no small talk. At least she didn't slam the door when she left.

I wasn't sure how long Gabriel would be in the ER. A lot of people were waiting, so I made a few work calls. I thought about calling Neil again, but just as I was about to, Gabriel walked in.

I smiled. "That was quicker than I thought." I dropped the phone in my purse.

He'd replaced his street clothes with scrubs. The cap on his head barely contained his mass of curls, some of which looked like they might escape at any moment. His deep bronze-colored eyes looked tired. I resisted an urge to hug him.

"Let's get that wrist of yours in a cast so you can take a shower." He walked to the counter where the gauze and clips were.

"Thanks so much for taking care of my wrist. And my mother. And just everything. You're amazing." *Shit, did I just say that?* My heart was beating too fast.

A faint smile edged his lips, and a slight pink graced his cheeks. "It was my pleasure."

I felt nervous sweat beads under my arms and around the back of my hair as he approached. Again, goose bumps ravaged my arms.

"Do you need help, Doctor?"

Jeez, Nurse Carmela was back. I wondered if she had hidden a GPS device on him.

"Yes, thanks." He laid out what he needed on a small aluminum tray table next to me. "It will go quicker with two of us."

I nodded, wincing when he touched my wrist. The nurse stood so close to him that it made me uncomfortable. I wondered what he thought about her. Do they date? Is there a history between them? She's definitely into him. I felt a strange tingle of jealousy.

Good to his word, he taped my arm so I could take a shower.

"Carmela, bring Ava to the doctors' lounge. She's going to take a shower. Get her a towel, please."

"Of course." Turning to me she said, in a completely different tone of voice, "This way, please."

I waited in the hallway for her. She came out of the room and zoomed past me. This time I was ready. I picked up my pace and stayed right on her heels. Nurse Carmela was beginning to grate on my nerves.

She threw open a door and pointed inside. "Here, take these." She handed me two pills in a small paper cup.

"What for?"

"Pain . . . ." She was gone. No towel.

Nurse Carmela acted like Nurse Ratchet. I threw the pills down the toilet and went in search of a towel, finding some in a cabinet in the hallway.

Ahhhhh . . . the shower was divine. Water and sewage treatment had resumed in the hospital a few days ago, as well as the surrounding area. I hoped it would be restored to my mother and the rest of the island soon. I could not leave her without power and water.

The shower energized me. It felt so good. Washing my hair was difficult with only one arm, but I managed.

After I dressed, humming a song, I checked my phone. Neil had called. No message. Once I couldn't wait to hear his voice. A long-ago memory flashed into my mind: Neil and I holding each other on the Wonder Wheel at Coney Island. Our hearts swayed with the ride. I could smell his rich cologne, and I closed my eyes, remembering. His exact words were lost but I still felt the love.

I attempted to blow-dry my hair with a hair dryer I discovered in the cabinet under the sink. At home I'd have styled it, but with one hand all I could do was dry and scrunch the curls.

I found a different nurse and asked her to let Gabriel know I would wait for him outside. He could call me when he was ready to leave. I was sure Nurse Carmela would still be hovering around and wondered if she stalked him like this every day. Shaking away my crazy thoughts, I returned my attention to Neil, calling him.

"Hey," I said.

"Ava, how are you? How's your mother?" he asked.

"Everything's fine. I hope to be able to come home in a week. I'm just waiting for my mother's water and electric to come back." I didn't tell him about my wrist.

"I'm so glad. I miss you," he said.

I did miss him. But did I miss the real version of Neil or just my memory of him—from when we'd first fallen in love, all those years ago, when we were young?

*

I rested my head on Gabriel's back as we rode home. It had been a long day. Our mothers made an amazing meal from the supplies I'd brought home yesterday. They fried the yellow plantains and pork chops and served them with freshly sliced avocados. Delicious. We ate outside on the picnic table. The citronella torches gave us light and discouraged all but the most aggressive mosquitos.

After dinner I said good night, barely able to keep my eyes open. My mother followed me home.

"Thanks, *Mami*, for such a nice meal."

"Come, let's get you in bed."

I started to protest but knew it would do no good. "I talked to Neil today." I wasn't sure why I shared that.

"Oh?"

"That's it? 'Oh?'"

Mami unbuttoned my blouse and helped me remove it. "What can I say? To me he had his chance a long time ago. What did he do with it? Aye? He threw it away."

"Now, *Mami*. That's unfair. His father forced him to break it off." I unzipped my shorts and shimmied out of them.

"So, he says."

I put my good hand on my hip. "What's that supposed to mean? I thought you liked him?"

"Funny, I don't remember you asking me what I thought about him." She picked up my clothes, folded them and placed them on top of the dresser.

Maybe I hadn't asked her. "I see you and Lola watching Gabriel and me. You want us to date. I know you." I stopped short of asking her about him. I didn't want her to know I was curious. I'd never hear the end of it.

She walked to the door. "He's the finest man I've ever known. You think about that."

Mothers! I dreamed of Ferris wheels and scooters until dawn.

Chapter 14

CHARLOTTE

"CHARLOTTE, WE HAVE to make deep cuts in the proposed budget for next year." My boss handed me back the initial analysis I'd prepared last week for the school board. Ted's face and neck were bright red. "I thought I'd made myself clear."

Shit seems to come in piles. I had barely stepped into the office before he started in on me.

"That damn board is looking at our salaries. We've been here a long time." He began to cough.

Dealing with the school board members, some of whom have no idea what they're doing, would give anyone high blood pressure. But lately it had become particularly discordant. They've insisted on huge cuts when there's no fat left on the bone—only academics. No art and music classes available to pillage.

I threw the proposal down on my desk. Only the first draft and Ted was already bellyaching. The budget always takes us six months with many revisions before the board approves it. He knows that. I wondered what had Ted so worked up.

The last ten years had been hard, with taxes going to everything but education. I slumped in my chair and wondered what had possessed me to take this promotion to begin with. I can't even blame it on my ex. I like to blame him for everything, but I'd been long divorced when this position came along. And damn, it's been nothing but a pain in my ass ever since.

Don't I have enough on my plate with Maxwell without this crap? I grabbed the proposal, flicking through it. I'd hate to lose my job. It's been one of the few constants in my life since my turbulent divorce.

Damn it—not now. My chest tightened. I rose, grabbed my water bottle, and went into the ladies' room. I was afraid that if someone asked me what was wrong, I'd cry. So, I sat on the ceramic throne and practiced my deep breathing from yoga class. *One . . . two . . . three . . . four . . . .* Inhaling to the full extent of my lung capacity. After twenty deep breaths I grew dizzy, which made me chuckle. Here I am, a grown woman sitting on a toilet, acting like a teenage girl smoking behind the stall door. All I needed was a cigarette and one of my friends and I'd be right back in high school. The controlled breathing had worked. My anxiety was gone.

Back at my desk, I attacked the figures with renewed rigor, calculating and recalculating. I even called a neighboring school board analyst to find out how she was structuring their numbers.

My neck was stiff by the time I finished. It was late, around six p.m. No noise came from the outer office. I must have been so engrossed that I didn't hear everyone leave. But my focus paid off—I had found some wiggle room.

I reached into my purse and applied a thick coat of gloss. My lips were so dry. I'd neglected them all day. Rubbing my neck, I glanced at my phone. Daisy had called six times. What was my harebrained college roommate up to now? I hadn't heard from her for months, even years, and then six phone calls in one day? But I wasn't surprised. After all, everything is a crisis to her.

Daisy and I had been roommates during our freshman year at Bennington College. We stayed friends after she dropped out at the end of that year. Even after I graduated and went home to New Jersey, we'd see one other once or twice a year.

I remembered how I'd tried to get her to stay in college, but she'd insisted she didn't belong there. None of her arguments made any sense to me. I found out later she had been dealing with her sexual orientation and an alcoholic mother.

I pushed Daisy's number. When she answered, I laughingly said, "Patience was never one of your virtues."

"Charlotte, she left me!" Daisy sobbed.

I straightened. "What? Who left? Speak up, I can barely hear you."

"Janice," she whispered. Then, "Janice," louder before she began to weep.

I thought back to the first time I'd met Janice. Daisy had invited me to a party in Montpelier hosted by a coworker.

*

Stevie Nicks' raspy and enchanting croon erupted from the speakers as I walked into the house in Montpelier. Even in Vermont, big hair reigned supreme in the 1980s and the air was heavy with hair spray.

Victoria, the hostess, handed me her "special party punch," as I entered her home. I thanked her and asked if she'd seen Daisy.

"Find the sexiest woman here and you'll find your friend."

I walked into a large room filled with marijuana smoke and people dancing. Squeezing through the crowd, I made my way toward the kitchen. I felt uncomfortable not knowing anyone there.

Finally, I spotted Daisy leaning on the refrigerator. She was wiping her nose constantly. Daisy liked her drugs. I had hoped that working would slow her down, but it clearly hadn't.

"Daisy." I yelled.

She waved with one hand and wiped her nose with the other. I pushed through a group of people who stood in a circle between us. Daisy grabbed me in a bear hug.

"You have to meet someone. Come with me." She pulled me along and up the stairs. "There . . . over there."

A woman with her back to us was speaking to another couple. When she turned, I was momentarily taken aback. Whoa. My shoulders drooped as I caught my breath.

Who are you? Her eyes held mine, her deep gaze piercing through me. I tried to speak but only nonsensical babbling came forth. She outshone everyone in the room with her fluttering eyelashes and penetrating stare.

Stammering, I took a step back. I was no match for her. But she reached out and stroked my arm. Electrical flashes shot everywhere. How the hell can a stranger make me feel like this? And a woman besides?

She had legs Tina Turner would envy, displaying them under a tiny black microskirt. Her flat stomach accentuated perfect curves. But it was her face, her sensuous lips, chiseled cheekbones and those eyes. I've never forgotten those eyes. Smoky gray like a harbor in Maine. You just fell into them willingly. Wantonly.

*

"Charlotte, are you there?" Daisy hollered.

Snapping out of my reverie, I replied, "Yes, sweetie. I'm here. What happened?"

"It's a long story. Can I come and stay with you for a week or so? I need to clear my head."

"Of course. Chad is coming on Thursday for a few days, so any time after Sunday is good with me. Let me know your arrival time and I'll pick you up at the airport."

"You're a lifesaver. Thanks. I need a change. I'll call after I make the arrangements."

*

Thursday finally arrived. A car door slammed around 1 p.m. and I heard a loud bark. I flew off the couch and swung open the front door, stepping right into my son's arms.

A monster of a dog jumped on the two of us, slobber and hair going every which way.

"That's a six-month-old? He almost knocked me over." I laughed. "Hey there, Tucker." I bent down and the dog smeared my face with the largest tongue I'd ever seen.

Chad roared with laughter. "Isn't he great? Look at the size of those paws." He held the leash tight. "I better warn you now, Tucker isn't well trained. I suggest hiring a trainer. I'll pay for it, Mama Bear."

"You mean he's going to get bigger? He's the size of a large dog now. How much bigger? And that musky smell—is that him?" I got a good whiff of Tucker as I bent down to pet him.

"Yeah, I haven't done a great job of grooming him." He took out his wallet and handed me his credit card. "Take this and put all the dog's expenses on it."

"No way. I've got this."

"I don't think you realize how expensive this dog is. It's as big as he is—huge, from the amount of food he eats, the grooming, the training, everything."

I ushered them both into the house. "Honey. I've got enough to take care of Tucker. Hanna, my friend from book club, has two large dogs and I'll ask her where to go for grooming, food, and training." I patted his back. "Let's get a bowl of water for our slobbering friend over there."

I watched as Tucker drank down the water in less than a minute. It fell off him like rain. The entire corner was wet, including the dog's chest.

Cleaning up the mess, I thought how my life was swaying off its nicely controlled path.

Chad took Tucker outside and I watched them from the kitchen door. What an amazing man my son had become. Smart, levelheaded, handsome. I guess all mothers feel that way about their children. But mine really is special. Both my sons are.

"I'm so happy I get a chance to see you," I told him as he and Tucker came through the door. "Why Kuwait?"

He shrugged. "Just another deployment. Don't worry, it's relatively safe."

"Hawaii was safe. Anything in the Middle East isn't. How long?" I prayed he'd only be there a few months.

"Not sure yet. Hopefully, not too long." He gave me a don't-worry wink.

We went into the family room and sat, reminiscing about our first dog, Sammy. Tucker either didn't like the mention of another dog or he wasn't getting enough attention. He jumped on my leather sofa into Chad's lap.

"Oh no, no, no. His nails will go right through the leather. Get him off. Please."

As Chad contended with Tucker, I called Hanna. "Help, I need a trainer!"

Hanna paused. "For Maxwell?"

We both laughed. I explained about my new roommate. By the time I clicked off, I had a trainer, a groomer, and a local pet store. My next call was to the trainer. I had taken a few days off work to spend with Chad. The trainer had availability the next day, so we set up an appointment. He also gave me tips on supplies for Tucker.

"Let's go, Chad, we need a few things for this monster pup of yours."

We headed out to the pet store. Chad was right, this dog was expensive. Later that night, it took both of us to lure him into the giant-size crate we'd bought. Tucker could no longer sleep with Chad.

"Sorry, buddy," Chad said, kneeling down to comfort his miserable pet. "Trainer said you have to get used to this archaic torture chamber."

"Don't worry," I told him, seeing he looked as upset as Tucker.

"He's a den animal and this metal monstrosity will help him feel secure in his own safe space, especially after you leave."

*

After three incredible days, Chad left for Kuwait on Sunday night. He thought it best if he took a cab to the airport. He knew me too well. I'd be bawling like a baby from the time we approached the airport to the moment I watched him go through security.

"Mama Bear, you are the best in the world." He hugged me tight. "Thanks for taking care of my little boy."

As he stepped back, I gripped him tighter. I forced myself not to get emotional, but a tear slipped from my eye. "I love you." I whispered in his ear and let him go. "Be careful." I clutched his shoulders with my hands. Looking at my beautiful boy. Desperately wanting him to stay.

I attempted to smile, but it felt awkward and contrived.

"I will." He lifted his knapsack and walked to the cab.

I'm going to wave goodbye and not stand here weeping. Tucker moved down the steps behind Chad. I pulled back on the leash. "No, boy, not today." The dog whined. I knew how he felt. Tucker and I stood there like good soldiers, me waving, him wagging his tail. Back inside I hugged the dog, smell and all, until my tears dried. "I'm gonna take great care of you. I promise."

*

I barely slept, tossing and turning all night, worried about Chad and wondering about my relationship with Maxwell. But by eight a.m., I was out the door and on my way to the groomer with Tucker. The groomer agreed to keep him until I picked him up after work. Daisy was due in that night and I was tired of that musky dog smell.

When I collected him after work, the transformation was unbelievable. He smelled great. I rushed home, showered, fed him and left to pick up Daisy at Newark Airport. Never an easy airport for pickups, I parked in short-term parking and went to the baggage carousel. She was waiting for her luggage to cycle. Her face was drawn and pale, her eyes downcast.

"Daisy!" I yelled.

She turned and rushed over, gripping me in a vise hold. "She left me! My God. She really left me this time."

"Hey!" I pushed her and held her back by her shoulders. "Let's get your luggage and go home. You can tell me what happened over a bottle of wine."

Daisy agreed. But she clearly couldn't wait. On the ride home, words flowed out of her nonstop, telling me what had happened. By the time we arrived, Daisy seemed talked out, exhausted. But I knew her better. She'd get a second wind and off we'd go down another line of incessant talking and theorizing.

"I put up with years of Janice openly flirting with everyone. Doesn't matter whether it's male or female. I couldn't take it anymore." Daisy paced my kitchen.

"Hold that thought. I have to get Tucker out of his crate and take him outside."

"You have a dog? I can't believe it," Daisy uttered excitedly. "Where is he?"

"Be prepared. This is a six-month-old super pooch." I laughed and we walked into Tucker's room.

He wagged his tail so hard I thought he would break the crate.

"Oh my, he's huge." Daisy squealed in a high-pitched voice that made Tucker even crazier.

When I unlatched the door, Tucker sprang from the crate and jumped up, putting his paws on Daisy's shoulders and licking her face. She shrieked with delight, making Tucker lap even more enthusiastically, until her face dripped with saliva.

Yuck! Love the dog but not that much. "Hey. Down, Tucker." I pulled his collar and yanked him outside before he could start peeing. Thank God the backyard was fenced in.

I grabbed a wet cloth from the bathroom and brought it to Daisy. "I'm so sorry. I'm not used to having a dog and he's a handful."

"Are you kidding? He's a delight," Daisy said.

"But you're covered in spittle." I scrunched my face.

"So what? Look, he wants to come back in." Daisy pointed to the sliders.

I went to get the leash like the trainer had taught me. It would limit his frantic activity.

"That's not necessary," Daisy uttered, shaking her hand no.

"Just till he calms down."

Daisy took the leash from me and sat on the couch, petting Tucker who sat by her legs. I opened a bottle of wine in the kitchen.

She motioned toward the bottle in my hand. "Do you have anything stronger?"

"You know I do." I opened a cabinet filled with various bottles of liquor.

"Vodka," she said, pointing at the Ketel One.

"Do you just want the bottle?" I asked. "Maybe with a straw?"

For the first time since landing, Daisy smiled. "No, silly. Do you have tonic or cranberry or any other mixer?"

Daisy took a large gulp of her drink and leaned back, letting the liquid do its magic. Unfortunately, it made her weepy. "You know I've been hopelessly in love with Janice since the day we met."

Tucker sensed her sadness and put his monstrous head on my friend's tiny lap. The scene was almost comical. This massive, hairy beast trying to comfort Daisy. She continued petting him with a rhythmic stroking that seemed to soothe them both.

"I never felt secure with her, ever," Daisy said in a muted voice. "You remember all those years I chased Janice. I gave up one day and attempted to get on with my life. It worked for a few years. Then out of nowhere she appeared at my doorstep. Like nothing ever happened."

Daisy had finished her drink, so I made her another. I sat across from her. "I recall how upset you were when you decided to go it alone. But I also remember how thrilled you were when Janice came back."

She took a large swallow of her drink. "Yes, I was ha . . . pp . . . y."

I moved to sit next to her, putting my arm around her shoulders.

"The first few years were wonderful." Daisy choked back tears. "But I guess old habits die hard. She started flirting again. And I mean aggressively."

I reached for some tissues and handed them to her. "Did Janice have an affair?"

Daisy shook her head. "No. At least, not that I know of."

"But it wasn't just flirting?" I asked, now confused.

"Janice didn't want to get married. She didn't want a child. But I really wanted a baby—my own or adopted. She wouldn't hear of it. So . . . ." Daisy began to whimper. "I gave up . . . having a child . . . for her."

Gasping for breath, Daisy wiped her eyes. "She just wants to have fun. The flirting doesn't mean anything." She blew her nose. "So why do I feel threatened?"

"I don't understand. Why did she leave? Did you have a bad fight?"

"Pretty much. You know how passive aggressive I can be. One day I snapped and started screaming about every perceived slight I'd stored up." Daisy rubbed her running nose. "She didn't say a word. When I finally stopped yelling, Janice stood and walked out the door. The next day when I got home from work, all her things were gone."

I gave her more tissues, putting both arms around her and squeezing, letting her cry in my arms. Tucker, however, had other ideas. He jumped into her lap, pushing me aside. Daisy wrapped her arms around him, burying her face in his neck. Tucker gave me a *Go ahead and try to dislodge me now* look. I slid back and let Daisy cry into the hairy comforter.

I wished I had the words to soothe my friend. But Janice wasn't the type to settle down. Wild, highly sexual, always on the prowl.

I almost got caught in her sensuous snare myself. I shuddered. I'd met my ex-husband, Grant, only a week later. Sometimes I wonder if that encounter pushed me into his arms.

*

I put Daisy and Tucker to bed and stayed up sipping a glass of wine in my family room. Tired as I was, I didn't think I'd sleep. I knew my thoughts would swirl around Chad and Maxwell until I would need a Xanax to calm me.

On the table next to me was the book club's selection for this month. It was god-awful. Had to be Madeline's pick. But I didn't want to be the one who didn't finish it. Some of these acclaimed books with rave reviews slay me. The sentences might be lyrical but sometimes the story gets lost. Or maybe I'm just a damn dumbass who can't figure it out. Either way, it was a tedious read.

Sure enough, within a half hour I was snoozing on the couch.

Light streaming through the windows woke me around six a.m. I decided to shower and start my day. I left Tucker in his crate until I was dressed.

Daisy was in the kitchen holding a cup of coffee when I finished. Tucker followed on my heels. He sidled up to her leg, wagging his enormous tail. I scooted him outside.

"Here." Daisy handed me a cup of coffee. "I put two sugars and milk in it. Do you still drink it that way?"

"I use artificial sweetener now." I took the cup from her. "But two sugars won't hurt me."

"You know those sweeteners are bad for you. Stop using them." She turned toward the sliding door, watching Tucker run around in the backyard.

Ugh. "Don't you know nothing's good for you? I'm so sick of these constant studies. They all contradict one other." I walked to the slider. "Tucker, come," I yelled.

He bounded into the house and I shut the door. Within a few

seconds I noticed a smell. A strong stench like poop. "Eww! What the hell is that?"

Daisy started to laugh. "You know nothing about dogs, do you?" She grabbed his collar. "Look."

I bent over and saw some brownish globs on his coat by his shoulder and trailing down his leg. "Are you kidding me? I just had him groomed yesterday. Christ, that stinks." I tore off some paper towels, wet them and put a little dish detergent on it.

"Tucker must have rolled in deer poop. He wants to smell like prey to mask his scent, not the groomer's fancy shampoo," she said, laughing hysterically.

"The backyard is fenced in. How did deer get in?" I looked through the sliders.

"Maybe it's from a smaller animal like a raccoon that can climb through the trees."

"Just great!" I uttered.

After I cleaned Tucker, I asked Daisy what she'd like to do today.

"I don't know. Sleep all day." She grinned.

"No way. Let's go to the gym. I have the day off. A good work-out will help your mood."

As we left the house, Maxwell called. When I got off the phone, I said, "Well, Daisy, the guy I told you about is coming for dinner this week."

A huge smile spread across Daisy's face. "That's great. I can't wait to meet him."

A month ago, I wouldn't have hesitated to have them meet. But Maxwell's uncertainty and aloofness were messing with my head. Now that he'd made me love him, I think he was unsure of his own feelings. Typical male bullshit. Jesus, this was not where I'd seen myself a few short months ago.

Chapter 15

BRIANNA

A SHIFT

"WHAT ARE YOU guys laughing about?"

Jane, Sandy, and Corrine were standing at Jane's cubicle, pointing and giggling at the computer screen.

Oh my! "I can't believe you watch stuff like this at work!" Shocked, I looked away. "What if Nicole searches your web history to see what you were doing when she was out of the office?"

"Bri, take a deep breath. It's my laptop, not the company's," Sandy said. "Besides, I've had a laugh or two with her about a few compromising positions."

Somehow, I doubt that. "Ah, well . . . . You know her better than I do."

Corrine pointed at me. "Look how red you are!"

Jane and Sandy snickered.

I touched my face. Not sure why.

Jane tapped me on the shoulder. "Hey, come on. Aren't you a child of the seventies or eighties? You know, the *free love* era?"

"You need to get your decades right. *Free love* started in the sixties." They were twenty years younger than me and I felt that dif-ference every day, especially in their ease with technology and their boundless energy. I felt tired and brain dead by the end of each day, while they were ready to go partying.

Why did I blush? It's not like I haven't seen erotic movies or pictures before. But never at work. Still, I'm too old to be this squea-mish about sex. Charlotte wouldn't have turned red, would she? I have to stop acting like a mother hen and be part of the group.

Later at dinner with Eric I mentioned that my coworkers were watching porno at work.

He smirked as he picked up my plate to bring it to the sink. "Did you see anything you'd like to try?"

"No. Of course not." I blushed, feeling embarrassed.

He pulled me up into an embrace. "I'm game if you'd like to try something new."

*

The charity event for the local museum was finishing when Jane came up to me. "Nice job, Bri."

I nodded. "I think it went well." Inwardly, I knew Nicole would find something to complain about tomorrow, but tonight I'd enjoy this as a job well done.

My elated mood as I drove home had me thinking about all sorts of things. Happy things. Maybe I *can* do this event planning thing as a career.

Arriving home, I found Eric sipping wine by the fire. He had a glass for me, and I was glad he'd waited up. Pleased with myself for the first time in weeks, I could actually enjoy his company without fretting about work.

As Eric talked about his day, I stared into the fire, thinking about him wanting to try something new. Be more adventurous. Me?

"Bri," he said.

I tilted my head toward him. Although I rarely initiated sex, the craving came over me fast and I wrapped my arm around his neck pulling his mouth to mine for a warm, inviting kiss.

He grinned. "Ah, Bri, you missed me."

Even though I had an early start tomorrow, I wanted to savor our time together.

*

The sun peeked through the curtains in our bedroom, waking me before the alarm. I stretched. Eric was sleeping soundly. Contentment radiated through me. Last August, when my youngest was packing to leave for college, I didn't think I could ever be this happy. It had been such a hard time. All I wanted now was to snuggle up with Eric and stay under the covers all morning. But we both had jobs to go to.

Sliding out of bed, I ambled grudgingly to the shower. I wondered what Nicole would find to criticize about last night's event. I was sure the client was pleased and would give her good feedback, but she'd still find something to complain about.

Nicole. My temples throbbed just thinking of her.

*

A chill had seized our beautiful town as I rode into work. Winter beckoned as the last of the fall foliage glided away. Chester's apple tree farms were already bare. The withered look of dormant trees always saddened me, but apple trees were especially creepy. The farms would make a great setting for a horror movie.

I slipped into my cubicle unnoticed and started up my computer, checking the company's calendar and assignments. I was booked for a luncheon hosted by the local Junior League in a few weeks. An appointment scheduled for tomorrow at 9:30 included Nicole, who was a member of the organization.

"Bri!" Nicole screamed through her door. "Get me the file for the Broad Valley Country Club."

I stood.

"Now," she ordered.

Nicole probably knew everything about the club by heart. Clearly, she just wanted to mess with me.

"Sit down," she commanded as I entered her office. A malicious grin crept across her lips.

Acid rose from my stomach. She loved to torment me because she could. I looked above her right shoulder close enough that she'd think I was looking at her but avoiding direct eye contact. Her shifty eyes made me nervous. I waited as she shuffled through the file. She studied something for a few minutes and finally plopped the Broad Valley Country Club file in front of me.

"Call the country club and confirm the date reserved for Junior League luncheon." With a wave of dismissal, she picked up her phone and turned to face the back wall.

I left her office, relieved. She'd never mentioned last night. Nothing good—nothing bad. Probably the best I could hope for.

Later that day in the lunchroom, June and Sandy talked about the upcoming Vegas trip. The firm's largest client hosted a two-day year-end party. *Alleluia!* I wasn't assigned to go. I'd heard from just about everyone how stressed-out Nicole gets during that event. Thank God, I wouldn't have to endure it.

*

Blissfully singing to myself on my way home, I decided to treat Eric to a nice meal and stopped at the store. Nicole was thousands of miles away. Tonight, I would have a relaxing dinner at home with my husband. I could hardly wait.

At home, I marinated the lamb I'd bought. Thinking about Eric made me smile. He'd be home from paddle tennis soon. Maybe I should change into a nice dress. *Or something more provocative.* One of my friends cooks her husband a great dinner and meets him at the door with a martini, wearing a short, sexy apron, high heels, and nothing else. The thought made me blush. *I couldn't do that.*

Shaking my head, I cut up vegetables to sauté for dinner. Just thinking about the apron and high heels gave me a warm, tingly sensation. Then I shuddered. *No, it's not me.* All these years of marriage and I couldn't remember doing anything so sexually suggestive.

My mind, stuck on thoughts of sex, led me to the computer as dinner cooked. Maybe I could be more adventurous. I googled: "Sex in Long-Term Marriages" and "Middle-Aged Sex." Boring. Next, I looked up: "How to put the zing back into your marriage." Still not helpful. I noticed my search brought up another site: *Will absolutely put the fire back into your relationship.* Curious, I clicked the link.

Shit, shit, shit—oh damn! An X-rated video started playing and my mouse froze. Some sort of S-and-M scene with whips and ear-splitting moaning. Hurriedly, I turned off the computer's speakers.

Slamming the control/alt/delete buttons did nothing. I yanked the plug out from the wall. *Damn it!* My cheeks burned just thinking about asking Eric to fix it, or worse, bringing the computer in for service.

After a few anxious minutes, I started the computer again. The site was gone. *Thank God.*

I poured myself a glass of wine and attempted another search, staying far away from links to videos. A few descriptions initially looked interesting but failed to excite me when I clicked through to the site.

Wondering why I was bothering with this, I noticed an article about building anticipation and started to read it when I heard the garage door open, I bookmarked the site and shut down the computer. Maybe I'll call Charlotte. She'd certainly have some ideas to give me.

*

Energized by a calm, tension-free work week while everyone else was in Las Vegas, I called Charlotte and arranged a dinner date. She would definitely have some pointers. *Jesus, what am I thinking? How do I even broach the subject?*

Charlotte dragged herself into the restaurant and plopped in a chair next to me. I was shocked to see her so bedraggled.

"What's wrong?" I asked.

She dropped her purse on an adjoining chair. "Nothing . . ."

Charlotte looked exhausted. Her bright red blouse clashed with her burgundy skirt. Our fashionista never mismatches anything. And while I've seen red and burgundy together on the runway, neon orange pumps and black pantyhose—never. Not even a teen-ager could pull off the color palette she was dressed in. But the real shocker was Charlotte's unadorned lips. Where was her ever-present tube of gloss?

"Is it Maxwell?" I patted her hand, leaning closer. "Out with it!"

She bowed her head. "Yes. His wife wants him back."

I realized I wouldn't be asking any of my silly questions. "Really, are you sure? I just don't see it."

Charlotte slumped back in her seat. "Yes, fairly sure."

"Don't give up on Maxwell." I saw tears in her eyes. "You love him. Don't walk away, fight for him."

*

My children came home Wednesday night before Thanksgiving and left on Sunday. Surprisingly, I had Friday off because not many events were planned during that weekend – people staying home with their families. The following month, however, was already booked solid with holiday events.

We saw a Broadway play and had dinner in the city on Friday. When we got home around eleven-thirty that night, the kids disappeared to be with their friends. Youth!

When Julianna and Logan returned to college, it no longer

bothered me like it had back in September. I guess I was learning to let go.

My cell rang within twenty minutes of the kids leaving.

It was Nicole. "Nice holiday? Good. You need to come in ASAP. We're busy, you know."

I kissed Eric and told him he'd have to figure out his own dinner.

"It's Sunday afternoon. Are you kidding?"

"Part of the job." I grabbed my keys and headed out the door. I'd known I'd have to work today, but I felt okay about it after my lovely days with Eric and the kids.

By the time I arrived at the office, the entire staff was seated at their cubicles. Our Thanksgiving holiday over, we were like accountants in April, heads down and crunching.

*

The five events scheduled for the week after Thanksgiving were equally divided among the event planners and their assistants. I only had to attend two of them, on Wednesday and Friday, and only one was with that bitch Nicole. I looked forward to doing some Christmas shopping and maybe coming up with some new twist to our lovemaking. Hell, I couldn't stop thinking about it. Why had I never thought to do this before?

Arriving home surprisingly early on Monday night, I sank into one of the kitchen chairs and sat still for a few minutes of quiet time. A flash of inspiration struck me, and I opened my laptop and started googling.

Two hours later, I was grinning ear to ear. I wasn't sure I could do this, but just maybe.

"Oh, baby, won't you be surprised?" I chirped out loud. *Hmm, can I really pull this off at his holiday dinner? Yes, I can. It's the perfect place for this little adventure.*

*

Luckily, Nicole wasn't at the first holiday event. We raised about five thousand dollars for the library and the patrons enjoyed meeting some local authors, sipping prosecco and munching on appetizers. Too small for Nicole to bother with, but it was the kind of event I loved—small and intimate.

She was at Friday's event however, in full critic mode.

"Bri, by now you should understand how the events work and what I expect to be done." Nicole fussed, rubbing at a spot on her sleeve. "Don't make me ask you again for something. Where is the full accounting of products used tonight?" She looked up from the spot, placing a hand on her hip.

"I sent it to you before the event by e-mail and text." I was weary of her condescending manner. I extended my phone and showed her the text.

"Well, I didn't get it." She walked away.

"Funny, it says *delivered* on my phone," I whispered, not really wanting to engage her. But she was driving everyone nuts that night, so I didn't feel singled out.

*

Over the weekend, I told Eric I was going Christmas shopping and drove to the mall to pick up some stuff: a new sexy teddy and a pair of high heels. *Oh my, I sounded just like Charlotte!*

Trying on teddies might not be quite as bad as bathing suits, but damn, the body's heading south faster than they're selling Spanx. Looking at myself in the awful fluorescent lighting of the dressing room, I distinctly remembered a scene in the 1980s show *Dynasty*. Joan Collins playing Alexis Carrington Colby, seducing a younger man. She was so sexy in her white negligee. Completely covered but so alluring. At fifty, Collins showed us all that age didn't matter. It came down to attitude. I've never been that comfortable in my own body. But buying a new nightgown is a bit of a thrill. Charlotte was right about buying sexy things—they do help inspire you.

When I arrived home, Eric had left for his paddle tennis match. My heart raced as I trotted upstairs with my packages, thinking about what to do and say for the short video I was contemplating. I knew I'd need to do a few takes. I closed the blinds and lit some candles. At my age, soft lighting was a must.

*

The week flew by in a swirl of events from the Ladies Auxiliary luncheon for the hospital to the Humane Society fundraiser. I was wiped out by the evening of Eric's partners' dinner on Friday night. I managed to find some time during the week to think through and prepare a few things for tonight. But I desperately needed a long shower to wake me up. I thought through the sequence one more time while showering. If it didn't turn Eric on, it sure was working for me.

We were a table of twelve, six of Eric's partners and their spouses at the beautiful La Belle Ristorante in a spacious private dining room, complete with bar and bartender. After a cosmopolitan for courage, I went to the bathroom and texted Eric.

You can't believe how flexible I've become from yoga.

Back at the table I watched as Eric checked his phone. He looked at me curiously but returned to his conversation with Anthony. I knew that at least half of the guests would be constantly texting and checking their phones, so we wouldn't stand out.

I giggled and turned to pretend to pay attention to my neighbor's conversation. But as I nodded and smiled, I was discreetly texting Eric again.

Do you know how sexy you are?

I waited a few minutes and sent it. I wanted to take my time with this and build the anticipation over dinner and dessert. Again, Eric glanced at me quizzically but said nothing.

I draped my arm around his chair back. My other hand slid down his arm, his shirt silky and smooth to the touch. He turned and stared at me, eyebrows raised.

I stood to go to the bar and asked everyone at our table if they wanted anything. It was just an excuse.

"Honey, I can get it for you," Eric said.

"No need." I turned and walked toward the bar and texted him again.

You know you're the handsomest man here . . . .

Were my texts affecting him the way I wanted? I wasn't sure. But they were certainly igniting my passion.

About twenty minutes later I sent another text.

We brought the SUV—lots of room in there.

This time I had his attention.

Eric leaned over and quietly asked, "Honey, what's up with you? We're at a firm dinner." He grabbed my hand and held it under the table.

I had a tough time texting with one hand, but I slowly tapped out:

Guess what I'm wearing right now—or not?

Eric looked at the text and squeezed my hand tightly. I moved our clasped hands to his leg and began to rub ever so slightly. He let go of my hand. I didn't want to embarrass him, just turn him on a little. I flashed him a knowing smile, my eyelids drooping ever so slightly.

Glancing at him through my eyelashes, I thought he was trying to read me, to stay cool and collected. But the glint in his eyes and the glow of his skin gave him away. His body radiated heat in waves; his hand was hot to the touch.

Dinner arrived. Halfway through dinner I texted again.

Hope you have lots of energy left. I have a few things planned.

Immediately after sending the text, I stood, excusing myself again and bent down as if to tell Eric something in his ear. He faced me, his ear slanted away from the table. I didn't say a word, though. Instead, I licked his ear and left.

When I emerged from the bathroom Eric stood in the small hallway leading to the restrooms.

"Bri," he whispered, pulling me tightly to him. "What's gotten into you? I've never . . . you've never . . . . What are you doing?" He covered my mouth with his.

His face flushed as I pulled away slowly. "This," I said and sashayed back to the table. The smoky taste from his whiskey lingered in my mouth.

Just as dessert arrived, I sent him the video I had made earlier in the week. Eric only watched thirty seconds before he clicked out of it. *Did I go too far?*

Eric stood, tapped my shoulder and pointed to the bar. I watched him get a drink, then go to the restroom. I hoped he was viewing the rest of the video. It's only a minute long. I couldn't believe what I was doing—and that I'd made a video—so exciting!

My phone binged. I read: **Let's get out of here. I want you!**
I texted: **Lead the way.**

*

Heavens, I guess I'm not as flexible as I thought I was. Our antics after Eric's holiday party left me tender yet satiated. What a night!

Inspired, we kept up our sexual adventures throughout the weekend. By Sunday night I was exhausted and sore. But I felt so alive. We were like honeymooners after twenty-five years of marriage. And this time it was all my doing.

The alarm rang on Monday morning. I hated leaving my warm,

safe place beside Eric. I was dreading the coming week, our busiest of the holiday season.

"Stay, Bri." Eric held the covers up, gesturing for me to climb back in. "You're killing yourself. For what? No matter what you do you're never going to satisfy her. She's just an intimidating bully who uses people and spits them out. Come on. Come back to bed."

"I wish I could." I kissed him and went to shower, exhausted before I even started the week.

Nicole yelled at me from her office as soon as I walked through the door. "Bri, why were you not here by seven? Every second is crucial this week. You know we have two events. You'll have to stay late tonight and make up for it. Get in here tomorrow by six-thirty." Nicole dismissed me with a wave of her hand.

I looked at my watch. It was eight a.m. No one had told me to be in two hours early. I sank into my cubicle chair. *Jesus. I can't do anything right.* I took a couple of deep breaths and closed my eyes, recalling Eric's warm embrace. That helped. Pacified, I opened my eyes and started work.

The luncheon went well on Tuesday. Half of us left early to put the finishing touches on the accountants' holiday dinner party at the Oak Wood Grille. While some restaurants go out of their way to make our jobs easier, others resent outsiders. The Grille was one of our favorite places. They're incredibly easy to work with.

As Jane and I placed the floral arrangements on the banquet room tables, the accounting firm's owner, Steven Lousse, strolled in.

"There's my girls," he shouted, approaching us. "The room looks good, but I'm not sure it's worth how much I paid for it."

Before either of us had a chance to respond he touched Jane's arm and slightly spun her toward him. "I hope you're changing into something . . . well . . . I know I can't say *sexy* anymore . . . . More alluring?"

Jane stepped away, saying nothing. He approached me. "You, too."

I looked him in the eye but said nothing. This guy was a jerk. I turned and walked to where Jane had backed away. Both of us wore slacks and blazers with simple blouses. My blouse was silk and Jane's an Oxford cotton—typical event ensemble. We weren't there as guests, after all.

"Where's that hot boss of yours?" he sneered. "She won't let me down."

"Nicole will be here by six before the event starts," I answered, placing the last of the floral arrangements on the tables.

"I'm going to the bar. Tell her to see me when she gets here," he bellowed.

"What an ass," Jane said after he walked away.

I nodded and left to speak with the chef. Nicole would be here within the hour and I wanted everything done properly beforehand. Henry Moore had only been the chef there for a few months. We reviewed the menu and timing of the dishes. He let me sample some of the cold appetizers. They were amazing. On my way back from the kitchen to the banquet room, I ran into Lousse again. He'd been drinking and was even more brazen than before.

"Hey . . . you . . . ." He pointed at me.

I glared but kept walking. As I passed by, he grabbed my arm. "What's the hurry, pretty lady? Stay and talk to me. I'm paying a lot of money for this event."

I took a step away. "Everything is ready. We're just waiting for your guests."

"Well, little missy," he said, sidling up to me. "I'll be the judge of that."

He moved so close that I backed up all the way to the kitchen entrance.

"You smell good," he muttered.

The kitchen had two doors directly behind me. One door opened out, the other in. The door I was in front of wouldn't budge.

I inched sideways toward the other door, but he closed the few inches between us, intruding into my personal space.

"Where are you going?" he slurred.

My heart raced as adrenaline kicked in. His hot breath assaulted my nose. I coughed. He grabbed my shoulders and slid his hands down my arms. I shivered, repulsed at his touch and his smell.

Tensing, I said loudly, "Mr. Lousse, step back. You're making me uncomfortable."

To my surprise he did. But then he turned angry. "You shouldn't tease, missy. Someone not as gentlemanly as me could get real mean."

"'Tease?' What are you talking about? I answered your question." He made my blood boil.

"Is that right?" He turned and headed back to the bar. "Tell your boss I want to see her as soon as she arrives."

I rushed back to the banquet room and told Jane what happened. "Has he ever talked to you like that?"

"What does it matter? He's an ass. Let's go stand by the entrance so we can guide people to the reception table," Jane replied matter-of-factly.

Did she not want to talk about it because he had accosted her before? Or didn't she find this type of behavior inappropriate? My composure surprised me as I followed Jane to the front. Shouldn't I be outraged? Instead, all I felt was numb.

Nicole briskly walked in, dropped her coat on the reception table, and started barking orders.

"Mr. Lousse is in the bar and wants to speak with you," I told her.

"Why? What did you do?" She placed both hands on her hips. "Really, Bri, I hope I can fix whatever you screwed up." She left in a snit.

If anything, I should be the outraged. Lousse's conduct crossed the line. The door opened and the first six attendees arrived. All smiles, we directed them to the banquet room, handing out table placement cards. Within a half hour everyone was accounted for and we started cleaning up the reception table.

"Bri," I heard Nicole hiss. "Jane."

I looked around. She was standing behind us, arms crossed tightly on her chest.

"Jesus, how long does it take to clean up a table? Move it. You should already be in the banquet room. Get going!"

I picked up the tablecloth, but she grabbed my arm. "Not you. Come with me."

I followed her outside. I hoped this wouldn't take long. It was freezing out.

"How dare you come on to a client? How stupid are you?" Nicole's face was scarlet. She stood ramrod straight with clenched fists. "Get your coat, you're leaving!"

"What? I never came on to him. If anything, he came on to me. Not the other way around. And . . . ." My thoughts jumbled mid-thought and I paused, wondering what to say.

"Now," she screeched. "Leave."

Anger ripped through my fog and I jabbed my finger toward her chest. "I would never come on to a client. Ever!" After months of her unsolicited and unwarranted crap, I didn't care if she fired me. I wasn't going down without a fight. I was innocent, for chrissake.

"Oh, please. He's a client. The client is always right, remember?" Nicole looked me up and down. "He's a man and needs a little flattery—a little stroking."

"He's lying." I took a step forward. "Go ask Jane what he said to the both of us while we were setting up."

"I'll speak with you in the office tomorrow." She abruptly swiveled and headed back into the warmth of the restaurant.

Needing my coat and bag, I followed her in.

Jane saw me grabbing my things from under the reception table. "What's going on?"

"That ass told Nicole I came on to him. Can you believe that?"

I shook my head. "I told her to talk to you about what he said to us earlier."

Jane twisted her hands together, looking everywhere but at me.

"Just tell her what happened. Okay?" I put on my coat. "I guess the good news is I get to go home early. See you tomorrow."

"Bye," Jane said in a small voice and went into the banquet room.

As I drove home, thinking over the situation made my skin crawl. It was wrong on so many levels. Nicole, of course, took the client's side. Didn't even ask for my side of the story. She must know the guy's a jerk from her past dealings with him. Yet she blamed me.

Anger and pain swirled through me and I slapped the steering wheel. They're both asses. Who talks to an employee that way? *I'm gonna tell her what I think tomorrow. Even if my job is on the line.*

I slipped into the house quietly, hoping Eric was asleep. I didn't want to tell him what had happened. I'd figure this out on my own. Strengthened by my resolve, I slept peacefully until three a.m. Waking with a jolt, my mind began to relive the night's events, my thoughts racing.

Flipping restlessly from one to side to the other must have disturbed Eric. He turned on his side, spooning with me until my heart rate slowed and sleep finally came.

I rose before the alarm, antsy and anxious. Beating Nicole into the office by a few minutes, I started organizing the last-minute details for tonight's event.

The hours ticked by and I wondered when Nicole was going to speak with me.

She finally called me into her office around four p.m.

"Close the door," she demanded. "We are letting you go."

She didn't even give me time to sit down. "What?" I said. "Lousse lied. You didn't even ask me my side of the story." Ire rose from my gut threatening to engulf me, but I managed to hold it together.

Rummaging around in a desk drawer like nothing she was saying was of any importance, she said, "No. It's a list of things.

You're just not organized enough to be an event planner." Shutting the desk drawer, she looked at me with a faint, self-satisfied smirk. "We wish you success in the future."

My head spun with things I should say, but nothing came out. Stunned. Speechless. I knew I'd regret not telling her off. But I just wanted out of there and to crawl into a hole somewhere. I'd never been fired from anything in my life.

Leaving her office, I spotted Jane by the break room. "Didn't you tell Nicole what that asshole said to us last night?"

"She didn't ask." Jane glanced nervously at Nicole's office.

"She just fired me." Tears welled in my eyes.

Jane looked uneasy. "I'm sorry, Bri. That sucks. But you'll land on your feet. After all, you don't really need the money."

I must have looked surprised. "What does that have to do with it?'

Jane started wiping down the already clean sink. "Well, we all don't have husbands who support us. Most of us need the job to survive."

"What does that matter? Truth be damned?"

"I'm really sorry, Bri. Good luck." Jane scurried out of the room.

I picked up my coat and left. I didn't bother with goodbyes. I sat in my car too stunned to start the engine. What should I tell people? The truth? But what was the truth? Eric had been right about Nicole. Her constant destructive criticism had eroded my fledgling self-esteem. And what if she were right? Had time passed me by? I took a deep breath and started the car. Mortified. I just got fired. Fired!

Walking into my house, I plopped myself in a family room chair. *Christ! What a year!* I damn well didn't deserve to be fired. I decided to speak with Nicole's boss.

I'd hoped this job would help me transition into my next chapter. Help me shift from full-time mom to businesswoman. Instead, it left me in a tailspin of anxiety, questioning everything I did.

I wiped away a tear rolling down my cheek. I knew the sting of the firing would fade like a cut, vanishing over time. But right now, it hurt.

Fuck. I threw my purse on the floor. I screamed, "Bitch! Bitch! Nicole, you're a heartless bitch!"

I stomped into the kitchen and opened the refrigerator. I needed some wine. I could hear Charlotte now: "What a nasty piece of work she is!" And Ava: "I'm calling my friend—her boss!"

That brought a smile to my face. My friends would circle around me and I loved them for it. *I'll reach out tomorrow.* I poured a glass of wine and went into the family room. Eric should be home soon.

Yes, I was strong enough to embrace the change, whatever that may be. But tonight, all I wanted was my husband's hug.

Chapter 16

HANNA

PIES—HUMBLE AND PIZZA

ASHLEY HAD FINISHED the first round of chemo and was starting to look and feel better. Mom and Dad were taking her and her husband, Josh out for a celebratory dinner the day after Thanksgiving. I offered to take Ashley's kids early on that Friday afternoon so she could relax before dinner.

Mark had been away for a week travelling in Asia for work. He'd gotten in late Tuesday night of Thanksgiving week and had taken a few vacation days to reset his rhythm back to East Coast time. His cheeriness irritated me when he finally woke up around 12 p.m. He might be refreshed by his break away from the tensions of our house, but I wasn't. Maybe I was just tired of being around my mother. I thought she'd be happier now that Ashley felt and looked healthier. But she still groused at me every chance she got even through our families' Thanksgiving dinner.

Before they left for Ashley's on Friday, Mother handed me Katie's freshly washed basketball uniform. "I got the stains on the front of her shirt out. I left you a note on the washing machine on how to get these types of splotches out of clothes. I think it was ketchup."

I took the folded uniform from her. "Mom, I told you I would wash our clothes."

"Well, at Katie's last game all I could see were those stains." Mom pointed to the front of the uniform. "Don't you care what your daughter looks like?"

"What? I couldn't see any stains on her uniform." I turned to walk away. *Jesus, she's harsh.*

"Call the eye doctor, then. You need glasses."

I slammed the door as I left to go pick up Ashley's kids, Bethie and Drake. I wanted to be out of Ashley's house by the time my parents arrived. I was grateful they had some errands to run first. I'd had enough. The kids were waiting eagerly by the door. I dropped Drake at our house. My cheerful husband was taking Drake and Brandon to see the latest Marvel movie at 5 p.m. I couldn't tell which of the three guys was more excited about seeing it.

Katie was thrilled to be playing in the Hoop Camp's playoffs that evening. She'd been active in the youth league since school began, having hounded her father all summer until he gave in and let her join. She'd definitely improved during the last two months and Bethie and I were looking forward to seeing her team, which was playing against a neighboring town.

Bethie hollered as Katie raced down the court in the second quarter and attempted a basket: "Go! Go, Katie!"

The only thing Bethie had inherited from her father was his dark hair. In every other way she looked and acted exactly like my sister. As Katie's team called a time-out, I asked Bethie, "How is school?" I stroked the back of her hair. At six she still allowed me to touch her. I missed that with my own kids.

"Huh?" Bethie tore her attention away from the court. "Good."

Afraid she was upset about her mom, I wanted to connect with her without talking about the illness. But now that I'd started a conversation with her, she must have seen it as an opening to ask me about it. "Mom will get better. Right? Like when you get a cold?"

150

God, what do I say? The truth. "We think so." I smiled faintly, hoping I was convincing enough. Hoping I was right.

Lucky for me, the whistle blew and Bethie's attention switched back to watching her cousin.

Katie's team won in overtime and both Bethie and I were hoarse from yelling.

My phone rang as we were buckling our seat belts after the game.

"Hey, how'd they do?" Mark's voice boomed over Bluetooth.

Katie screamed, "We won!"

"That's great. Congratulations. I'm going to be at the next game. I promise," Mark told her.

"Don't worry, Dad. Bethie was there, cheering me on." Katie grinned ear-to-ear at her cousin and then high-fived her.

"How was the movie?" I asked.

In unison, Brandon and Drake said, "Great."

Mark asked, "Do you need me to pick up anything for dinner while I'm out?"

Katie shouted, "Pizza!"

"Yeah, pizza." Bethie bounced up and down in her seat.

"Yes. Yes. Yes." I heard in fast succession. It was unanimous—among the kids, at least.

"Well, you all know what Grandma thinks about pizza." I countered, hoping Mark would have the good sense not to chime in.

"But Grandma is taking our parents out," Bethie volunteered. "She won't be at dinner."

My niece was starting to figure out how the world works.

"Okay," I agreed.

The excited hoots and screams from both cars almost deafened me.

"I'll pick up two pies on the way home," Mark said, after the kids piped down. "Anything on them?"

"Get one plain and one with sausage," I instructed. "But don't forget the salad. Please. And you know I'll never hear the end of this."

Friday had been our pizza night since Katie was four. We always bought a salad or antipasto with it, my compromise to add some good nutrition to the meal. Of course, Mother would never allow pizza at the dinner table. So, we hadn't had it for months. The kids complained, but they couldn't imagine the dragon my mother would become if she saw that crispy crust, bubbling cheese, and savory tomato sauce. *Hmm. Maybe I've missed it, too.*

I decided that whatever pizza we didn't eat, I'd throw away and chuck the boxes in the outside garbage bins. That way I wouldn't have to hear about it from my mother.

I set the table with paper plates and lots of napkins. When Mark arrived, he put the pizzas down on the island next to our kitchen table. The kids jumped up and dove into it, grabbing slices.

"Hold up. Salad first. Then you can have pizza."

Grumbles everywhere, even from Mark. I opened the container with the salad and passed it around.

Just as the kids settled down and started eating salad, the front door opened.

"Hello," I called.

My father answered, "Just us."

My heart sank. *Trouble!*

I tried to intercept them before they came into the kitchen. "Why are you home so early? Is everything okay?"

But I was too late. Both parents had entered the kitchen.

"What's this?" Mother zeroed in on the pizza.

I felt like a teenager caught hosting a party for the entire school, beer cans and crumpled chip bags littering the floor. "Nothing. We're having dinner. Why are you home so early?" I moved closer to her and whispered, "Is Ashley okay?"

Mother's face turned beet red. "How many times do I have to tell you?" She snatched both pizza boxes from the counter and marched to our garage door. Stunned, I stood by motionless as my seventy-year-old mother rushed out of the kitchen. In two seconds flat, she'd opened the door and was in the garage, balancing both boxes in one hand.

I grasped what she was up to and ran for the door. "Don't you dare!" I screamed.

But the dogs beat me there, barreling into the kitchen from the family room, wagging their tails, wanting to be part of the excitement. I tried to push them out of the way, but Rusty sat right in front of the door, drooling in anticipation. "Move," I shouted, but he just looked at me, a puddle forming under his panting mouth. *Ugh!* I grabbed his collar and yanked him out of the way.

By now, Mother was standing over the outside garbage bin, brushing her empty hands together as if to signify a job well done. The dogs made a beeline for her, hoping for some food.

"Where is the pizza?" I hollered. But I already knew the answer.

"Where they belong." She pointed at the bin.

I pushed past her gripping the bin lid and looking in. Not only were the boxes in there, but she had opened them and shaken out each pie. No way to salvage them now.

"What have you done, Mom?" Both hands moved to my hips, squaring off for a fight.

Mark ran to the garage, his face red. Dad followed.

"That stuff will kill you! I've told you over and over!" Mom's face was flushed, and her eyes narrowed.

"You have no right to take food off of my table and throw it away." My voice rose an octave on every word. I put my hand up on Mark's chest as he strode forward, hoping to prevent him from lashing out. "This is my mother. I've got this," I told him.

"Be responsible. Giving children such crap only sets them up for problems later. I've taught you better than that." She stood defiant; her arms crossed.

I wanted to slap her. But Mark's red face made me switch gears. I needed to calm everyone down. "Mark, can you go and make sure the kids are okay?" I cast my most pleading look at him. I knew he was pissed, but we'd agreed when we first got married that we'd handle our own families. I'd received that advice from a friend who had ended up in marital therapy. She explained what her therapist had told her, that families each have their own culture, their own way of doing things. It's much easier for a child to deal with their own family than for an outsider to do so.

"Enough, Helen!" my father shouted. He grabbed her hand and pulled her into the house. I followed, looking at the wide-eyed kids. Bethie was crying and Katie was trying to comfort her. I hoped my mom saw that.

But Mom and Dad were already out of the kitchen, moving up the stairs. Their bedroom door closed.

*

I dreaded getting up the next morning. But I had to face Mom sooner or later. Mark was still asleep even though it was almost nine on Saturday morning. After we had calmed the kids down last night, we took them out for pizza. I couldn't swallow a bite.

Mark and I stayed up late talking in the family room. We left the TV on so no one could hear us.

My mother had crossed a line, but I didn't want there to be a permanent rift. Determined to talk it out with her, I grabbed my bathrobe and washed my face, taking a few deep breaths before heading out to the kitchen. The house was quiet. Even the kids were still asleep. I went into the kitchen and saw a note on the counter.

The note was scribbled in Dad's messy handwriting.

Hanna, we left this morning to go back to California for a week.
I thought we could all use a break.
Dad

My hand shook as I dropped the note. I felt awful. Mom must be a nervous wreck about Ashley, and she hadn't been able to slow down since she got here. This was all my fault. I knew she'd go nuts over the pizza. I should have talked everyone into something else. Something she would have approved of.

My stomach ached. Poor Mom. Poor Dad. That's a long flight only to turn around in a week. I wasn't sure how they'd managed to book a flight to the West Coast so quickly. Dad must have paid a bloody fortune.

Relief began to mix with my sadness. I had my house and my life back. A little peace. I let everyone sleep in and made pancakes and sausages and cut up some cantaloupe. Mom wasn't here to critique my choices. After all, the incident last night had been ugly, and the kids had still been shell-shocked at the pizza parlor. We didn't volunteer an explanation and they didn't ask.

The kids woke up first and were delighted by breakfast. They ran to wake their Dad. He staggered into the kitchen in sweats, his hair askew, yawning.

"Good morning, honey." He sat at his usual seat and sipped the hot coffee I poured. "What's all this? Are you rebelling on purpose? Please, no more episodes like last night."

"My parents left for California early this morning."

Mark almost spit out his coffee. "What? Why?"

"I have no idea. How did they get a flight? I hope they're not sitting at the airport waiting for standby."

"Wow. I wasn't expecting that." Mark plucked a sausage from his plate and popped it into his mouth. "It's sure good to eat whatever we like again, though."

I smiled and took a deep breath. I would call my parents later and make sure they'd arrived home all right. Dad always steps in just when Mom goes too far. He was probably up half the night making arrangements.

"Remember, sometimes a little separation is a good thing," Mark said.

"I know, I know, your three-day rule."

The kids laughed and we all ate our unhealthy breakfast in perfect harmony.

*

After Katie's team lost the playoff game the next Saturday, we consoled her by watching silly TV shows, eating popcorn with *yellow globs*, and even had ice cream after dinner. If Katie had to lose, at least we could cheer her with normal family activities, ones that weren't limited by Mom's dietary restrictions.

We went to our favorite Sunday morning breakfast place after church. Packed as always, we loved Marilyn's small-town ambience. We knew everyone in the restaurant and spent the time waiting to be seated by catching up on the local news. My mouth watered for my favorite western omelet. No egg white omelet with veggies today.

Once seated, Katie looked around and spotted her teacher seated five booths away. Immediately she launched into a story about what happened in class that week.

Listening to my daughter reminded me just how different my childhood had been. We never went to restaurants. I don't remember telling my mom what happened during my school day. We always had something to do—no time to just talk. I was glad I'd created other memories for my own kids.

The restaurant door opened, and I felt cold air on the back of my neck. I turned toward the chill and my heart stopped. Jim held the door open for his daughter, Gracie.

Katie waved at Gracie, who was a year younger. They knew one other from playing on the same summer soccer team that Jim had coached.

"Mom," Katie whispered. "Grace was in the girls' room on Friday, crying." She looked over her shoulder at her. "I asked her what was wrong. All she said was it was her mother."

I wondered if Gracie knew everything. Apparently, she knew something.

"I think her parents are getting a divorce." Out of the corner of my eye, I saw Gracie stride over to our table. *Oh no.* I tried to remain stoic and prayed my cheeks hadn't turned red.

Gracie reached across me and high-fived Katie. "Hey," she said.

"Hey," Katie returned.

Jim approached. "I'm sorry for the intrusion. Gracie, let the Feldons eat in peace. Come on. They're cleaning our table now."

"That's okay," I said, a grin plastered on my face. "Jim, this is my husband, Mark. Mark, this is Jim Snyder." The two men shook hands. A lump caught in my throat. God, this was awkward.

Katie said, "Dad, he's our soccer coach and Mom's running coach. And this is Gracie." She pointed at her.

Okay, this is enough. Go away now. The guilt over that damn kiss with Jim last summer was killing me. Should I tell Mark? If I did, what would happen? If I didn't—would he find out somehow and make things worse?

"Nice meeting you," Jim said to Mark. "Enjoy your breakfast. Come on, Gracie."

I exhaled. I thought about going to confession, but I wasn't sure confession would save anything—least of all me.

*

Dad called me a few times during the week they were in California. Neither of us said anything about the pizza incident. I wanted Dad to bring it up as I was still upset over it. But I didn't know how to start the conversation.

My parents returned the following Saturday. They rented a car at the airport and drove to our house, arriving around nine p.m. I really wanted to talk to Mom, but they insisted they were tired and wanted to get some sleep before seeing Ashley the next day.

In the morning, I caught them leaving early with filled coffee mugs. "Hi, Mom and Dad. Can you give me ten minutes and I'll be ready to go with you?"

"Enjoy your family today. It's Sunday. We've got this," Dad said, following Mom out of the house.

Okay, Mom and Dad. Let's just ignore the elephant in the room. Mom clearly didn't want to speak with me. So damned awkward.

After a full day feeling fidgety and anxious, I decided to go to Ashley's. Maybe helping my sister together would smooth the way to a conversation with Mom. When I arrived, the house was immaculate and a covered pan on the stove tickled my nose with warm spices. Nothing to do.

I walked into the living room, where Dad was working with Drake on some math homework. "Hi. Looks like you have everything under control." I smiled and placed my hand on my dad's shoulder.

He patted my hand with his. "We do. You didn't have to come today. You should be with your family."

"I'm going to the grocery store. Do you want anything?" I asked.

"That's your mother's domain. Go ask her. She's in Ashley's room."

Looking around, I wondered where my brother-in-law and niece might be on a Sunday afternoon. "Where's Josh?"

"He took Bethie to her friend's home. He'll be back soon. Do you need him?"

"No. Just being nosy."

Dad smiled and returned to Drake and his math problem.

Entering my sister's room, I heard Mom and Ashley speaking softly over the running water. Mom was assisting Ashley in the shower. Not that she needed it. Mom treats Ashley like an invalid.

My heart sped up. "Hi, guys. Mom, do you want anything from the grocery store?" I yelled so they could hear me in her bathroom.

Mom walked into the bedroom. "No. Thanks. Your father and I are going later." She dropped a folded towel on a chair, turned, and promptly returned to the bathroom without ever making eye contact with me.

She's the one who threw out our dinner in the garbage but *she's* the one with the attitude? "Okay. Ashley, do you want anything?"

Ashley entered her bedroom in a bathrobe with a towel wrapped around her wet hair. While she was pale, she didn't look as weak as she had a few weeks ago. She sat at the foot of the bed. "Mom's cleaning the bathroom." She pointed through the door and rolled her eyes.

"I figured. Can I get you anything?"

"Ice cream. I'm dying for some ice cream. The drugs make my throat sore."

"We both know that's not happening tonight." I bent to whisper in her ear. "Look at what happened at my house. We'll sneak out this week and go to Taylor's Ice Cream downtown." I snickered like a ten-year-old pulling something over on her mother. "Just don't spill anything on yourself. Old Eagle Eye would zero in on that in a minute."

Ashley smiled. "You promise?"

I nodded as Mom entered the room. "Okay. I'll see you tonight at home, Mom." I kissed Ashley on the cheek and left.

*

The house was peaceful for the rest of the day until my parents arrived home. As they came in, the dogs happened to be in the house instead of in the backyard. The commotion they caused agitated my mother so much that she escaped to her room. The dogs didn't care; Dad was talking to and petting them—and letting them lick him all over. He loved animals, especially dogs. He walked them every day he stayed with us. Long walks where he allowed them all the time they desired to sniff and explore. I think he looked forward to it as much as the dogs. After all, it gave him some quiet time.

The dogs finally settled down and Mom reappeared. I knew she would have to. She'd want her groceries in their proper places, the space she'd carved out in my pantry and cabinets. They had bought so much. What was she going to do with all this food?

When the last item was stored, Dad grabbed the dog's leashes.

"Hey, I'd like to go with you," I said.

"Sure. They're your dogs." He hooked up both dogs and gave me Rusty, the Saint Bernard who, though bigger, didn't pull as hard as the Lucky, our crazy Labrador. Mom had said more than once that he could use some Ritalin for his hyperactive behavior. We didn't care, he was so damn lovable just the way he was.

About a mile into the walk, I said to Dad, "I feel bad about what happened with Mom and the pizza. But I don't know how you stand her OCD or insanity or whatever excuse she uses for her behavior."

Dad said nothing, just continued walking. I always admired my parents' devotion to one other, but his silent defense of her was really pissing me off.

"You can't get a word in edgewise with her. She talks over me, spinning the same story year after year until she exhausts herself or me in the process. She doesn't listen to a damn thing I say." I stopped. I wanted Dad to talk about this. I was frustrated and tired, too. "I know you make excuses for her. Friends and family say she's a perfectionist, but that's no excuse." I punched the air with my free hand, infuriated that he wouldn't engage—and agree with me.

"Honey, your mom means well. Clearly it doesn't always come across that way," He wrapped his arm around my shoulder as we descended the slope at the end of my cul-de-sac. "Your mom loves you and only wants the best for you." He released my shoulder.

I halted, not wanting to accept this lame excuse. It had worn thin. "I know Mom had it tough watching her own mother die. But Bri and Charlotte both lost parents young and they don't act like her."

Dad looked old to me today. The stress of the last few months had caused cavernous furrows to cross his brow. "Everyone reacts differently to tragedy."

I threw up my arm, exasperated. "Dad, you're just blind when it comes to Mom. We can't control life or its outcomes. She needs to understand that."

Lucky started barking and pulling Dad on the leash. A neighbor's dog was roaming its property, hemmed in by an invisible fence.

"He's just letting us know another dog is close by." Dad bent down, petting him. "Good boy."

"Dad!"

He turned and studied me with his kind, caring face. "I know you're frustrated, honey, but give her some leeway. She's devastated by Ashley's illness."

And I'm not? I stood stock-still, fury seizing me. If I opened my mouth, I'd say something I'd regret. So, I said nothing. I spun and started climbing the hill.

A memory flashed in my mind of a time when Mom put me on a diet. I was twelve. I had gained weight around my stomach over the summer and by the time school started, I had packed on an extra ten pounds. While the other kids ate hamburgers and French fries, my school lunches consisted of salads and carrots that Mom stuffed into Tupperware containers. She made me walk with her every day after school, so fast that I panted to keep up. She weighed me once a week, grimacing every time the scale didn't move. Finally, by the end of the year, I grew two inches and the extra weight vanished. Of course, she took credit for it. It couldn't have been the growth spurt.

My muscles tensed with indignation. I heard Dad breathing right behind me.

"Honey, stop for a minute. Let's talk," he said.

I halted, pressing my lips together as I tried to calm down.

"What's really the problem?" Dad lay a hand on my shoulder.

"What's the problem?" My tone hardened. "This is the problem." I pointed at him and back at myself. "I want to understand why . . . you let her abuse us." I pulled hard on the leash as Rusty started dragging me after a squirrel who'd popped out of a nearby bush.

"What? Come on— abuse?" Dad maneuvered to stand in front of me and the dogs, locking eyes with me. His diction was clipped, short and hard. "She's harsh, maybe, but not abusive."

Rusty lunged forward, dragging me to the bush where two squirrels were bouncing their tails up and down, almost toying with him. They dove under the winterberry plants lining the property. I clutched the leash tightly with both hands and bent my knees to prevent him from shooting into the bush.

Lucky either smelled the squirrels or picked up on Rusty's excitement. He leapt, yanking Dad off-balance. I grabbed his arm to steady him.

We reined in both dogs and moved on up the block. It gave us both a few minutes to chill. I noticed Dad's stance soften.

When he spoke, his words flowed like looped cursive writing, floating and calming. "I know her words were hurtful, my sweet Hanna." Dad grabbed my free hand, adding with his soothing bed-side manner, "I spoke with her many, many times about the way she addressed you and your sister." He looked at the ground, hunching his shoulders. "I'm sorry you feel I let you down. But I can tell you she loves you with all her heart."

Wow . . . What a relief that he understood and advocated for us. Even if we didn't know it at the time when it would have made a differ-ence. The day closed in on me. My dad, so caring and compassion-ate, shouldn't have to take the brunt of my fury, my hurt. Tiredness settled over me. I just wanted to curl up in bed and take a nap.

*

Determined to have this out with Mom, I plotted when I could get her alone. I thought the best time would be when the kids were doing their homework, Dad was out walking the dogs, and before Mark got home from work. But she must have felt me lurking and always managed to slip away on some errand before I could corner her. By the end of the second week, I gave up. Why bother? Nothing would change.

Ignoring the issue, however, didn't help. I woke in a sour mood the next morning and needed more than a wimpy walk with the neighbors, which was more about sharing gossip than getting exercise. After the kids were carted off on the school bus, I set a brisk pace. Amanda and Laura rushed behind me, yakking about the upcoming children's art show. I increased my speed and before I knew it, I was jogging.

"Hey, wait up, Hanna!" Amanda yelled. "Jesus, this isn't a running club. Walk, please."

"Sorry," I yelled, slowing down. I wanted to run for miles. The anger fueled by Mom and fear for Ashley's life created a toxic soup in my mind and I needed to expel it. My legs kept moving faster, almost of their own accord. My friends struggled to keep up.

"Tomorrow we're walking. If you want to run, go by yourself." Laura was panting when we made it back to the bus stop.

"Yeah, okay," I said. "I'm just itchy this morning. Sorry."

I left my friends and walked to my driveway. Still agitated and uneasy, I paused at the top, turned abruptly to my left, and started running. I ran for at least five miles. I knew I'd pay tomorrow with sore calves and cranky knees. But I needed to move to get a grip on the acid in my system.

By the time I made it home, I was utterly exhausted. Walking into the house, I found myself alone with my mother. I started to say something to her, but now I felt calm and happy. Why spoil the mood? What's the sense anyway? I smiled at Mom and went to shower.

After I dried my hair, I dressed and applied some light makeup. When I returned to the kitchen, Mom had set out two steaming herbal teas on the table.

"I'd like to talk to you. Please sit," Mom commanded.

Shock registered first, then anxiety as irrational fears overtook me. Was she going to threaten to take my kids away? Because in her eyes I was an unfit mother? My hands shook as I picked up the tea. *Shit. Why would I ever think that?*

"Hanna, I'd like to apologize for the night I threw out your dinner." Mom looked down at her tea. "I had no right to do that." She shot me a beseeching glance.

Exhaling, I steadied myself. Relief spread through me, squelching my crazy thoughts. My mother apologizing? Could this actually be happening?

"I . . . I . . . just want Ashley to be okay." Stumbling through the sentence, she put both hands over her face, crying with a low moaning wail.

I stood and wrapped my arms around her, her body so fragile despite her steely personality. "It's okay, Mom. Don't cry."

But it still wasn't okay. Now was my chance to have a serious conversation with her, but I didn't know where to start. I sat down at the table in the chair on the opposite side.

"Hanna, all I ever wanted was for you to be healthy and happy." Her mascara had smudged under her eyes. My mother had never lost control like that.

My shoulders slumped. "Mom, I know, but . . . Well, it's hard to live with you. You refuse to compromise. It's your way or nothing." I drew a shaky breath. "Ashley and I are grown adults, yet you're still telling us what to do in our own homes. You're obsessive about food and not in a good way."

Mom reached across the table and tucked a wayward hair behind my ear as if I were still a child. "Do you know how many diseases result from poor nutrition?" She held up one finger. "First, there's diabetes," She held up a second finger. "Then heart disease."

I reached over and clutched the fingers to stop her from counting. "Mom, I know all this. I can recite it in my sleep. You've been lecturing us since I could understand and probably before that." I let go of her hand and leaned back in my seat.

"Then why would you eat pizza? And give it to your children?" Her brows tightened and her nostrils flared.

I sighed. "Because a little fun food isn't all bad."

"The statistics say otherwise." Her tone was controlled, all emotion flattened.

Inhaling a deep breath, I said, "Look, both of your daughters and your grandchildren are good, nutritious eaters. Occasionally, we allow ourselves a pizza or ice cream. I don't need to deprive my children or myself. I'm a firm believer in moderation."

She swiped away my comments. "That's just rubbish."

Looking down at the table, I countered, "Mom, did you know what a crazy frenzied look you have in your eyes when you talk about food?" Slowing down my words, I added, "It's illogical to think that you can control our health and our lives by feeding us what you believe is some all-healing nectar. Honestly, it's a fixation with you."

"It's not illogical, but scientifically proven." Mom raised her chin, her tone dismissive.

Damn it. "You threw out my family's dinner screaming at the top of your lungs. That's anything but logical." Anger stirred in my gut. She always goes too far and then brushes it aside.

She rubbed the back of her neck, suddenly looking deflated. "Well, maybe sometimes I come across a little strong . . ."

I could barely control the rage screaming in my head. "What? 'A little strong'?" I stood and paced around the table. She watched me, warily. "Shit! You're intolerable!" The gall of her sitting there, pretending she was this noble mother with only her daughters' best wishes at heart!

"Hanna, language. And really, just because I want to keep you healthy, you act like you spent your childhood chained to a bed." She pushed the chair back as if to end the conversation.

Chained to a bed? "You're not going to get out of it this time, Mother. I'm going to tell you what I feel, and you're going to listen. Or you can find another place to live." Shaking, I sat back in my seat. I'd had enough. Clenching my right hand under the table I began, "Just because you're not a textbook abusive parent doesn't mean that you didn't inflict damage on us both."

"What are you talking about? I did no such thing." She stood in a huff.

I glared at her. "Sit down or leave."

She sat.

I inhaled deeply, heart pounding in my chest. "Your constant control over every aspect of our lives was incredibly harmful. No matter what we did, it was never good enough."

"Totally ridiculous!" She swiveled away from me.

"You never listened. I would get two words out of my mouth and you'd take off on a tangent and suddenly everything was my fault. And your issues with food were the worst."

She tapped her fingers on the table in a staccato rhythm. "Listen to how angry you're getting just because I tried to feed you well, to keep you healthy. You think I'm some kind of monster? This is ludicrous."

"'Ludicrous,' huh? Do you know that in high school Ashley was so stressed out about what she should and shouldn't eat that she ended throwing up her food after most of her meals? Do you know what that's called, Mother? Bulimia!" My cheeks burned. "And maybe the damage that caused is making it harder for her to recover from the cancer now!"

The conversation ground to a halt.

She shook her head wildly back and forth, as if trying to shake away my comments. "Stop it." Mom held up her hand. "How could you?" She stood, then sat, looking like a caged cat. "Stop." The weight of my accusation seemed to crush her, and she crumbled onto the table, sobbing.

Shit. Why did I do that?

We said nothing for what felt like five long minutes.

"I didn't know." Mom lifted her head to look at me. Her face was red and puffy. "I'm sorry." She touched the cross around her neck. Her tearstained and swollen face pained me.

"No, Mom." My chin trembled. "I'm sorry. I shouldn't have said that."

"I just tried so hard and I guess it was too much. I want you to understand why." She took a deep breath and sat straighter in her chair. "Every night when I close my eyes, the last thing I see is my mother's face. Not my beautiful mother but a woman who was ravaged by cancer." She choked out the words. "Her skin hung off her. Only a few strands of hair remained on her head. Her body was covered with sores and lesions." Mom clutched the cross around her neck and rubbed it. "We were so poor, and food was scarce. One day, she was so sick she couldn't keep any food or water down. I helped her walk the three blocks to a free clinic. We waited for hours. A cancer patient throwing up wasn't an immediate life-threatening situation." In a matter-of-fact way, she added, "It was the 1950s, you know."

Acid started to rise from my gut.

"When we finally got to see a doctor, he told Mom to try to eat fresh fruits and vegetables. That it might help." She raised both hands in a helpless gesture. "We couldn't afford them."

Mom had never told us the details of Grandma's death. "You must have been so scared."

"Of course, I was scared. There weren't many jobs for a twelve-year-old over the summer, but I found one as a mother's helper for a neighbor down the street. I bought my mother fresh fruits and vegetables with the little money I made."

She stared off into space, quiet for a minute, then resumed. "I worked all day for Mrs. Davis ironing clothes, feeding her children, and cleaning up after them, then rushing home at dusk with whatever fruits and vegetables were left over at the local market." She smiled. "By the middle of August, Mom's complexion was actually rosy. My hopes soared. But by the beginning of September when I returned to school, she got worse again. I hated school after that, didn't want to go. I only wanted to work and be able to buy good food for her. But Mom wouldn't hear of it and made me go to school."

She sank further down in her chair. "By October, our money had run out. I remember holding Mom up and walking her down the hallway to a neighbor who had a phone. She called Mom's sister, Marion. Aunt Marion came the following day, and we left our cramped little room to live in her home." She shook her head at the memory. Her fingers pushed hard on the cross, almost crushing it.

I piped up, looking into her face, which was splotched from crying. "That must have been a relief."

"Sort of. I never really felt like I belonged there." A slack expression crossed her face. "Mom died a few months later. I got Aunt Marion to give her fresh fruits and vegetables, but the doctor said that the cancer had spread too far."

"I'm so sorry, Mom."

"I know you think it's ridiculous, but I really believe that good nutrition can prevent illness. So, when the two of you were born, I was determined never to lose anyone I loved again. I researched and studied about nutrition and prepared good food no matter how tired I was." She started weeping again. "And . . . and I made sure you both had the best food possible."

I began to say something, but Mom started wailing. "All my hard work . . ." Mom banged the table hard with both hands. "And she got cancer anyway!" Tears overtook her. "It's so wrong!"

I thought my heart would burst. I moved next to her and put both arms around her, leaning her head onto my shoulder.

I kept embracing her until she cried herself out. I was grateful no one was home. The brutal sadness she felt overshadowed my hurt. Her daughter had contracted the same illness that claimed her mother despite all her best efforts.

"Shhh, shhh . . . Ashley will be okay, Mom." I totally believed it. "She will, you'll see." I smoothed my mother's hair down just like she had done to me so many times before.

Mom was clearly terrified. I hadn't realized how much. Maybe I should have.

Before Dad returned with the dogs, Mom and I freshened up. We said nothing about our talk to anyone. Instead, we enjoyed dinner with the family that night.

Sleeping proved impossible, however. I tossed and turned. How would I feel if Katie were the one fighting cancer? I should have talked with my mother years ago.

Mark turned over on his side, snoring softly. Curls sprang up off the back of his head. I wanted to reach over and touch his face, but I didn't want to wake him. Instead of needling him last year and bottling up all my resentment, I should have talked to him about how his constant traveling and lack of help with the house and kids made me feel. Instead, I almost had an affair.

It was time to get my own house in order.

Flipping over on my side, I realized I hadn't been to confession since the beginning of summer. *My damn guilt over Jim.* I couldn't remember ever going so long without it. I decided I'd start there, first thing in the morning.

*

I waited for the priest to arrive. It was early and no one else was there. I knelt in a pew and prayed. I began a long, silent soliloquy that spanned the last year. Everything I could think of that I felt bad about. I heard the priest behind me. I rose and entered the confessional.

"Bless me, Father, for I have sinned . . ."

Chapter 17

MADELINE

EVERYBODY PLAYS THE FOOL

I JUMPED UP OFF my chair. "What the hell are you talking about?" I raged at our attorney, Arthur Goldstein.

"Madeline, sit and be quiet. Let him talk," Stan growled. "I need to understand what's happening."

I sat back in my chair. My nerves stretched thin as adrenaline pumped hard through my veins.

"As I was saying, your partner, David Shepard, was indicted for wire fraud and for assisting in the preparation of false tax returns." Goldstein put down the letter from the U.S. attorney's office and picked up the subpoena for Stan's records.

Stan's face was pale, and I noticed sweat on his forehead. "When do I get my records back, Arthur? I can't run my business without them. There are quarterly tax returns due soon. And thanks to the media coverage, I'm losing clients daily." Stan lowered his head.

"So far, you haven't been charged with anything." Goldstein rummaged in the file and pulled out an inventory of files from the U.S. attorney's office and handed it to Stan.

Stan stood and paced the office. "I haven't done anything wrong."

Goldstein motioned for him to sit, which he did, staying on the edge of his seat.

"Did you know anything about your partner's schemes? Anything at all?" the lawyer asked.

Stan bounded back out of his chair. "No. Nothing. I would never do that." He started pacing again, arms flailing.

"Did you work with any of his clients? Or did you work on any of his client's returns or do any other work that was associated with him?" Goldstein persisted.

"No," Stan bellowed. "We have two separate CPA businesses. We only partnered through our joint management company, sharing the office expenses, including the rent. We both have our own LLC's for our respective accounting companies."

Goldstein closed the file on his desk. "That's good."

"Arthur, can't you get Stan's files back?" I pressed him. "What's the holdup?"

"The IRS and the U.S. attorney's office are reviewing Stan's documents under a microscope." Goldstein looked at me, seeming annoyed, then turned to my husband. "Stan, are there any . . . irregularities . . . in those documents?"

"Hell, no." Stan flopped into his chair, wiping sweat off his forehead.

I've never seen Stan so flustered. I often have trouble controlling my emotions, especially when I get angry, but not Stan. I wanted to reach over, to hold his hand and tell him we'd get through this.

"Okay. I'll contact the prosecutor." Goldstein rose and walked around his desk toward us. "Stan, steel yourself. You got swept up in this mess and it's going to take time to sort it all out. There's nothing you can do about it."

Stan rose slowly, stooping forward to brace himself on the back of his chair. He straightened, looking directly at Goldstein. "Tell them I have a company to run. I need my clients' documents back. This is killing my business."

"I will." Goldstein patted him on the back and escorted us from the office.

I drove home. I didn't think Stan could focus on anything but this right now. His friend, his partner, had not only buried himself and his family out of sheer greed, but had also jeopardized our family. Stan's hopelessness came at me in waves. And for once, I didn't know what to do.

*

The next morning, Stan left early to go work. I watched him leave from our bedroom window, choking back tears. *How do I help him? There must be something.* I opened my laptop and started searching—for what I wasn't sure.

My cell rang an hour later. I hesitated when Bri's name came up.

"Madeline, how are you? How's Stan? What can I do? Do you need Eric's help?" Bri's words fell over one another in her eagerness to help.

The tension in my spine relaxed hearing how concerned she sounded. "Hey, I'm glad you called. I could use a friend. Want to grab a drink when you get out of work?"

"I can meet you right now or anytime that's easiest for you," Bri replied.

I sighed. "I don't want you to get in trouble at work. After work is fine."

Bri hesitated. "Madeline, I got fired a few days ago. I didn't want you to worry about me while you're going through this mess."

Anger broiled under my skin. "What the hell? Has the world gone crazy?"

"It's for the best, believe me. My boss was a horror. My only regret is I didn't tell her off. I played it too nice, as always. Sometimes I wish I were more like you and spoke my mind."

"Thanks—I think." Standing, I walked to the window and

looked out. "Let's have lunch. That way I'll be here when Stan gets home tonight."

*

We met at a small restaurant in Morristown. I didn't want to stay in Chester where people knew about the indictment. It was in all the local and state papers, published with a picture of David, Vivian, Stan, and me at last year's charity dinner for the hospital. That damn picture! Last year I was pleased at how nice we all looked. But under these circumstances, we looked guilty simply because we looked rich.

Walking toward the restaurant, I passed a woman I had worked with on the PTO at the high school. She and I had crossed swords once or twice. I winced as I saw the light of recognition cross her face.

Sure enough, she jumped at the chance to be nasty. "Jeez, Madeline, do you think you could keep your husband out of the papers for just one day?" She and her equally annoying friend walked on, tittering.

You're lucky I'm not my normal self. I could slice and dice you in little pieces, starting with that bad dye job and haircut. I clenched my fists in silent rage, then made myself turn away.

I relaxed when I saw Bri, giving her a bear hug before sitting down. I took a few deep breaths and opened the menu. When the waitress came by, I ordered a pinot grigio and a salad. I'd drink the wine but wasn't sure my stomach could handle food.

"I'm so sorry, Madeline. I don't even know what to say," Bri consoled me.

"Stan didn't do anything wrong. It was his partner in the management company who was charged." I gulped my wine. "Remember that day we saw him at that restaurant with that lawyer? I wonder if he knew then that trouble was on the horizon."

"Does Stan have an attorney? If not, Eric could refer him to some good ones."

"Stan has hired Arthur Goldstein. But never in my wildest dreams did I think we'd need an attorney for a criminal investigation."

"Goldstein is renowned. You have great representation." Bri sipped her iced tea.

"I don't know what to do. How to help. I never figured that Stan, my honest Abe, would ever have legal issues. This came out of left field." I paused. "And Stan is . . ." I choked up, ". . . devastated."

Bri reached her hand across the table and grasped mine. "I'm here to help in any way I can. I'm so sorry you're going through this."

"I know. Thanks." I struggled to continue and turned the conversation to her. "What the hell happened to you? Fired? I worked with you on all sorts of events and you're really good at them. She must have felt threatened by you."

Bri smiled broadly. "I doubt it. But thanks for making me feel better."

"Anytime. You know that."

Bri told me what happened at the event with the client and her boss's reaction. I asked her what Eric thought.

"He thinks at the very least it's harassment," Bri said. "Of course, he wants to sue. I'm just not sure what I want to do yet."

Talk of lawsuits got me thinking about Stan again. "Never in a million years did I think this would ever happen to my husband."

"You two have been together a long time," Bri said.

I sipped my wine and watched it settle back to the bottom of the glass. "Yes, we go way back."

"You met in college, right?"

Maybe she was just trying to distract me from thinking about this absurd lawsuit. It was working. "Well, it was a long time ago . . ." I started. "We were both juniors at the University of Virginia . . .

*

My manager told me to call Stan Miller and have him come in early to cover my shift. I'd asked for the weekend off to attend my cousin's wedding. Although, I barely knew the guy, he agreed.

Stan told me he'd be at the bookstore by 3:30. He didn't show up. I began to panic more every minute he was late. At 3:45, I paced by the doors. Where the hell was he?

Stan finally showed up at 4:02. I almost decked him. Instead, I blurted out, "You're such an asshole! I'm going to miss my bus!"

He apologized, saying something about his car breaking down. I pushed past him, running with my backpack and suitcase for the bus stop seven blocks away.

I found out later that Stan's car had broken down and he'd walked three miles to get to work. He left his car at the side of the road with a note that he'd deal with it after he got out of work that night.

The following Friday, Stan came in early and handed me a huge bouquet of flowers. "I'm sorry. I hope your plans weren't ruined."

By now I knew the whole story and was glad to have a chance to apologize. "No, I'm sorry I was such a bitch . . . ."

*

It was as if that memory had happened yesterday. Like how his face flushed when he handed me the flowers. He was so sincere.

Bri listened to my story, nodding every once in a while.

Warmth curled around me and I closed my eyes for a moment, imagining Stan's embrace. "That's how we met." I smiled at my kind friend. "I had a lot on my plate in college and tended to lash out when I got stressed." I motioned for the waitress. "I guess I still do."

"It couldn't have been easy for you. Your childhood. But you got past it and made a better life for yourself, for Stan and for your children." Bri soothed me.

Thinking out loud, I said, "How could anyone think that a man who'd walk three miles for a person he barely knew because he'd made a promise would ever do anything illegal?" I hid my face in my hands. Bri reached over and patted my shoulder.

*

Every night, Stan came home and closed himself off in his office. We didn't eat dinner together nor did he eat any of the meals I left for him. The more days he locked himself away, the more worried I became.

Both our daughters called every evening to speak with their father. He refused to take their calls.

After a few days of this, I decided to act. Pounding on his office door, I shouted, "Pick up the house phone. Your daughters want to talk to you. They're worried sick. What the hell are you doing, shutting out the people who love you? Pick up the damn phone!"

It took a few extra rounds of pounding, but he finally did speak with them.

Stan had no excuse for not communicating. Even my cousins called, offering to bring over dinners, asking what they could do. It was comforting to see the family rallying around us. But even after that call with the girls, Stan isolated himself. It was only a few weeks before Christmas. The storm cloud wouldn't dissipate, it just hung there like a dirty sheet on a windless afternoon.

I thought about calling Dr. Mann, the psychologist who helped Sarah during a particularly hard time in high school. I doubted Stan would have anything to do with a psychologist right now, but maybe it would help me. I called and made an appointment.

I met with Dr. Mann twice and she gave me some good advice. I was determined to follow it. Anxiety ate at me all afternoon as I waited for the hours to pass. I would try to engage Stan tonight when he arrived home. Normally I act like a bull in a china shop, speaking my mind, but Dr. Mann and I agreed that this situation needed a softer approach.

*

I heard the garage door open and knew Stan was home. I looked at my hand. It was shaking. I centered my breathing and poured us two glasses of wine, setting them on the countertop. The door from the garage opened.

"Hi, honey. Sit and have a glass of wine with me," I said softly.

Stan shook his head, face drained. "I'm just going to my office." He started to walk by me.

I grabbed his arm. "No, you're not. Please sit down and talk to me."

He hesitated, then pulled out the counter chair and sat, body slouched like that of an old man. "What do you want, Madeline?"

I gently told him why I was concerned and how his behavior was affecting me and our family, all the while praying Dr. Mann knew what she was talking about.

Stan lowered his head. I was afraid he was going to retreat into his office and shut me out again. Instead, he gulped down half of the glass of wine I had poured for him. "I'm such a failure. How could I have not known what was happening?" He threw back the rest of the wine.

I kept my voice soft and even. "You weren't involved with his work or his clients. This has nothing to do with you."

"Tell that to my clients. I got another letter today asking for their files back." Stan furrowed his brow, his breath rapid and unsteady.

I thought he might be hyperventilating. I watched him, keeping myself still with an effort.

Then he struck the counter with his hand. "Don't you get it? I was the one who suggested to David that we team up to share expenses. I did this to myself. I never suspected anything shady about him."

Stan jumped up, opened the liquor cabinet, and poured a good slug of vodka into a glass. He pounded down at least half of the liquor in a single swallow. "You know, it hurts. I thought we were friends. He's probably been playing me all along. Damn it." He knocked back the rest of the vodka. His eyes were damp, and a tear escaped. Angrily, he struck it away with his free hand.

Watching my husband crumble in front of my eyes tore me apart.

"In the name of God, how do I turn this around? I'm fifty-six, Madeline. How can I support the family now?" He let the glass clatter on the counter and covered his face with both hands.

Touching his shoulder, I said, "You are the smartest man I've ever known. You'll be cleared by the attorney general. We'll put all this behind us." I inhaled, wrapping my arm around his shoulder, wanting more than anything to shelter him from his pain. "We have money saved and we can sell this house and downsize. Don't worry. We'll find a way."

"Mads, David was my best friend. How could he do this to his family? To us?" He stood, pacing the kitchen, picking up the vodka bottle and pouring himself another glass. "Jesus, how blind can I be? I never saw this coming. Any of it. He took total advantage of me." He shook his head as he sat back down. "None of this would have happened to you. You would have seen right through it."

"Are you kidding? Anybody can be deceived. Haven't you noticed how hypercritical and suspicious of everything I am? Where do you think that came from?"

"You mean your parents?" Stan asked, his words slurring. "Somebody else?"

Jesus! Was this what it had come to? Vodka after wine? "Let me make you something to eat, okay?"

"No. Just another drink!"

I watched the remnants of my wine slide down the glass ignoring his request for another drink. "Remember me mentioning Patrick, my first boyfriend?"

"Why? What in the hell does that have to do with David?"

Should I tell him this? Dr. Mann had thought it was a good idea, to show him that he wasn't the only person who had ever been duped.

"Everybody has been fooled or used by someone." Shifting in the chair, I faced him. "I never told you much about Patrick. I hate thinking about it. Too humiliating."

Stan rose again to bring the bottle of vodka from the cabinet to where we were sitting. "I'm gonna need more of this. A lot more!" He poured a full glass. "Okay. So, what—he deceived you? I don't understand."

"I told you that Patrick Harrison was the adjunct professor in my English literature class, didn't I?"

"Maybe . . .not really." He rubbed the back of his neck. "He's that guy you dated in your freshman year?"

I knew I didn't want to tell him this particular story while he was on his way to getting drunk. "What are you doing?" I asked, exasperated. "If you just want to drink, we can talk another time."

"No, sorry. I'm not drunk, just a little tipsy." He smiled for the first time in days, a little euphoric from the booze. "Go ahead."

"You sure?" At his nod, I continued. "Okay. Patrick was quite handsome, and the female students all came early to class to sit up in front."

"Including you I suppose?" He fidgeted with his now-empty glass.

"Yes, including me." I didn't tell him that Patrick had looked like a rich preppy Ralph Lauren model, standing out in a sea of wrinkled shirts and bow ties. Nor that outside of a few dates, I'd never had an actual boyfriend before. All I wanted back then was to leave home and never return. I worked two jobs in college to help defray my student loans. Having friends—girls or boys—didn't interest me. They'd only divert me from my goal.

Stan stared at me; impatience clearly written across his face. "Well?"

I closed my eyes. Lurking at the edge of my memory, Patrick stood at his office door at the university . . .

*

"Madeline, I'd like to go over your essay. Can you stay for a few minutes?"

"I have to go to the bookstore. I work there right after class." I licked my slightly parched lips. Was there a problem with my essay?

"When do you get out of work? I'll meet you and we'll review your essay then."

Wow, taking his own time to help me. *"Are you sure? I don't get out until nine p.m."*

"Great, meet me at Sherry's Bowl in the restaurant."

I left work a few minutes early so I could freshen up. I'd been up since five-thirty a.m., so I desperately needed to.

Arriving early, I sat in a booth and watched as he came in. My heart pounded in my chest. Patrick, dressed in jeans and a T-shirt that showed off his muscles, strode to the table. Instead of sitting across from me, he sat next to me.

It took a minute to process this intrusion of my space. His tantalizing musk with its undertones of citrus sent shivers down my spine.

He grinned, maybe reading my startled expression. "It's easier to work side by side."

I barely nodded.

"You have excellent writing skills, but they need honing. Let's go over your paper."

He opened the cover of the essay. I was embarrassed at the mass of red lines and letters everywhere.

"Doesn't look like I'm a good writer from all those marks."

"Like I said, you need honing." *He inched closer in the booth until our legs touched.*

My breath caught. My heart beat so fast I thought he could see it under my shirt. I don't remember a word he said that night. By the end of it, he had wrapped his arm around my shoulders. Was he going to kiss me? He didn't.

*

180

Stan's irritated voice snapped me back to reality. "Really, what the hell does your dating life have to do with this situation? Honestly, Madeline, not everything is about you." Stan reached for the vodka.

I wrenched the bottle out of his hands. I don't ever remember Stan being this nasty. His face so tight and red. "Calm down. Now. I'm trying to tell you something painful from my past. At least listen."

His face softened. "You're right. I'm sorry."

I cleared my throat. "I met Patrick a few times a week for the first month of classes for instruction. He'd get really close to me physically and then back away. One minute I thought he liked me and the next I didn't. Finally, one night he did kiss me. Do you know what he said?"

Stan straightened in his chair. I had his full attention now. "That you're a great kisser?"

"No, honey. He told me that I needed practice. And he'd be happy to instruct me."

"What a jerk!"

"It gets worse." For years, I looked back at that first kiss in horror, trying to erase both it and Patrick from my mind. Therapy helped. But at the time, I thought I was in love. Sometimes, when I least suspect it, the faint scent of citrus can send me reeling back there.

The wine worked its magic and I relaxed, drifting back to that large auditorium and my English literature class . . .

*

Patrick manipulated me for the next few months by pursuing then ignoring me. He made me wait endlessly for him and gave me the silent treatment for any infraction. He made me beg for his attention. By the time we slept together, I was so nervous about pleasing him that I never considered my own pleasure.

But by the end of the semester, he was done with me and on to the next shiny new toy. I barely saw him except in class and he made it clear

I wasn't to approach him there or even during his office hours. I started chewing my fingernails, something I hadn't done since second grade.

One day I called in sick from the bookstore and knocked on his office door. No answer. As I walked away, I heard giggling. I stopped, but it went quiet again.

Suspicion overwhelmed me. I tried a few doors till I found one open and slipped into a dark room, leaving the door slightly ajar. I wanted to see who came out of his office.

A few minutes passed. What the hell was I doing? This was ridiculous. I put my hand on the doorknob but stopped when I heard voices. Patrick and a woman.

"That was great. As always. Same time next week?" she asked.

"Yes, sweetness. Till then," Patrick answered.

Tension pinched the back of my neck. He'd called me *sweetness.*

I pushed the door open ever so slightly, maybe an inch or two. They were walking a few doors down the hallway, oblivious to me. Standing close together, they whispered, staring into each other's eyes. When she turned and walked toward me, I slipped deeper into the dark of the room. I knew her. She sat behind me in class.

I fell against the wall, stunned. How could he betray me like this? I loved him. He knew that. What had I done wrong?

The next day as I approached Patrick's desk after class, he held up his hand like a stop sign, saying in front of the three girls speaking with him. "Not now, Madeline. I'm busy. If you need to talk about class, call the department secretary and arrange an office hour."

The girls snickered as I left, head drooping.

What the hell was going on?

Humiliated and confused, I accepted an invitation from my roommate to go out drinking that night. We walked by a couple groping on a side street as we approached the college bar. Something was familiar about the man, but I couldn't make him out in the dimness of the alley.

The couple emerged from the street as we waited in line. No wonder I thought there was something familiar! It was Patrick and yet another girl . . . Jesus, she sat two seats away from me in class! I cut in front of my friends and pushed into the bar, not wanting Patrick to see me. I knew he wouldn't come in. Too public. What a prick!

*

Stan's booming voice interrupted my reverie. "What the hell, Mads. That's not you. I don't believe it. We met two years later and if I'd tried anything like that, you'd have kicked my ass. No. That's not you." He shook his head wildly.

"Well, believe it. Look what I grew up with. How much self-worth do you think I had?" I shrugged. "There's more . . ." I closed my eyes, letting the painful memories flood over me.

*

A B-. I couldn't believe it. I threw the paper with my grades on the floor. Jesus Christ, what else was this man going to take from me? I had to maintain a B or higher in every class to continue my desperately needed scholarship. Nauseated, I paced my room, finally curling up on my bed in a fetal position, crying.

Somewhere during that sleepless night, anger gripped me. I had sworn, curled up in my mother's car years ago, that no one would ever control me again. Yet here I was.

No, not this time. I took all my papers to the head of the department to contest my grade.

The department head told me to speak with the teacher first. I made an appointment with Patrick. When I walked into his office, I had to stop myself from imagining all the places he'd had sex with other students or how luscious his lips were.

Forget about my broken heart, I told myself sternly. My only goal was to get that B that I deserved.

"What do you want, Madeline?" Patrick sneered.

"I need you to change my grade from a B- to a B. I brought all my

183

papers with me and they average to a B+ or an A-." I placed everything on his desk.

"Yes, but your in-class performance was subpar." Patrick handed me back the papers.

Stunned, I looked him in the eyes. "What are you talking about? You ignored me every time I raised my hand."

The asshole had played me. Something snapped.

"You will change my grade, or I'll tell the head of the department about all your sexual conquests. Some right here in this room." I spread my arms wide.

"Seriously? You have no proof." He flicked his hand.

"Do you think for one moment that I won't go and ask every single woman in the class about their relationship with you?" I hissed. "How many of those women are angry with you right now? There must be at least one other and that's all I'll need. What do you think the head of the department will think of that?"

A hot flush rose to Patrick's cheeks. He stood. "That's blackmail. The school won't tolerate that."

"Go ahead. Try me." I stood tall. My arms folded across my chest. I refused to lose my scholarship to this dick. Not today. Not ever.

The next day, my grade was changed to a B, securing my scholarship.

*

Stan slapped my arm. "Now that's the woman I know."

"There." I raised my hand. "See? Even I got duped." Clearing my throat, I added, "Listen, what's happening to you isn't fatal. You'll survive. We'll be okay. You have to stop dwelling on it. It's over. Move on."

He took a deep breath, pushing the vodka glass away. "You're my rock, Mads. I don't deserve you."

Wrapping both hands around his, I said, "Oh yes, you do. Patrick taught me what love wasn't. You taught me what love is."

Chapter 18

AVA

Deseos

Let there be light! When the power came back on, *Mami* and I danced through the house and out to Lola's. I had lived without power for two weeks, but they had survived the blackout for more than six. Relief washed over me. I needed to go home but couldn't leave her there without electricity and water. I hoped water would soon follow.

A celebration was in order that night. We decided to drive into town. The road was dry, and they had started to repave it closer to the city. *Mami* made me ride as a passenger on Gabriel's scooter while she took Lola.

The whole town was in celebratory mode. One of the restaurants had opened last week when power and water was restored. But we opted to eat in the square where José Andrés still had a makeshift kitchen. We took our paper plates and found a table.

A feisty salsa beat filled the air from a boombox a few tables over. As night fell, musicians played in the square, which filled with couples dancing just like the first time we had eaten in town.

"Does this happen every night, Gabriel?"

"What?" He tilted his head.

"The dancing?"

"No, I've seen it maybe a handful of times when I slept at the hospital." He looked out over the crowd. "But it's a beautiful night and that's always something to celebrate."

My mother's words echoed in my head. *He's the finest man I've ever known.* I barely remembered meeting him when I was a teenager. We'd vacationed in Puerto Rico and stayed at my grandmother's home and visited with our cousins. Our parents often went out with Lola and her husband, but our two families only gathered a few times. If I remembered correctly, Gabriel was in middle school then, maybe five years younger than me.

"Did you go to college and med school on the island?" I asked.

"No. I went to NYU for both." He stood, picking up our empty plates and heading to the bins at the side of the makeshift dining area.

I never knew he was in New York when I lived there. When he returned, I asked, "Did you always want to be a doctor?" I winced, realizing I sounded like a bad prospect at a speed-dating event.

He smiled. Was he thinking the same thing? "Since I was a teenager, I guess."

Gabriel watched our mothers dancing together. They motioned for us to join them. "Water should be back on in a few days and then I'll have to return to New York. How about you?"

"Yes, as soon as it comes back, I'll head out myself." I sighed, a little sad at the prospect of leaving.

Our mothers dragged us to the improvised dance floor. He danced with his mother and I with mine. The song ended and a slow song started. Both of our mothers bolted off the dance floor, leaving Gabriel and me standing there.

"Would you like to dance?" He reached out his hand.

I took it, moving closer to him and draping my uninjured arm on his shoulder. I looked up into his bronze eyes and the hair on my arms stood at full attention.

Knowing our mothers were watching from the sidelines, I fought the urge to nuzzle my head on his shoulder. I didn't have to see them to know they'd be giggling like schoolgirls.

He drew me closer, and we swayed to the music. His lips settled by my ear and he whispered, "I remember you, Ava. You were a goddess to me when we were younger."

My pulse started racing.

Goddess? I barely remembered him. A flick of a scene here and there, but nothing more. I honestly didn't know what to say. I drew a long shaky breath.

He laughed. "My brothers and I were all in love with you and I don't think you noticed any of us."

"Oh, stop. We were just kids. What did any of us know?" I said in a wobbly voice, stealing another glance at him.

His eyes glowed. I could see he was about to say something but must have decided not to. The song ended. He spun me once around and guided me off the dance floor. Our mothers scattered quickly, like mischievous teenagers when they see a police car.

As we returned to our table, he said, "I've worked with Aiding the Children before. It's a wonderful organization. What do you do for them?"

"Not much. I just provide some transportation and translation services for the Spanish speaking patients." I shrugged.

He edged closer to me. "It sounds like you do a lot."

"There's nothing like helping a child. How could I not?" I sat.

He straddled the end of the picnic bench opposite from me. "I feel the same way."

Our mothers brought us over two cold beers and went back to dancing.

Gabriel took a swig of beer. "My mother tells me you are divorced and dating someone."

Direct. Wow. How come I haven't been able to ask him anything?

When have I ever been this tongue-tied? "Yes, that's right." His eyes were so expressive. "How about you? Married? Children?"

Tingles crept along my skin as I waited for his reply.

"I was married and have one child, a daughter, who is in her last year of college."

Now what? Say something. But what?

I looked out on the dance floor and spied Nurse Carmela. *Jesus.* "Isn't that your nurse?"

He looked at her. "She's a nurse, but not my nurse."

"She always seems to be around."

"Yeah, I'm aware." He looked away.

I was riveted at the sight of her swaying to the music, however. She was a hell of a dancer. Halfway through the song I noticed Gabriel watching her. Nurse Carmela certainly knew how to entice, and I felt a pang of jealousy. *How ridiculous am I being?*

When the song ended, she sashayed toward us. "Oh, hello, Dr. Ruiz," she cooed, batting her eyelashes, standing mere inches away from him.

She was dressed in a clingy red dress with a high slit on one side and four-inch heels. I couldn't figure out how she didn't break an ankle dancing in those.

He backed closer to me, using me as a shield. "Carmela. You remember Ava?"

"Sure." She slid even nearer to him. "Would you like to dance, Doctor?"

He immediately said, "No, thanks. We're getting ready to leave."

Our mothers must have seen this encounter and decided to intervene. They walked back to us.

"You two dance well together," my mother announced as they both sat, completely ignoring Nurse Carmela, who refused to take the hint and leave.

A long, awkward moment of silence. Finally, Gabriel introduced her. "Nurse Carmela, this is my mother and her neighbor, Ava's mother, Mrs. Delmar."

"Such a pleasure to meet you, Mrs. Ruiz." She barely nodded to my mother.

I almost laughed out loud, probably from nerves at Carmela's obvious sexual appeal, but I could see how uncomfortable Gabriel was. Had they been involved previously? Was she stalking him? I secretly hoped she would trip and fall from her too high stiletto heels.

I stood. "Is everyone ready to go?"

Both mothers jumped up, picking up on Gabriel's vibe.

"Will you be in work tomorrow, Doctor?" Carmela asked breathlessly. "I'm working the morning shift."

"Yes," he said, dismissing her. "Have a good night." He turned quickly and walked toward the parking lot.

We followed Gabriel. The back of my neck burned. Nurse Carmela must be watching our every move, sending laser rays of hatred in my direction. I wondered what she'd think when I threw my leg over the back of Gabriel's scooter.

But I quickly forgot about Nurse Carmela as Gabriel and I headed home through the rhythmic twists and turns of the torn-up road. When he stopped in my driveway, I popped up from the seat and quickly swung my leg over, stepping on an exposed tree root coming through the blacktop. Totally off-balance, I felt myself fall before Gabriel grabbed my arm and pulled me into him. Neither of us moved. My heart leapt in my chest. I raised my head and looked directly into his intense bronze eyes. My mind raced, darting like a hummingbird. Time ceased and the air changed between us. We stayed entranced until I finally broke eye contact, gulped a breath of air. "Thanks, I'm okay" I whispered.

As soon as they arrived, both mothers demanded to know more about that crazy woman in the red dress. I left Gabriel explaining and walked into our house for a drink. I needed one. My hands shook as I relived those last few exquisite moments. *God, why didn't he kiss me? Shit, is that really what I want?* Maybe I'm reading too much into this. I rummaged around in the liquor cabinet and found a bottle of tequila and a glass. I threw back a shot. The liquid settled me down. But I could still smell his citric cologne mixed with anti-septic. I downed another shot.

Hearing laughter outside, I walked to the door: "Anyone want a drink?"

We opened a bottle of prosecco I'd put into the refrigerator this morning. We sat at the picnic table enjoying the crisp, cold bubbles.

Sitting across from my mother, I could read her thoughts as she looked back and forth from Gabriel to me. I jumped in to divert her before she could say something I'd regret. *"Mami,* I still think you should come back with me for a month or so. You, too, Lola. Come back to civilization. I have plenty of room and you can both spend time with your families in the States."

"Mom, please. Go with Ava. I can't stay much longer, and I don't feel good about leaving you here." Gabriel grabbed his mother's hand. "Please."

"But, what about our chickens?" *Mami* threw her arms up.

"Those damn chickens again!" *I knew it was more than that.*

"Si. And what about our homes? *Nos roban.* There are gangs stealing from abandoned homes. They'll take all our stuff."

"Mami, please."

She stood. "You don't understand." She wrapped both arms around her chest. "This is my home. I'm not leaving."

Lola jumped up next. "Me, either."

They chattered in rapid Spanish, arms flying everywhere, then stormed into Lola's house.

I felt bad. "I should go speak with my mother."

Gabriel stood. "Yeah. Me, too. Listen, let's try to talk them both into going back with you. Even if it's only a week. Anything to get them out of here."

I watched him walk away. A warm, pleasant sensation surged

through me. I stood, transfixed. I closed my eyes and heard him whisper in my ear. *Goddess*, he'd called me. What the hell was happening to me?

I walked into Lola's house and saw him speaking with his mother. I searched for mine, who was sulking by the kitchen counter. As I approached her, she jabbered in nonstop Spanish, telling me that I didn't understand anything.

"*Mami*, come home with me for just a week or so and bring Lola. Don't you want to see all your grandkids? Doesn't Lola want to see hers? You can come back here anytime you want. By then the water should be back on. Please."

My mother looked at the ground. "How? I have animals to take care of."

"Will you come if I can find and pay someone to take good care of them and watch your home?"

"Only if Lola comes." *Mami* recrossed her arms. "There better be no dead chickens when I return. You understand me?"

"Yes, *Mami*." Relief spread through me. *Finally!* "I'll make all the arrangements."

She went to confer with Lola as Gabriel came over to me.

"Success," he said.

"Yup," I uttered. "Please feel free to come to my house anytime you want to see your mom."

He nodded. "Thanks, I'd like that."

Me, too!

*

It took a week to get everything in order so we could leave the island. Gabriel had a patient who would look after our mothers' properties and the chickens. I hired a locksmith to install more secure locks on both homes. My mother still worried about looters, so I engaged an alarm company to wire and monitor my mother's and Lola's homes.

"Let me reimburse you for the security company at least, Ava," Gabriel said, driving us to the airport.

"No, that's all right. I only paid till the end of the year. It wasn't a lot of money. You've done so much for my mother, it's the least I can do." I looked at his hands on the steering wheel. While not as smooth as other surgeons, he still had long, sensuous fingers.

He tilted his head toward me. "Thank you."

Our mothers had stopped speaking in the back seat, listening intently to our conversation the way they'd eavesdropped on us every time we spoke. I was sure they'd critiqued each one. I could only imagine what my mother would say to me once we were alone at my house.

Gabriel parked the car and helped me with all the suitcases. He said goodbye at security. Once we were through, I looked back and saw him still standing where we had parted. He waved and left. A twinge of sadness overcame me. But our mothers started asking a million questions about nonsensical things, distracting me.

I sat on the aisle in the plane and closed my eyes, faintly listening to their nonstop chatter. I believed they thought that no one understood them when they spoke in Spanish. I had made that mistake myself once too often and now know better.

I relaxed, drifting into a daydream of a woman in a red dress dancing with Gabriel. That made me edgy. I forced my thoughts to return to Neil. I remembered how, when I'd been young and brokenhearted, I had searched for him in crowded New York streets, hoping beyond all hope that he'd see me and recall how much he'd cared for me. Decades had passed without us meeting until that awful day that Paul, my ex-husband, had arranged to sell our management company to Neil.

My eyes shot open and my body twitched.

"Ava, are you all right?" *Mami* shot me a concerned glance.

"Yes. Just dreaming about getting pecked to death by chickens." I knew that would shut her up.

"Funny. I get it. You don't want to tell your mother." She turned back to Lola.

I pulled my iPhone out of my bag and connected the earbuds to listen to a book. Anything to stop my thoughts from overwhelming me. But my mind kept returning to that fateful day.

*

"Sell, we need to sell the company. We don't need two businesses. I want to enjoy my life, not work all the time." Having told me this, my husband, Paul quickly arranged for the sale. Barely two weeks went by before he had a buyer and a closing date.

The deal came together so quickly that I grew suspicious. Plus, Paul gave me excuse after excuse when I asked to review the documents before the closing. But when the buyers came into the conference room and I saw Neil, I knew something was desperately wrong. How could Paul have contacted Neil, of all people? Neil, my first love?

I refused to sign the papers.

The last straw came when Paul appeared at my door drunk and bleeding from a beating, blaming me for stopping the sale. He desperately needed to sell the company to cover his gambling losses. This had happened once before in our marriage and I wouldn't put up with it again. I was done.

We sold the company within a few weeks to another firm from Queens.

*

I looked out the airplane window watching the lights from the city far below and thought about Neil. Seeing him that day had revived all those feelings I squelched long ago. He'd lived in my mind as the love of my life, exalted above all others. Initially enamored, I rejoiced at his being back in my life, believing my dreams had come true and the man I'd once fallen madly in love with had returned.

Slowly, however, my fantasy faded like a bright rainbow after a storm.

I reacted to Neil's intensity by trying to slow the relationship down, refusing to spend every minute together. Newly divorced, I needed some breathing room. But every time I pulled away, he just pushed harder.

And now I was on my way home. To him? The thought of him didn't cause that flutter of excitement. I just wasn't sure anymore.

Switching from the audiobook I was listening to, I immersed myself in e-mails, hoping my work would distract me from my emotions.

Mami nudged my arm. "Ava, I hope you're not going to work the entire time after you dragged me away from my home."

"No, of course not." I closed the lid of the iPad. *Ugh!* This may be a long visit.

*

Neil wanted to pick us up from the airport, but I managed to push off our reunion until the next night. Right on time, the doorbell rang. Both mothers stood in the kitchen waiting to greet him.

"*Mami*, you remember Neil. And this is Lola Ruiz, my mother's neighbor and dear friend."

Neil handed each a bouquet of flowers and opened an expensive, chilled bottle of champagne he'd brought "to celebrate Ava's homecoming."

My mother's eyebrows rose when he reached in the right cabinet for the glasses. I stifled a laugh.

"To three beautiful women," Neil toasted.

After we finished our first glass of champagne and small talk subsided, Neil and I went into the family room carrying a second glass, sitting together on the couch. The mothers stayed in the kitchen, dissecting everything about him in rapid-fire Spanish. I hoped he didn't understand, but I'm sure he caught a word or two.

"Darling, how is your wrist?" He gently touched my hand. "I told you I should have been there. This would never have happened."

I shrugged. "It's not so bad. Just hard getting dressed."

"You need a man in your life. And I know the perfect one." He clinked my champagne glass with his.

His comment set my teeth on edge. "I'm fine, really." I sipped my champagne and listened to my mother, trying to hear what she was saying.

He inched closer to me and grasped my hand. "I really missed you these last few weeks. I just want . . . us . . . . Let's move in together."

"What?" I wanted to slow things down, not speed them up. No way was I ready for that.

Conversation from the kitchen immediately ceased. Out of the corner of my eye, I saw both mothers tiptoe around the kitchen island so they could hear better.

Momentarily stunned, I inhaled sharply. "Let's take our drinks out on the deck." I shot my mother a fraught look as I grabbed my coat and went outside.

The brilliant day was turning into a dreamy twilight with a light breeze, but I suddenly felt fatigued. *Move in together? Absolutely not.*

"We can keep both places. I'll work from here and we can stay at my apartment in the city and take in plays, dinners, whenever you feel like it." He put his glass down on the table and stretched an arm around me, kissing my forehead. "I'm so happy you're home." Neil brought out a small box with a bow on it, his eyes wide and eager.

My stomach flip-flopped. No, it couldn't be. I glanced up and saw *Mami* and Lola plastered to the window behind me. I waved my hand behind his back to shoo them away. They didn't budge.

"What's this?" My voice shaky.

"Just a small token of my love." He beamed with excitement.

Panic gripped me. *Dear God, what if it's a ring?*

"Open it."

My hand trembled as I tried to untie the bow. My mind worked overtime to think of what I could say to him. When I removed the top of the box, an elegant diamond solitaire pendant nestled against dark velvet. I exhaled.

"Neil, it's lovely, but I can't accept such a lavish gift." I handed him back the box.

He laughed. "Of course, you can." He took the necklace out of the box and reached around me to put it on.

I touched the pendant. "Really, it's far too extravagant."

"Let's get out of here. I want to celebrate. We're going to spend the rest of our lives together."

"Wait!" I commanded. "I'm not ready for that kind of commitment." Resentment brewed deep within me. "I've told you this repeatedly. You need to listen."

Neil started to say something, then stopped.

A memory flashed into my mind of a much younger Neil telling me he was leaving for California. His features had been drawn into the same expression he was wearing now. The one that's been seared into my psyche all these years. Seeing it again only solidified my resolve to determine my own fate.

"You need to listen," I repeated.

His eyes scanned me, trying to read me. He must have seen that I was serious and sighed. Awkwardly, he placed his arms around me. "I've waited this long. I can wait until you're ready."

Maybe I'll never be ready.

"Let's get some dinner in town." He guided me toward the slider.

At least *Mami* and Lola had the sense to disappear. I wondered how much they'd heard.

We drove in silence to the restaurant. As we passed the Black River, the setting sun illuminated the stream of water in a fiery red with ribbons of gold.

The restaurant, Redwoods, while busy as usual at this time of night, always seemed to find me a table whenever I came in. Tonight, was no exception and the hostess sat us at a small booth by the bay window.

He looked at me, his eyes seeking mine. "Do you know how lucky we are to have found one another again? This rarely happens." A satisfied look crossed his face, almost as if he had planned it all.

I had to make him hear me. "Yes, it is rare. And I'm thrilled we've had this chance. But we've only been back in each other's lives for a few months and you're already talking about moving in." I felt a lump at the back of my throat and took a large gulp of water. "I don't understand the rush. I can't do this now. Please. I want to take this slowly."

Neil released my hand and leaned back in his chair. Was he angry? I sensed he might be.

"Besides Alysia is moving back home for a spell until she figures out her career." I motioned for the waiter.

"What?" Neil slapped his hand on the table. "Why are you letting your adult daughter move home? She needs to figure her life out on her own. I don't understand all these parents that let their kids move back. It's ridiculous. They need to grow up."

His mansplaining made my blood boil. This from a man who never had a child. Doesn't know jack shit about them. "Like you? Abandoning me the moment your father demanded it because you didn't want to get cut off from his money?" My face burned. Furious to my core, I snagged my purse from the back of the chair and stood.

Neil grabbed my arm as I walked past him to the door. "Oh God, Ava. I'm so sorry. That was an awful thing to say."

I stared at his hand holding my arm.

He released it, clasping both hands together on the table like in prayer. "I just don't want to waste a minute without you. I'm a complete idiot." He hung his head.

Weighted down. That's how I felt. Us. Together. Always. I took a deep breath and sat back down. My anxiety notched up. "Listen to me. I don't want a forever-after deal right now. If you persist in moving so fast, in judging my relationship with my family, we can end this tonight." My voice had raised a few octaves and people were turning our way.

Neil's face reddened but he measured his words. "Whoa. Wait a minute. I told you I was sorry. I'm a moron. Please, honey, it was just a stupid comment. I don't have kids—what do I know? Forgive me." His eyes pleaded with mine. "Please."

Somehow the rest of dinner went smoothly. I kissed Neil good night at the front door, explaining that he couldn't possibly stay while my mother was here. I would come into the city for our next date and we could stay together then.

"Tomorrow," he said, but then added, "or whenever is good for you."

The house was dark except the under-cabinet lights in the kitchen. I went to turn them off and jumped. *Mami* was sipping a glass of milk reading a book.

"Did you wait up for me?" There wasn't enough light to read anything.

"Yes, as a matter of fact I did." She closed the book.

"What's up?" I knew exactly what she was going to say.

"He's all wrong for you. And you know it."

The only sound in the room was the hum of the refrigerator.

"You're not that desperate young girl anymore. You've made a wonderful life for yourself and your children. There's no hurry. Wait for the man that deserves you." She stood. "I've said my piece. Buenas noches." She patted my arm as she made her way out of the room.

*

Since we'd gotten back together during the summer, Neil and I had spent most of our time at my house. But with my mother staying with me, I decided to take Neil up on his offer to spend Saturday with him, returning home on Sunday. I knew we'd get no privacy otherwise.

He told me to dress casually, to bring a bathing suit and a change of clothes for dinner. He had the whole day planned. I couldn't figure out why I needed a bathing suit in November but brought one anyway.

I'd been in Neil's apartment a few times, but we were usually on our way somewhere else. While he finished packing his bathing suit and a change of clothes, I glanced at the framed photos on a bookshelf in his living room. One in particular caught my eye.

"Where did you get this picture?" I yelled so he'd hear me in the next room.

"Which picture?"

"Oh, come on, you know. The one of us." I picked it up. I didn't remember ever seeing it. Neil had this huge smile in the picture, with lots of soft curls accenting his handsome features. I looked about twelve years old.

He came into the room smiling. "Do you like it?"

"Yes. I want a copy."

"Remember Jerrod and that party we went to on the Upper East Side in the eighties?" He picked up the picture and pointed to the house in the background. "A friend of his shot this and gave it to Jerrod, who sent it to me a few years ago when he was clearing out his parents' home for sale."

I touched my youthful face and saw in the picture the girl I craved to be, partying in a swanky town house on the ritzy side of town. My aspirations had been so clear then. Success. Nothing but success. Never to worry about money again. To live like Neil and his peers.

I looked at him. "It's amazing what's buried in our parents' basements. All these long-forgotten mementos." I didn't mention that I was no longer the girl in the photo.

"Let's go, our car is here," he said, returning the photo to its shelf.

Off we went downtown. We stopped outside a hefty brick industrial building with an impressively large sign above the door that read: Brahmin Ancient Baths.

"Why are we here?" I asked, curious.

"Oh, you will love it. They have ten different thermal baths we can enjoy and then I've booked us a couple's massage. And believe me, they're to die for." He rubbed his hands together in excitement, then took the stairs two at a time, opening the door for me.

The place was magnificent. Dark, sensual, aromatic, quiet. Everything you hope for in a spa. Two attendants gave us a tour, and then one escorted each of us into the large bath and changing area. Slippers and robes were provided.

We had an hour before our massage, so we met in the larger bath area and slid into the tub. With only a few other people around, it felt incredibly private and intimate.

The water was an aquamarine color with light eucalyptus and citrus scent misting up from the heated water. "My God, this is relaxing," I said, stretching in the water in sheer bliss.

"Isn't it great? I'm a member. That just means I pay a monthly fee for a single visit. Each additional I pay for." He cupped water into his hands and wiped his face to clear the sweat. "Let's head to the cooler bath. I'm starting to overheat."

I laughed. "I'll follow you."

Even though I was no longer striving for the luxuries I once lusted for, a good spa day is always a fabulous extravagance. I thought, *On Monday I'll arrange an appointment here for Mami and Lola. They deserve it after all they've been through.*

By the time we headed to our massages, I was calm and completely content. Luxuriating in the bath, we talked about news events, my mother's stay, and the restaurant he'd picked for dinner. Nothing about us. I hoped this good feeling could continue for the whole day.

By the time we arrived back at Neil's apartment I felt a touch sleepy from the massage and the champagne we'd drunk in the car on the way home. But Neil was amorous, coming up behind me and rubbing my arms. I welcomed his touch. In my relaxed state, I melted into him, turning off my mind and its constant ruminations on our relationship.

Our first few intimate times had been awkward for me. I persisted in feeling like I was cheating on my husband, even though we were divorced. Getting over years of loyalty still took time. Even with Neil, the man I'd been dreaming about for years.

He whispered into my ear now, "Come, let's continue that massage." He caressed my neck and ears, sending his hot breath sizzling down my shirt.

Passing by the bookshelves, I glanced once again at our youthful selves. So full of life and love. He walked me into his bedroom, pressing himself up into my back, then spun me into him. He smelled of eucalyptus and citrus. I unbuttoned his shirt and ran my hands slowly over his chest. It still glistened slightly with remnants of massage oil. He bent forward, kissing me hard.

Wrapping my hands around his neck, I flashed back to a younger Neil at his parents' Hampton beach house. Entwined in one other, my hands playing with the curls that fell on the back of his neck.

I opened my eyes. The curly locks from the photo were long gone. A sigh escaped me.

He closed the curtains and moved to the bed, motioning for me. He draped me in his arms and we kissed. His lips were persuasive. His mouth tasted like champagne, the expensive kind he'd indulged us with on the drive home. He stepped back and pulled off my shirt, his hands hot from need.

We looked into each other's eyes for a moment. His smoldered. This had been my fervent dream once, to be with Neil again. As he stepped closer, I pushed my leggings down and lay on the bed, watching him undress.

Sliding into bed, he pulled me to him. A quiet moan escaped my lips.

"Ava, I've missed you so much." He whispered into my ear,

kissing and caressing. His whole body, heated to sauna level, warmed mine immediately. His need excited me.

"I missed you, too." It was all I could manage. I buried my head in his neck and let myself succumb to his need. His touch was steeped so long in my memory that its familiarity instantly aroused our long-ago rhythm.

I closed my eyes. My head, light with bubbles from the spa and champagne, made his kisses even sweeter. Oh, how I remembered him. I rolled back the years and fell again into young Neil's arms. The need grew so much stronger, the intensity overwhelming. We just couldn't keep our hands off one another.

My mind circled back to our familiar cadence, finding every note, every chord slowly building toward that final progression.

"Ava," Neil whispered, his voice still husky.

I opened my eyes and came bounding back to the present. Crashing through the years and all the tears I'd shed, through marriage and children, to this place I had so longed for all those years ago.

"God, it's good having you back from Puerto Rico," he murmured.

I touched his flushed cheek and smiled warmly.

Sleep overcame us and we napped for an hour. We decided to eat in and canceled our dinner reservation. Neil placed an order for takeout while I showered. I dried my hair humming, feeling light and easy.

Waiting for dinner to arrive, Neil made a business call from his office. He left the door slightly ajar and I could hear the conversation on speaker.

He lashed out at the person on the other end. "I told you I don't care about those evictions. Move them along. That's what I pay you for. The project must be completed on time or there are penalties. Do you understand?"

I heard papers being rustled. Neil opened the door, his brow furrowed tightly.

"What's wrong?" I asked.

"Nothing. I need to light a fire under my attorney to get a project back on track. That's all." His brow softened and he walked to the bar, pouring us some wine.

"You're evicting tenants from a building?" I understood the legal necessity of this step from my younger days of dealing with real estate and management companies. But I never liked it.

"Yes, but we're giving them a fair market price for their units." He sipped his wine. "You'll like this. It's from Tuscany."

I felt uncomfortable. "Maybe they like where they live."

"It's a ramshackle old building that's starting to crumble. They'll be better off somewhere else."

"But . . ."

The doorbell rang. "Great, dinner. I'm starved," he said.

He talked a lot during the next few hours about his plans for this new monster skyscraper and other business dealings. I remembered being so enthralled with a younger Neil, listening intently, almost memorizing his words as he talked about his business dealings. Back then, I was so impressed that someone like him would even look at me.

But now, not so much. As I grew older, my hunger for power and money had waned. How much does one person need? I wanted to give back to the community and help others. I didn't see that desire in Neil.

He must have drunk a full bottle of wine during his soliloquy. He yawned once, then again. And again.

"Go to bed. I'll clean up."

"You sure?" He yawned through the words.

"Yes. Go. I'll be in in a minute."

After straightening the kitchen, I poured myself a glass of wine and went outside on the terrace. Neil's penthouse overlooked Central Park. I thought about the people being evicted as I lounged on this massive balcony sipping wine. *Wait for someone that deserves you. Mami's* words cut through me.

Neil was softly snoring when I slipped into bed. I lay awake for a long time, my mind whirling. When sleep finally came, it brought transient glimpses of our past life: being young at Neil's beach house, having my first glass of champagne with him, Broadway plays, his black Porsche, dancing, fun, then pain. So much pain. What was my subconscious telling me?

As light dawned, I found myself riding on a scooter with Gabriel as he skirted potholes and fallen branches, his curly hair sliding up my nose and me laughing. I remembered following him around the town square while he checked on people, making sure their injuries were healing. He shrugged off any mention of payment for his services. He only cared about their well-being. My heart swelled at the thought of his altruism. Then the scene faded away and I fell back into sleep.

I heard my mother's voice, but I couldn't understand her. She was speaking fast, and I struggled to comprehend. She seemed to be telling me something—over and over, but I still didn't realize what she was saying. Then I saw her in slow motion and mouthing the words: *He's the finest man I've ever known!*

Chapter 19

CHARLOTTE

NOSTALGIA

"Wow. I could spend days here." Daisy circled around the salad bar squealing in delight. Chester's ShopRite had reinvented itself to compete with the more expensive and chic grocery stores in the area. Now it had aisle after aisle of crisp produce, prepared meals, fresh flowers, and even sushi chefs.

The sweet smell from the bakery behind us and the hardier scent of rotisserie chicken off to our left made my mouth water. I hadn't eaten since seven a.m. and it was now after three.

Daisy picked some legumes, flax and chia seeds, tofu, and something that stated it was *sprouted and fermented plant food.*

"Daisy, please get whatever you'd like. I'm sorry, I should have asked you what kind of food you wanted before you came."

"No. I've liked everything we've eaten. I just thought I'd make you a meal before I return home. Do you know where the organic olive oil is?"

Judging from her ingredients, I wasn't sure what kind of concoction she was making. "I believe it's in aisle nine." I pointed. I had olive oil at home, but not organic. "Meet me in the next section. I have to get some pasta."

She scurried off.

"Hold on," I said, looking at her items in my basket. "Are you a vegan now?"

"No. I still eat meat, just not that often."

When she returned, Daisy prattled on about eating everything organic. But I was barely paying attention, thinking about Maxwell. I kept twisting my necklace around and around while staring at the different types of rigatoni. I was planning to buy some spicy Italian sausage along with tomatoes and fresh parmesan cheese for the pasta dish I would prepare for tonight.

"Charlotte, what are you staring at?" Daisy bellowed. She held two packages of sausage, one in each hand. "Look, I saw these at the end of the aisle with the olive oil. Will they do for your dish?"

"Sorry," I said, blinking back into consciousness. "No, but thanks anyway. The butcher here makes a great traditional Italian sausage. But you must ask for it at the meat counter at the back of the store. Come, we'll go together." I grabbed a package of pasta.

"Is something wrong?" she asked.

"No. Just trying to focus on buying everything I need for dinner tonight," I lied.

Daisy helped me finish the dinner prep, so I had extra time to get ready. I used every minute of it. Letting the warm spray of the shower relax me, I thought back to the Saturday before Maxwell's kids arrived. It had been unseasonably warm that day despite a cold front set to swoop in later on. We ate a light meal on his dock and watched the sunset. Its vast hues of magenta clashed, growing darker and more turbulent. That night we slowly caressed each other into ecstasy. *God, I miss him. I miss us.*

I sensed something was off ever since that meeting with his children. I felt it down to my core. The look on his face when he said,

I really hoped the kids would've accepted you more. That remark still stung. What had changed?

Sighing, I closed my eyes and reached deep within myself. *No, no more running from man to man.* Maxwell was the one. I just hoped that we'd get through this.

Shaking off my despair, I picked up my blow dryer. Determined to look my best tonight, I fussed over my hair and makeup, adding a touch of drama around my eyes and a layer of red gloss on my lips. *As good as it gets*, I thought, turning out my bedroom light.

*

The doorbell rang at seven-thirty sharp. I inhaled deeply. We hadn't seen each other since that awkward meeting with his kids two weeks ago.

I opened the door. Maxwell looked sharp, dressed in a wool gray-on-gray checked sports coat, jeans, and a white button-down. As I shut the door, I noticed my hand was shaking.

Daisy barely let him get into the family room before pouncing. "Hi, I'm Daisy." She clamped her arms around his neck and squeezed, giving him a power hug.

Maxwell stood awkwardly trying to balance. His coat slung over his left arm and both hands were full, one with a bottle of wine and the other a flower arrangement.

Tucker had an excited full-body wag going on. I had forgotten to put him on a leash, which the trainer had suggested I do when people visit. Unable to control himself, the dog leapt up, slapping a wet one on Maxwell and pushing him into the wall.

"Oh no." I pulled Tucker down. "I'm so sorry." I dragged Tucker into the kitchen and put the leash on him. "Are you okay?" I asked, over my shoulder.

"Yes, I'm fine. No worries," he said, wiping his face. "He's huge. How are you going to handle him when he's full grown?"

I petted Tucker's head. "I'm hoping he'll be back with Chad in a few months."

"Charlotte, you didn't tell me how good-looking Maxwell is," Daisy effused as she stepped around the island.

Maxwell blushed, handing me the flower arrangement.

I breathed in the scent of roses and carnations. "Thank you. They're lovely." *Ah*, he remembered me telling him that a hostess appreciates flowers already cut and in a container.

I handed Daisy the leash and replaced the centerpiece on the kitchen table, which was already set for dinner. "What do you guys want to drink?"

"Vodka and tonic," Daisy said.

"That sounds good." Maxwell nodded.

God, he really does look good tonight. I brought them their drinks. "When would you like to eat?"

"Whenever." Daisy made herself comfortable in the leather high-back chair in the family room. Tucker happily followed her, still tethered to the leash. Once Daisy settled into the chair, Tucker laid his big head on her lap.

"Any time that's good for you," Maxwell said, standing. "Can I help?"

"No, it's all done. Just have to cook the rigatoni." Filling the pasta pot with water, I asked, "How about we eat in an hour?"

Fussing in the kitchen, I listened as Daisy espoused her knowledge about global warming and organic food. The open floor plan of my town house allowed me to work in the kitchen but still engage in conversation with guests in the family room. Maxwell listened to my friend politely and made a comment or two.

When Daisy and Maxwell finished their drinks, I took that as a cue to bring out the antipasto with my grandmother's secret dressing, setting it on the counter. I poured three glasses of red wine.

I motioned with my arm. "Come, have something to eat."

Sipping my wine, I thought it paired perfectly with the anti-pasto. Thank God for the wine steward at the liquor store.

"Charlie, this is lovely, and the wine is superb. My compliments to the chef." Maxwell winked at me and clinked my glass.

"That's adorable," Daisy cooed.

"The antipasto?" I asked.

"No, silly. He calls you Charlie." She was waving her wineglass around like a baton and I thought for sure she'd spill some. I was glad I'd gotten some extra seltzer from the store – I might need it to clean the stain. "I've never heard anyone call you that. I love it." She raised her glass to Maxwell.

The wine settled my nerves, but I decided to wait until dinner was on the table before I have another. Daisy, however, replenished her glass with a large pour.

"Charlie tells me you were roommates in your freshman year. Where do you live now?" Maxwell asked.

"In Rutland, Vermont." Daisy slowly churned the generous slug of wine in her glass with one hand and ate the antipasto with a fork directly from the dish, ignoring the small plate I'd placed by her hand.

"Daisy, you're about to spill your wine," I cautioned her.

She glanced at the swirling liquid and placed it on the counter. "Did *Charlie* tell you that my Janice left me?" She drew a deep breath, then launched into the story.

By the time she finished, her bright, happy face had become dark. Her mouth turned downward and her eyes seemed focused on someplace distant.

Maxwell looked at her sympathetically.

I walked over to Daisy and put my arm around her. "Can you help me with the pasta?" I thought perhaps giving her something to do would distract her from her sad thoughts and hopefully cut down on her drinking.

She cleared her throat. "Yes, of course. Wait. What?"

I guided her to the pot and asked her to stir the boiling pasta every minute or two, so it wouldn't burn.

"Okay. How about another wine?"

I would have refused, but Maxwell poured her another glass and asked about the breakup, about Janice, and what she would do now. He ignored the frown I directed at him.

Daisy, totally engaged by his questions, left the pasta pot and sat down next to him at the island.

Maxwell told her about his breakup with his ex-wife.

For the first five minutes of his trip down memory lane, I was as engrossed as Daisy. Maxwell and I hadn't really talked much about his marriage.

"You know it's okay to be sad," he said. "My therapist offered me sage advice at every session. You should find someone and go. Don't try to get through this by yourself."

I never knew he had gone to therapy. Was he still? I stirred the pasta, listening intently. Noticing only a minute left on the timer, I turned it off, not wanting its shrill to interrupt.

Daisy looked riveted by his every word. "What sage advice did your therapist have?"

"One thing that no one believes when they're going through it is that it won't always feel as bad as it does now." Maxwell patted her arm. "And they're right. The pain subsides and life continues." He looked at me. "Sometimes for the better."

That's the man I fell in love with. My heart fluttered.

Daisy reached for the carafe and emptied it into her glass. Then she took a large gulp.

"Oh, God," I mumbled.

By the time dinner was ready, Daisy could barely stand. Maxwell held her arm and guided her to the table. I didn't offer any more wine. We all still had some in our glasses and I wanted to cut Daisy off. Tucker curled up at her feet, probably hoping for table scraps.

Returning to Maxwell's earlier comment, Daisy slurred, "Is that it? That's all you've got—you won't hurt so bad in a month?"

Cringing with embarrassment, I tried to think how to extricate Maxwell from this conversation. Before I could, Daisy began to cry.

Maxwell reached over and cupped her hands. "The way you talk about her, are you sure this is really over? Can't you work it out?"

Daisy shook her head. "Don't think so."

Maxwell suggested couples' counseling. "Sometimes it works."

"Did it work for you?" Daisy blew her nose.

Clearly not. What kind of question is that? Daisy was ruining my night with Maxwell. Why did I think introducing them was a good idea? I should have gone out with him alone.

"No. But my wife was in love with someone else." Maxwell looked at the table. This clearly still hurt him. "I found out in a therapy session. It was like getting hit with a bat in the gut."

"I *know*," Daisy cried, tears welling up again.

Maxwell rubbed his hands together, making me grow more anxious with each rotation. He cleared his throat. "We continued for another ten sessions. I don't know why, but I thought maybe, just maybe, we could work through it."

Work through what exactly? Is he an idiot? His wife tells him she's in love with someone else and they continue for ten more therapy sessions? For what? Delusional. But knowing this made me nervous. He must have really loved his ex to humiliate himself so. *Oh, God.*

I tried to block out what Maxwell was saying by pushing food around my plate. Anger seeped up from my gut. All this reminiscing about Maxwell's ex-wife was grating on my nerves. "You know, we've all been hurt. But that was a long time ago," I said sharply.

Maxwell frowned and Daisy stared at me. My cheeks flushed.

Realizing I'd sounded too harsh, I added, "Daisy, I know that your pain is fresh and raw, and I know it helps to talk. But maybe we can move to another topic just for a little while?"

"Sure," she slurred. "Whatever you want."

What could I say? What would lighten the situation? "Have either of you read any good books lately?" I fumbled, grasping for straws. "We need new ideas for our book club." I cut my sausage and ate a small piece.

Both only shrugged.

Hmm. "I heard on the news that we're in for a snowy winter. At least, that's what they're predicting. Daisy, how about in Vermont?"

She shrugged again. "Don't know."

How awkward was this? I should never have tried to change the subject. "How about those Giants?" Even I knew that was lame.

Daisy reached down and petted Tucker. Maxwell stared at his dinner plate.

We finished dinner in silence.

I cleared the plates with Maxwell's help. I didn't trust Daisy to carry anything. Instead, I sat her at the island while I made her a cup of her favorite herbal tea.

She sobered up a bit and decided to head to bed.

"Do you need some help?" I asked. She still looked out of it.

"No," she muttered as she bounced off the kitchen wall into the archway of the foyer.

I followed her down the hallway to her bedroom.

When she reached her door, she turned toward me. "I'm fine. Really. Go enjoy Maxwell. He's quite the catch." She pinched my cheek. "You're a lucky girl." Daisy closed her bedroom door.

I rested my forehead on the door, not feeling lucky at all.

I found Maxwell sitting in the family room. I grabbed my wineglass which was still half full and lit the gas fireplace. I sat next to him on the couch. "Would you like coffee, tea, water?"

"No. Thanks." His tone sharp as he swiveled aggressively toward me. "Your friend really needed to talk. She's hurting. Why on earth would you shut her down like that?"

Grimacing liked I'd been punched; I didn't know what to say. "I've been listening to Daisy for days and I guess I wanted us . . .

well." My heart sped up and I felt heat in my cheeks. I blurted, "It wasn't Daisy's story that bothered me. It was yours. Talking about your ex with such devotion, and how much it hurt you. I mean . . . ." I snapped up my wineglass from the table, holding back tears. "How would you feel if I talked like that about my ex?"

Maxwell just stared into the fire.

What the hell is happening? Who is this man? He'd been so attentive and loving these past few months, never even uttering a harsh remark. Clearly talking about his ex brought back old memories and wounds. Was I jealous or irritated? Probably both.

"Charlotte, I think that I should go."

What happened to calling me Charlie? Shocked, I opened the front door for him.

He kissed me on the cheek and left.

*

The smell of coffee woke me. Pain emanated at my temples. Pounding thrusts every ten seconds made it difficult to open my eyes completely. I slowly sat up in bed. The hammering expanded around my entire head. *Crap.* I saw the bottle of Scotch or what was left of it on my nightstand. *Oh God!*

My tongue stuck to the roof of my mouth. I desperately needed water. I inched up and held on to the wall until my feet responded. The kitchen seemed a long way off. I crept into the bathroom and filled a paper cup with tap water. I drank five of them before my stomach began rumbling. I held on to the sides of the sink with both hands as a dizzying wave hit. When my balance returned, I looked at the mirror. An old drunk stared back at me, eyes swollen and dark. Mascara weeping down her cheeks. Hair stuck to one side by some spilled Scotch. *What a damn mess!* I turned on the shower and inched in. The water hurt initially like little pellets sticking my skin, but within a minute the warm water soothed me, lessening the pain.

As I crept into the kitchen, Daisy screeched, "Good morning!"

I wrapped my arms around my ears. "Shhhhh!" Her voice reverberated through the room, bringing a fresh wave of nausea with it. I held out my hand for her to stop.

"Charlie, what's the matter?" she whispered, rushing over to me.

I pointed to the faucet and mouthed *water* as I slowly positioned myself at the kitchen island.

"You barely drank last night. Don't tell me you have a hangover." Daisy opened the cabinet and grabbed a glass.

I'd wrapped my wet hair in a towel, but strands escaped the turban, dripping water on my shirt and the chair. I drank the water Daisy handed me.

"Do you want another?"

I focused on her. "Yes."

"Maybe wine doesn't agree with you." Daisy handed me the water.

"No. It wasn't the wine. I drank almost a half-bottle of Scotch after Maxwell left. Abruptly." I cradled my head in my hands.

"Why did he leave? We had a wonderful evening." Daisy sat down next to me.

Anger rose in the pit of my stomach. "He left because of you." I knew the moment I said it that I shouldn't have. The hurt on Daisy's face made my heart sink. I added, more softly, "I didn't mean that the way it sounded."

Daisy looked away.

I sipped the water. "Maxwell got angry when I wanted to change the subject. He thought you needed to talk about your breakup and that I wasn't being a good friend." I inhaled deeply, holding back my emotions. "It wasn't your breakup that bothered me, it was his." Just saying those words out loud was enough. I started to cry.

Daisy jumped up and hugged me. "I don't understand. Why would talking about his ex-wife make you so sad? It's long over."

"Is it?" I wiped my eyes with my sleeve.

"Talk to me. What's going on?" She sat down next to me.

I stammered, barely able to speak.

"Start talking," Daisy commanded.

"Wait." I held up my hand. "I need some aspirin." I finished my water and reached into a bowl on the countertop, thinking it was granola. I needed food in my stomach. The oat mixture tasted like paper with an acerbic aftertaste, some prickly pieces irritating my throat. *Shit!* "What is that?" I pointed at the bowl, coughing. I wobbled to the sink for water to flush it down.

"Grain-free vegan granola." Daisy took a handful and popped it in her mouth. "You have to get used to the taste."

"How can you have grain-free granola? Granola's a grain." I shook my head and went to the bread drawer, pulling out an everything bagel. "I'll stick to real grains."

Daisy shook her head as I lathered butter on my toasted bagel. "It's a good thing you work out because you'd have weight issues with that high carb diet of yours."

Keeping my opinion to myself, I took an exaggerated big bite. After I finished half the bagel, I swallowed two extra strength aspirins, hoping they'd rid me of this monster headache.

Daisy busied herself around the kitchen, making breakfast. "You look like you feel better. Do you?"

"A little."

"Okay then, spill it. What the hell is going on?"

I wiped my mouth. "I don't know. That's the problem." I told Daisy about meeting his children and how different he'd been toward me ever since. "The kids want their parents back together and apparently the ex-wife is no longer with the man she left Maxwell for."

"Doesn't she live out west?"

"Yes, but still. He's changed since his kids' visit. I just can't explain it. Call it intuition." I shrugged. "I don't know."

"Don't worry about it. He seems crazy about you." Daisy wiped down the island. "What do you want to do today?"

I stood, moaning. "This is the worst hangover I've ever had."

Daisy smirked. "No, I don't think it is."

I rummaged around in my addled brain until I remembered what she was talking about. Heat rose on my face. *Jeez. Not this again.* I really didn't want to hash this out yet again. We'd done it so many times before.

Daisy, staring at me, said, "Yup. That time."

One night, one incident, one person that had forced me to take a hard look at what I wanted. It was just one stinking little detour that challenged who I thought I was. It all went back to Janice and that damn party so long ago.

*

Janice's touch sent electrical charges throughout my body. I had to meet her, Daisy said. She captivated the room, oozing sex appeal with every arch of her brow or gesture of her hand.

"So nice to meet one of Daisy's friends." Janice purred. "Come sit with me." She looked at Daisy. "Daisy, dear, go get me the bottle of tequila on the dresser over there." She pointed. "And a few of those paper cups."

Janice tilted herself so the arm of the couch supported her back and slowly crossed her legs barely covered by her microskirt.

Daisy bumbled over and almost spilled the tequila. "Oh, sorry. Want me to pour us some?"

"No, honey," Janice hummed. "I've got this. Why don't you find Chip and get a joint from him? Tell him I want the good stuff. He'll know what I want." She gave me two cups and poured a generous portion of tequila in each.

"To you." She held up her cup to toast me.

"Shouldn't we pour one for Daisy?" I asked.

"Don't worry. I'll pour her one when she gets back." She took a section of her hair and moved it behind her ear, then chugged the half cup of tequila. "Now you."

I tried my hardest to chug it, but I kept coughing. It took me four gulps to get the half a Solo cup down. Damn, it burned.

"I see you're a novice," she murmured, placing her empty cup on the floor. "Such a lovely necklace." She touched the charm and then followed the chain around my neck.

Her touch was light and exhilarating. I wanted to say something smart or witty, but the tequila hit me harder than I thought, so I just rested my head against the back of the couch. I closed my eyes and let myself drift.

"I've got it," Daisy blurted in a high-pitched voice.

I snapped out of my stupor.

Janice lit the joint and passed it to me. I took a toke and handed it to Daisy. The pot was smooth as the three of us alternated smoking it. I'd only smoked pot a few times and never touched any other drugs. Just wasn't interested. The other few times I tried it, it had made me giddy, but this time I felt relaxed. Light-headed.

After ten minutes, Janice sent Daisy on another errand. As soon as she left, Janice held out her hand. "Come with me," she murmured.

Janice ushered me into a small room with a full bed and dresser in it. She closed the door, revealing a full-length mirror. Janice came up behind me and slid her finger next to my mouth.

"Shhhh," Janice said. She lit another joint. I had no idea where it came from.

"Here." She handed it to me.

I giggled. "More?" I took a large hit.

"Sure, let's have some fun." Janice stayed behind me, massaging my shoulders.

I looked in the mirror. My head felt light and I didn't know how much longer I'd be able to stand. Too much pot, too much liquor.

I swayed left to right. Words swirled around my head, but I couldn't catch them to form actual sentences.

"Let's make this a night to remember," she whispered into my ear

and pulled me toward her. She kissed me. A long, liquid, lingering kiss I felt down to my toes. Every part of my body tingled, waiting for her.

Janice took my hand and sat me on the bed. She took off my blouse and gently massaged my breasts.

Bam, bam, bam. "Janice, Charlotte, are you in there?" Daisy squealed.

"W . . . ." I tried to answer, but Janice covered my mouth.

"Shhh," she whispered, smothering me with velvet kisses. "Don't you want me to kiss you all over?"

I fell backward onto the bed. "Yes," I remembered saying, "Yes."

*

Tucker barked at a squirrel outside and it startled me back to the present. Looking at Daisy, I knew my face was flushed. "I don't know, this Scotch headache feels a lot worse than that tequila one all those years ago." Damn. I'd downed almost three quarters of a bottle of Scotch. At my age, the effects would hang around for a few days.

Walking into the family room, I curled up on the couch. "Will you ever forgive me for that night? I know we've talked about it a lot, but I've never felt . . . well, that you've forgiven me."

"I have." She came into the room and sat opposite of me. "Really. It was a lifetime ago."

"I'm sorry things didn't work out with Janice. But maybe Maxwell is right, and you should try counseling." I took the throw off the back of the couch and draped it over me. "I never meant to mess things up with you two all those years ago. I got so drunk and high I don't even remember what happened. I basically passed out."

"But she chose you first, not me." A tear rolled down her cheek. "It's her choice that still hurts."

Sitting up increased the throbbing in my head, so instead, I reached out my hand. "I'm so, so sorry." It made me sad to think I hurt her even if it was years ago. She had clearly been smitten with Janice. As Daisy's friend, I should have stayed away from any involvement with her. Drunk or sober, I shouldn't have let it happen.

"She knows she can have anybody she wants." Daisy pet Tucker as he lay his head on her lap. "I was always jealous."

"She is sexy. Damn sexy. But she still needs love. And you, Daisy, are the epitome of love. I think you should try working out your problems." Maybe I should take my own advice. "Call her and go to couples' counseling."

"Maybe, just maybe," Daisy said.

I watched the dog close his eyes in sheer delight as she rubbed his head. "Tucker will be devastated when you leave."

Daisy laughed long and hard.

*

She squeezed me tight and hugged Tucker goodbye.

"Call me when you get home," I said, kissing Daisy on the cheek. Our week together had flown by. "And let me know if you straighten things out with Janice."

"I will." She walked down the steps handing her suitcase to the car's driver standing by the open trunk. She started to open the door but looked back and said, "You should do the same with your life. Maxwell is worth it. Don't let him get away."

"You're right." I waved. Tucker whined, so I took him for a short walk around the neighborhood. I had to face this thing with Maxwell and not pretend everything was fine.

When I got home, I called to invite him to Bri's holiday party, but he didn't pick up. I left a voicemail.

Daisy had already stripped the bedding and put it in the laundry room. As I threw the sheets into the washer, I thought back to that night with Janice and about how it might have inadvertently led me into Grant's arms.

Janice's seduction had thrilled me. Up until then, I'd followed in my lifelong friend Bri's footsteps. Always conscientious, doing the *right* thing, respectful, a basic do-gooder. But facing temptation, my soul tried to break free of constraints and I gave in to my passion, plunging into unknown waters.

The next morning, I felt ashamed and scared. This wasn't me. I would never disregard a friend's crush. And Daisy was clearly smitten with Janice. The excitement of my night with Janice had worn off; in its place was sheer humiliation and a wicked headache.

Blaming it on alcohol and pot was feeble. I had decided to succumb. How could I have been so callous? How could I have done that to Daisy?

I met my ex-husband a few weeks later. He initially reminded me of my father, who had died when I was a teenager. Both my parents died within a year of each other from illnesses. The loss had been almost too much to bear. Bri had helped me then. She too had lost her parents when she was very young. But that hollow, numb feeling was always there.

Grant had seemed like someone my parents would have approved of; safe and reliable. But the warning signs were there. Right after we married, he didn't return my phone calls, made excuses to leave the house on errands at odd hours, needed total privacy for business calls and spent a lot of time at the gym.

In the end, Grant had numerous affairs, even with so-called friends. His shockingly heartless response when I finally confronted him was to *just get over it.*

What the hell am I doing thinking about all this old shit? Shaking myself out of this morbid mood, I heard my cell ring and ran to it hoping it was Maxwell.

Holy crap it's Nathan, my on-again-off-again lover. I let the call go to voicemail, then I listened.

"Hello, my dear Charlotte. I'm here on business and wondered if you'd like to get together for dinner. Heading into meetings. Text me. I've got reservations for eight p.m. at the Bedminster Inn."

Does he expect me to just show up after all these months?

But if Maxwell doesn't want to return my calls then . . . the hell with him. I felt wanted again for the first time in weeks. This is what I should be doing. Having fun with an interesting man and not waiting around the house for Maxwell's call like a lovesick teenager.

I showered and dolled myself up and headed out the door by seven-thirty. It would take about a half hour to get there. I realized I had forgotten to text Nathan back but since I was driving, I thought I'd just surprise him. I got there a few minutes early and parked myself, choosing not to valet.

About five minutes later, Nathan pulled into the parking lot and up to the front door. I watched as he got out of his car looking as dashing as ever in a silk sports jacket, probably a Tom Ford.

He had a small discussion with the valet. Time collapsed and I remembered our last night together—satisfying only in its shallowness. A heavy weight descended on me as I watched him go through the entrance. No. I didn't want this. Not anymore.

I texted Nathan that I just received his message and had plans for tonight. Maybe next time.

Damn you, Maxwell. You came into my life and messed everything up. I was doing fine without you. Now look at me. Sitting alone in a parking lot, sad and frustrated, missing you.

Chapter 20

STACI

ANTICIPATION

L UNCH WITH MOTHER. How nice! Some would think my life with her would make a hilarious sitcom. Me—not so much. We never shared the same sweet bond I had with my father. They say you marry one of your parents. Well, I picked the wrong one. Mother was a mirrored version of my ex-husband. Both toxic. Two in one lifetime. How fortunate.

Hanna and I always commiserated on our mothers. I called to tell her about my lunch today and we swapped mother stories. At least she now understands where her mother's OCD originated. I don't think I'll ever be that lucky.

I'd learned never to be stuck in a car with Mother. Instead, I'd meet her at the restaurant. I related totally with teenagers, but I'd never be able to just slip in earbuds when I wanted to ignore my mother. She'd never let me get away with it. At seventy-six, Mother still played golf and doubles tennis and was sharp as a razor.

Mother goes by the name Poppy. It makes no sense. She was born in Brooklyn in 1941 to Italian parents who lived in an Italian neighborhood. Why adopt a preppy name straight out of Greenwich, Connecticut? No one knows her name is really Polissena.

Today we met at Broad Valley Country Club, where I was still a member. I hadn't asked to continue my membership after the divorce, but George said I should. Ever so concerned about appearances! Mother was just the same. She had insisted we have lunch there. I'd have been just as happy at Panera Bread. Happier, maybe.

She found me in the dining room. "Darling, you're looking a little pale," Mother said, coming up behind me and delicately air kissing my forehead.

Always so positive. She managed to determine my pallor in the nanosecond she kissed my head. "Nice to see you, Mother."

"That's it? After—what has it been—three months?" She placed her purse on a chair and sat down opposite me. "Really, honey, this divorce was a bad idea. I think you should call George and tell him you made a mistake. I'm sure he would welcome you back with open arms. This was a foolish decision on your part. You know, you're not so young anymore." She paused, maybe wanting to continue, but thinking better of it.

"Really, Mother? You say that to me after everything I went through with him?"

She just stared at me, eyebrows raised.

Seething, I wanted to hit back. "Maybe you're having trouble remembering the events. You know," I reached out, patted her hand and murmured, "because of your age." Maybe that was hitting below the belt, but I was sick of justifying my every action to her.

Mother jerked her hand out from under mine.

I sat back. *I want to go home.* I should have made another excuse not to meet. But my sister, Savannah, had pleaded with me. She needed a break. My sister's children were younger, so Mother spent a great deal of time with them. Just as she had when my boys were young. I knew all too well what Savannah was going through. At least her husband was supportive, helping with the kids and my mother. I never had that. Mother and George always double-teamed me.

"Don't you worry about my memory. It's just fine. You should be more concerned about your own behavior." Mother lowered her voice, "George called and told me you were sleeping with a laborer. What in the world were you thinking? In the home where you raised your sons!"

My blood boiled. "Oh really? Is that what he said? And why in the name of God are you even talking with him? *I'm* your daughter. *I'm* the one who's been hurt. Yet you're siding with him—the way you always do!" I'd had enough. I stood.

"Stop! Don't go. I haven't seen you since last summer," Mother pleaded.

I slowly sat again, wishing with all my heart my father was still alive. He always found a way to make it easier to be around Mother. Maybe this was my challenge now, to find some common ground. I'd avoided her since my divorce. She and George nagged me in stereo about everything and anything. I took a deep breath, waiting with trepidation for what she'd say next.

"That's better." Mother nodded. "Remarks about memory are quite hurtful to older people. But I forgive you."

My leg bounced under the table. I picked up my water glass and noticed my hand shaking. I put the glass down. "The fact that you're siding with George hurts me, you know. But I forgive you too."

Mother fixed me with a steely glare. "Why would you sleep with a painter? Are you lonely? Why don't you try one of those dating apps?" She leaned in closer and whispered, "Or a vibrator."

Oh dear God, this is worse than I thought it would be. "I didn't sleep with a painter or a worker or anyone George said I slept with. Really, why do you insist on siding with him? And anyway, if I did, who cares?" My leg shook so hard that my upper body was now bobbing.

Mother took a deep breath and blew out a noisy stream of air. She picked up her menu. "I'm hungry. Let's order."

Our lunch conversation consisted largely of how my nieces and nephew were doing. Until she ordered coffee.

"So, what exactly are you doing with that plumber?" She reached for her purse to put lipstick on, blotting it with a napkin.

My head fell. "I have to go."

"Where? To do what?" She replaced her lipstick in her bag. "It's not like you work or have kids or a husband at home." She looked smug, as though she'd just won a point in some bizarre game.

"I have to finish a blog post I'm writing for Brook's decorating company." I motioned to the waiter.

Mother shook her head. "Why bother? You're too old for a writing career. George gave you plenty of money. I swear I just don't understand you. You had everything."

"For the last time, I had nothing. Why do you equate possessions with love? Who cares how big your house is? Or how many properties you own? I want to love and be loved and grow old with someone." My voice rose. "I've had it all—the house, car, jewelry, designer clothing, and I paid for every bit of it with pieces of my soul. George never made me feel anything but inferior. Nothing I did was ever good enough."

Mother rubbed her thumb and forefinger together gesturing a small violin. "Staci, you're so dramatic. He was only trying to help you."

"Toxic, Mother. He was toxic. But, hey, he's single now. If you like him so much, ask him out on a date!" Her mock sympathy so typical.

Seething, I dropped my napkin on the table. "I have to go. I need to finish Brook's blog before I leave for Vermont tomorrow— you know, to see my plumber, painter, laborer, whatever. Goodbye, Mother. Hope the rest of your day is just peachy."

By the time I got into my car I felt awful. Why was she so blind? Why does she push all of my buttons?

*

Lake Champlain glistened like tiny diamonds as the plane circled for a landing. I couldn't wait to see John again. It had been three weeks since he visited me in Chester. The idea of attending a wedding with him, however, made me nervous. After all, I didn't know his friends. *Ugh. What if that awful Maryanne is there? When we first met, she accosted me in the bathroom, for God's sake, telling me that I was definitely not the right person for John.*

The rehearsal dinner and the wedding were being held at the Burlington Country Club. I'd rented a room at the nearby Marriott. Convenience wasn't the only reason. I wanted to be on neutral ground, not to stay at his home with all those memories. I wanted him all for myself.

John met me in the lobby at seven p.m. for the rehearsal dinner. Seeing him in a suit almost knocked me over. Wow, does he clean up well. He wrapped me in his arms, and I breathed in his essence.

"You look beautiful, Staci." He hooked my arm as we walked to the parking lot.

I was worried I'd have to heave myself up into the cab of his trunk with a tight dress and four-inch heels. But he unlocked the door to a 1967 Porsche Carrera and my heart starting pumping. *Yahoo . . . this was going to be fun—riding around in this beauty with my favorite race car driver.*

The car reminded me of a day I'd spent with my family a long time ago. Dad had asked a friend who owned a red 1966 Thunderbird if he could borrow it. He wanted his family to go in style to the new balloon festival in Readington. The top was down, and Savannah and I were squished in the back seat, our hair flying every which way. At twelve, I thought my dad was awesome. He always thought of fun and exciting things for us to do that didn't cost a lot of money. As we drove through the parking lot people stopped us and asked about the car. I felt special that day—just like I did today. Floating back and forth in time, I didn't realize at first John was talking to me. Then I heard him say "Natalie and Sophie."

"What? I'm sorry, did you say something about your daughters?" I dismissed my memories, giving him my full attention.

"Both of them will be at Jessica's wedding and tonight at the rehearsal dinner." He downshifted, gliding into a curve.

OMG! I'll meet the daughters tonight. I should have asked. What an idiot! I thought he wanted to move slowly in this relationship. Now I'm meeting his family and friends.

Taking a deep breath, I replied, "That's great." My stomach tightened with dread. It was all so new. If his girls didn't like me, any hope of a long-lasting relationship was doomed.

"Do the girls know about me?" I cringed, waiting for his answer.

John slowed and put on the blinker. "Here we are."

Was he deliberately ignoring the question? I couldn't go in there without an answer. "John, do your daughters know that I'm coming tonight?"

John got out of the car as the valet opened my door. He hooked my arm and whispered in my ear, "Don't worry so much. The girls will love you."

I was still processing this new information as he ushered me in. Fast. Too fast. I looked down at my dress. *Crap! If I'd known, I never would have picked this one. It's way too tight.*

We stopped to check our coats and turned toward the dining room.

"Dad," I heard ahead of me. Before I looked up to see where the voice was coming from, a young woman threw her arms around John and gave him a big kiss on the cheek.

"Hey, Nat. When did you get in? I thought you were going to call for a ride from the airport." John gazed at his daughter with deep affection.

Giggling she said, "Dad, I'm staying at Ella's. I told you that. I knew you had a date tonight, and I didn't want to . . . well . . . you know . . . get in the way."

John's face reddened. He started to say something then stopped.

Letting go of her father, she turned to me. "Hi, I'm Natalie." She held out her hand with what looked like a welcoming smile.

I shook her hand. "Hi, I'm Staci." Natalie was a female version of John with his dark hair and green eyes. Her bubbly personality was barely contained in her thin frame.

"Dad, we're in the Post room tonight for dinner and tomorrow the reception is in the Champlain room." Natalie twirled around, grabbing John's arm again. "We're not sitting at the same table. You can get your place cards over there." She pointed. "I'm so excited. I can't wait to see Jessica in her wedding dress tomorrow." The door behind us opened and she must have spotted someone. "It was nice meeting you," she threw over her shoulder as she hurried off.

"That's my Nat," he said, watching her go.

"She's lovely. I wish I had her energy." We picked up our place cards and entered a small but beautiful dining room. My stomach tightened seeing so many new faces. The far wall was covered with floor to ceiling windows overlooking Lake Champlain. I walked over to them and caught the sunset while John got us drinks. Nothing like the dazzling sight of the sun sinking below the water to settle my thoughts.

"Are you Staci?" a young voice behind me asked.

"Yes," I answered, turning toward her. She looked so much like the picture in John's family room of his deceased wife that it brought me up short. Her blond hair swirled around her shoulders and her eyes were a bright blue. "Ah . . . are you Sophie?"

"Yes. It's a pleasure to meet you," she reached out her hand.

Her posture was perfectly straight, her manner friendly but more reserved than her sister's. I shook her hand. We stood there while I tried to think of something to say. I was momentarily tongue-tied.

"How was your flight?" Sophie asked after what seemed like an eternity.

I guess John had told his daughters about me. *That's good, I think!* "Quick and easy. Only took a little over an hour."

John came over with our drinks. "Hey, honey." He handed me my drink and then hugged Sophie with his free arm, kissing the top of her head.

"Dad." She stepped back and looked him up and down. "Don't you look nice!"

For the second time in fifteen minutes, John blushed. It was good to know that he wasn't always so confident.

"Did you meet Staci?" he asked.

She nodded toward me. "Yes."

"How was the rehearsal?" John asked her.

"Fast. That minister had us in and out in half an hour. That drink looks good. I'm gonna go get one. Nice meeting you." Sophie walked away.

Relief spread over me. I'd met both daughters without saying something stupid or tripping over anything.

"See. I told you they'd love you." His eyes glowing with delight.

"John, 'love' is a strong word. Let's be happy for right now that they don't seem to hate me."

He threw back his head and laughed causing me to laugh. I grabbed his hand and inhaled deeply; the air seemed lighter in the room.

We sat at a table of eight. Everyone except me had known John his entire life. They drilled me. Where was I from? Where had I grown up? What did I do? Did I have kids? I gulped my drink while the interrogation continued. I looked around the tables for any sign of that nasty Maryanne and was relieved when I didn't see her.

Finally, the bride and groom and both sets of parents came into the room. My breath caught. *Oh dear God!* There in a teal blue silk dress was Maryanne.

"John, isn't that the woman and man who came over to our table last spring at dinner?" I knew it was. I never asked whose wedding we were going to because I didn't know any of his friends—except for Carl and Maryanne. And as luck would have it—this was their daughter's wedding.

"Oh, that's right, I forgot you met them at the restaurant." John took a sip of his wine. "Jessica and Sophie have been best friends their entire lives. Sophie is her maid of honor."

Men just don't think to share details. I would have told John if one of my sons were in the wedding party. Maryanne's influence on his life was coming clearer to me. She'd been an integral part of John's family for decades. She even named her daughter after John's deceased wife, Jess. This didn't bode well.

The festivities began and I tried to pay attention or at least look like I was. John's attentiveness tonight reassured me somewhat, but that nagging feeling held tight. I planned to slip out to the ladies' room during the speeches. I convinced myself that Maryanne couldn't follow me there then. My plan worked.

During dessert, Carl and Maryanne came to our table and spoke with us all.

"It's nice to see you again," Carl said to me. Maryanne nodded my way but said nothing. She quickly turned her attention to the woman across from me. After a few minutes, they moved on to the next table.

Maryanne didn't seem so hostile toward me tonight. Thank goodness. Maybe whatever ax she had to grind with me was gone.

John was saying his goodbyes and I volunteered to get our coats. By the time we got into the car, I was relieved and happy. My feet hurt from my high heels, but I had made it through without incident.

Back at the hotel room I uncorked a bottle of chilled white Burgundy I had pillaged from George's wine cellar. I poured and placed the full glasses on the coffee table across from the couch. I moved his suit jacket to the chair. His scent drifted up and I inhaled deeply, remembering the last time we were in this hotel together. Excitement flared through me. I slipped my shoes off and settled back, thrilled to have John all to myself for the first time that day.

He sat next to me. I sipped my wine, hungrily watching him as he told me stories about the men at our table. A memory flashed into my mind of him carrying and lowering me into the bed. A burst of heat surged through me. *Oh . . . how I want him.*

"Do you have friends from childhood?" John asked.

"What? I'm sorry. I . . ." Straightening, I smiled at him.

"Am I boring you with my old stories?" His eyebrows rose in amusement. "What were you thinking about?"

Shit. Busted. "You could never bore me." I stood abruptly. "More wine?" I wavered a bit in my bare feet. Not sure I needed any more wine.

"Ah . . . ." He glanced at his glass. "Maybe a splash."

Don't let me spill it. Don't let me spill it, I chanted to myself and managed to pour both glasses without mishap. Elated, I turned abruptly and stubbed my toe on the leg of the coffee table. I doubled over but straightened right back up.

"Staci, you okay?" John asked.

"Yes," I managed, hopping on one foot. "I'm such a klutz." I hobbled over to the refrigerator and replaced the wine bottle.

"Let me see that toe," John cajoled. "I have the perfect cure." His eyes glinted and his mouth slowly curled upward.

"What might that be?" I sat next to him.

John stood. "Move down and put your legs up on the couch."

I quickly complied, curious.

He picked up my feet and slid underneath, placing them in his lap. "Perfect. Now, which one hurts?"

I giggled and pointed.

"Okay, we won't touch that one right away. Let the pain fade on its own for a while." He started to tenderly massage right below the ball of my foot. Slowly, as he kneaded my arch over and over with both hands, one foot at a time, I relaxed and leaned back on the couch's armrest.

My feet sizzled under his warm, gentle touch. Pedicures never felt like this. *Hmm . . . so nice.*

"Does your toe still hurt?" he asked.

I sighed instead of answering.

John grinned. When his hands roamed up my calves, a delicious shudder shot up my body. I closed my eyes.

"You're good at this," I whispered.

He said nothing, continuing to knead and caress my thighs. His touch was suddenly almost unbearable in its tenderness.

His hot breath tickled my ear. "Thank you for tonight . . . for meeting everyone . . . ." His massaging hands continued their upward climb.

Stop talking and kiss me already!

His body melted against me. His lips, hot and needy, found mine. Nothing could compare to this . . . to him. I couldn't restrain myself any longer, a moan rolling up from my soul, escaping my lips, igniting my desire.

"Staci," John muttered, kissing my ear.

I covered his mouth with mine, exploring, longing so hard for this man.

John pushed himself up and held out his arm for me. When I stood, he swept me into his arms. We kissed and undressed, grabbing, holding, and caressing one another before falling into bed.

Savoring every moment, the pleasure pure and explosive, I floated dazzlingly back into the warmth of John's arms. Winded, I stared at his handsome face as he stroked my hair. Couldn't we stay here forever?

*

The wedding was beautiful. As I watched the young couple, so full of promise, make their vows, a tear traveled down my cheek. I always cry at weddings, wishing I might have had that fairy-tale ending rather than the bitter road George and I had gone down.

Rain began to fall by the time we arrived at the reception. My thoughts turned again to Maryanne. I decided to just stay out of her way and hope she was so engrossed with her daughter's wedding that I could slip by her without incident.

John and I spent time with his daughters at the cocktail hour. Natalie told some silly stories from college, while Sophie gave her advice—sounding more like a mother than an older sister.

After the initial wedding dances, we sat with the same couples from the rehearsal dinner, which made it easier on me.

I wanted another drink rather than the wine being served at the table. So, I excused myself and went to the bar. Maryanne caught my eye and started to walk toward me. I grabbed my drink and made a beeline back to my table. She probably wouldn't say anything in front of John.

The band started playing and John asked me to dance. "It's a slow song," he whispered in my ear.

Snuggled in his arms, everyone else fell away. I loved his smell, how I fit nicely into him, his warmth. After a few turns, I looked up and out of the corner of my eye I noticed Maryanne standing by the dance floor with a group of friends. Maybe I was being paranoid. She was laughing and enjoying her daughter's wedding. I put my head back on John's shoulder.

After the wedding cake was served, I headed to the ladies' room. Knowing Maryanne's MO for cornering me in the bathroom, I looked around for her first. Sophie and Natalie were there washing their hands.

"Hi, Staci. Are you having fun?" Natalie bubbled.

"Yes, I am. The wedding was really beautiful."

"Didn't you just love Jessica's wedding dress?" Natalie praised it. "Oh, I can't wait for my own wedding."

Sophie giggled. "You need a husband first."

The girls left but I heard Natalie's voice outside the door talking to someone. I emerged from the stall to wash my hands and Maryanne stood at the sink, arms crossed over her chest, waiting for me.

"We have to stop meeting like this." It was the only thing I could think to say.

"You think you're real funny." She looked me up and down, raising her voice. "How dare you show up here at my daughter's wedding! What gall!" She threw both arms up in the air. "My daughter was Jess's godchild, for Christ's sake." Maryanne pointed at me. "She's even named after her. And you pick *this* event to throw yourself all over John? Jess must be turning in her grave. It's . . . sacrilegious!"

Stunned, I took a step back.

Maryanne advanced. "How could you disrespect us like this? You won't get our John. Mark my words!" she spat, her face crimson.

Just as I was about to say something, anything, Natalie walked into the bathroom. She must have heard some, if not all, of the poison Maryanne was spewing at me. My eyes filled. I pushed past Maryanne to reach the door. I needed a breath of fresh air and headed out to the veranda.

John appeared a few minutes later, looking concerned. "Is everything all right? Natalie said that you and Maryanne were . . . well, having words. What happened?"

I wasn't sure what to say. I knew that if his friends didn't like me, I wouldn't stand a chance. Not a long-term one, anyway. "I'm not sure really. I think she just misses her friend. Jessica." *Crap, why am I so nice? This woman has been nothing but a bitch to me.*

John froze. *Double crap. Why'd I mention his deceased wife? Now he'll be thinking of her all night.*

My shoulders sagged. Drained, I walked back inside and went to get my coat. I pulled out my phone, thinking maybe I should get a ride back to the hotel and let things settle down, that maybe he'd want some space, especially after I'd mentioned his wife.

As I scrolled for the app, John came up behind me. "Staci, I'm sorry about Maryanne. She can be pretty protective, I guess." He shrugged. "I'm still not sure what happened, but I'll speak with her tomorrow."

I wasn't sure I wanted him to do that. She would give him an earful, telling him why our relationship won't work. Would he listen to her? Would he start to doubt what we had? It's just so new and with John asking to take it slow, whatever that meant, I couldn't tell if we were strong enough together to withstand that type of attack.

The guests were all leaving the reception. "Come on. Let's get the car," John said.

The rain that had started earlier in the day had grown even stronger, with high, gusty winds sweeping the torrents from one side of the driveway to another.

Halfway to the hotel, John's phone rang. He asked me to pick it up from the cup holder and push the speaker button. His Porsche was an older car without Bluetooth. The name on the screen was Nick Turner.

"Mr. Marshall," he said without preamble, "with all the rain, the tractor got stuck on Chappy hillside. We tried to shift it, but it's too dark to see anything and . . ."

"No. Leave it alone. I'll be home tomorrow and will take care of it then." John ran his hand through his hair.

I sucked in a deep breath. Relieved. He would stay with me tonight even after the episode with Maryanne. Even after being reminded of Jess.

At the hotel, we skipped drinks. I changed into a nightgown and saw John texting in bed. "Is there a problem?"

"No, just Nick letting me know the night tasks are done." He pulled the blanket down on my side of the bed. "My arms need you."

I wanted to dive into them but knowing me I'd miss and hit him in the face. So, I gently climbed into bed and into his arms. My body molded into his.

A tingling started in the pit of my stomach. John ran his hands over my sides and back, stroking. Maryanne and his daughters and his deceased wife faded from my mind. All that was left was John, the two of us swirling in our own vortex where nothing else mattered.

*

I sprang out of bed and opened the blinds. Yesterday's rain was now just a memory, a brilliant, bright blue fall sky greeted me. John was in the shower. I thought about sneaking into the shower with him, but that would mean blow drying my big bushy hair. I decided to take one after him and put on a shower cap, so he didn't have to wait too long. Pulling out my clothes, I checked my flight for tonight and packed everything I didn't need today.

"Good morning." John came up behind me with a towel draped around him. We kissed, a long, slow, gentle kiss. "I have to go to the farm this morning and get that tractor out of the mud. Would you like to come?" he asked. "I'll bring you to the airport after a late lunch."

"That sounds great." I jumped into the shower and surprised myself by how fast I got ready.

We grabbed a coffee and Danish from the complimentary breakfast at the hotel and got to the farm before eleven a.m. "Sunday, the farm staff is off. I'm going to see to the cows first and then get the tractor out of the mud," John said.

We walked to the larger barn. I followed him as he checked the cows' water and food.

"I've read that tariffs and low prices are wiping out some dairy farms across the country. Has that affected you?" I asked.

"It's really tough making a profit now," he replied as he checked on the cow's feed. "There's more to it than just low prices and tariffs.

I've diversified with different products and I'm holding my own for now. But there will probably come a time when the girls and I have to make some sort of decision." He motioned for me to follow.

I said nothing. What could I say? We left the large barn and entered a smaller one.

"Let's take the ATV." He pointed to a blue vehicle in the corner of the barn. "This will be faster than saddling two horses and I think you'll like it better." John started up the ATV and headed out of the barn. "Can you drive one of these?"

I shook my head.

"It's easy. I'll show you and you can drive this back and I'll take the tractor. Sit in front of me."

I climbed in front. *"Easy," I've heard that before.* Like the time I went skiing in Lake Placid with George who said that the black diamond route down was easy and that they hadn't marked it right. He wasn't much of a skier, so like a fool I followed him. Huge moguls and a sheet of ice faced me. I managed to get down the slope, but I never forgot the fear. So no, I no longer believe it when someone says *easy*.

Mud thick around the tires from the drenching rain of the day before splashed onto my jeans. The bumpy ride made me glad I'd zipped my phone into my coat pocket. John snuggled tightly into my back and instructed me how to drive the ATV. I enjoyed every minute of the ride. By the time we got to the hillside, my jeans were coated in mud.

The tractor was on top of a hill with a large piece of machinery attached to it. It looked like it was dangling down the slope.

"I'll have to call Nick. There's no way this is a one-man job." John reached into his coat for his phone.

"Wait. Can't I do something?"

He inspected the tractor and the attached plow. The tractor tire was caught in a deep rut on top of the hill. "Maybe." He climbed on the tractor, started it up and told me he would put the gear into low and turn hard right to try to get out of it. "Staci, stand over there by those trees."

Standing between two huge oak trees, anxiety crept up my spine. Nothing to worry about, I told myself. John knew what he was doing. He jerked the steering wheel all the way to the right. The noise hurt my ears: a mixture of grinding and growling, growing into an almost deafening scream as he accelerated. The uneasy feeling settled into my stomach and this morning's Danish didn't taste so good anymore.

"Shit!" I heard John yell.

He turned the wheel slightly left, then the tractor turned over on its side. It took one second.

I stood frozen. Waiting for John to pop up. He didn't. "Oh my God! Oh my God! John! John!" I ran to the tractor, terrified I'd see him mangled and torn apart. There was blood on the plow. I looked down the slope. John lay a few feet below on his side. I ran to him. I wasn't sure if I should move him onto his back or not. His forehead was bleeding; he must have hit his head. I lay my face next to his and placed my finger under his nose. Was he breathing? He was.

I yanked out my phone and dialed 911, scared that there'd be no service here.

It rang. How would I explain exactly where I am?

"Nine-one-one. What is your emergency?"

I screamed into the phone and the operator quietly convinced me to calm down for John's sake. I told her everything I knew and wasn't sure any of it made sense. I gave them the address of the farm and described as much as I could where we were. Once I knew help was on its way, I cried, and the operator did her best to soothe me.

It took forever. I kept checking his breathing. Thank God, he still was. I realized that the tractor wasn't sputtering any more—had John managed to turn it off while falling? Did it have some kind of cutoff switch?

At last, I saw the ambulance traversing over to us. The EMTs jumped out.

"How long has he been unconscious, ma'am?" one of them asked.

"About twenty minutes, maybe more." I stepped away and let them treat him.

A neck brace and backboard secured John's head and spine and they administered an IV. One of the attendants asked me if he took any medications. I didn't know. One of his daughters might. I gave them their names.

My whole body trembled. One of the paramedics wrapped a blanket around me.

"I'm coming with you," I said.

They nodded and I climbed into the ambulance.

An hour must have elapsed from the time of the accident until we were in the emergency room in Burlington. I waited, pacing back and forth. John's daughters were on their way. I felt sick.

I pulled out my phone. "Bri," was all I got out of my mouth before I started to cry. I cried so hard that I made no sense. I tried to listen to her questions, but I just had to get it all out.

"Staci, calm down. Are you all right?" Bri said over and over. "I have you on speakerphone, Madeline is here with me."

I walked outside and paced again, up and down the emergency parking lot. I begged Bri to come be with me.

"Um . . . well . . ."

I heard Bri speaking with Madeline. Then she got on the phone. "Staci, it's Madeline. Calm down and tell us what happened."

Madeline's commanding voice did the trick. I took a deep breath and told them both what happened.

"I'll come up today. I just need to get some clothes," Madeline said. "It'll do me good to get away for a day or so."

I didn't understand why she sounded so eager to come. Deflated, I thanked her. Why couldn't Bri come? I couldn't imagine Madeline being any help at all. She'd just make me feel worse.

I went back into the waiting room. A nurse came and asked if John's daughters had arrived yet.

"No, but I'm sure they'll be here soon."

Both daughters arrived forty-five minutes later, together with Carl and Maryanne. *Oh no! Crap. Not her, not here.* Maryanne had her arm around Natalie, who was crying. Sophie had her arms wrapped tightly around her coat. She looked forlorn, shaking. Hesitantly, I approached them.

"The doctor hasn't come out yet, but the nurse said he would speak to us shortly." The girls stared at me wide-eyed. I wasn't sure why they looked so shocked.

They left the waiting room to inform the nurse they'd arrived. Maryanne approached me. "You again. I bet you caused this accident. You know nothing about farming and probably put John in harm's way."

I turned away.

"At least wash their father's blood off your face. The girls are traumatized enough!" she yelled.

So that was the reason why the girls had looked at me like that. I fled the waiting room for the bathroom. *Jesus, how could I be so stupid? She's right. I should have realized John's blood had crusted on my face and clothes.* My reflection in the mirror shocked me. My clothes were caked with mud and blood and dirt smeared my face and clumped in my hair. I quickly washed up and tried to drag a brush through my hair.

I saw a vending machine outside the ladies' room and rummaged around my pockets, finding a few singles. I bought water bottles for the girls and headed back to the waiting room. I hoped the doctor would tell us something soon. How many times in book club had we read books where the heroine finally meets the man of her dreams only for one of them to die? *Why in the world did I think of that?*

I sat separately from the others. I wanted to comfort Natalie and Sophie, but Maryanne stayed glued to their sides, sitting between them both. Despite what the nurse had told us, it felt like hours before a doctor finally came out.

A nurse led the doctor over to Natalie and Sophie. He said, "Your dad has a closed traumatic brain injury. The bleeding has stopped from a gash over his left eye to his ear. But there was no fracture of the skull."

Natalie started to cry.

The doctor added, "We're monitoring any swelling he may develop. We'll know more in the next twenty-four hours."

Sophie asked, "Can we see him?"

"Family members only. He's unconscious. Don't try to wake him," he said. "Follow me."

Natalie and Sophie complied.

I left the room and stood outside in the hallway. I didn't want to talk to Maryanne. I'd been cooped up with her for five long hours, which felt more like fifteen.

As more of John's friends arrived at the hospital. Maryanne took it upon herself to inform them of his condition and always snidely pointed at me when she finished. As much as I didn't want to be around her, I also didn't want to leave in case the doctor returned with more news. I knew no one would bother to inform me of what was happening. Maryanne would be delighted to keep John's condition to herself and his daughters had chosen to stay in the hospital room with their father.

At some point, my nerves fried, I escaped again to the bathroom. I sat on the toilet seat and tried to remember the mindful mantra I had learned when I sought therapy after my separation from George. But this was so much worse. It was like I was stuck in a Victorian novel, scorned as an outsider. Eventually, my butt numb, I rose, stretching my glutes. I slowly walked back to the waiting room.

Where was everyone? The waiting room was empty. I quickly went through the emergency room doors looking for the doctor or the girls or somebody. My heart accelerated with every step.

I heard Natalie's faint voice and followed it to a curtained-off area. The curtain was slightly ajar, and I peeked in. John had tubes and lines everywhere and machines were blinking, but he was awake. My relief was so intense that I almost fainted.

His room was packed with people, but somehow, we locked eyes and he said softly, "Staci." He tried to move his arm, but it caught on a line.

I walked in. Everyone moved aside. I sat down next to him on the bed. "Hi," was all I could say. Tears welled in my eyes. I clutched his hand.

The glow of his smile warmed me. His eyes flickered and he closed them, lapsing into sleep or unconsciousness. I hoped it was sleep.

Natalie started to cry, and a few tears fell on my own cheeks. I stood.

"You shouldn't be here!" Maryanne shouted, rising from a chair. "This is all your fault."

"What are you talking about?" I countered.

Just then the curtain was pulled all the way back and there stood the doctor and my uptight friend Madeline. Dressed to perfection in a suede jacket and pants with a silk blouse, her hair shone like she just came from the hairdresser. How did she manage to look like that after a six-hour drive?

"Doctor, this woman has no right to be here." Maryanne pointed at me. "She caused the accident."

"And you are?" Madeline asked in an aristocratic voice.

"Me? Who the hell are you?" Maryanne retorted, hands on hip.

The doctor entered the room and looked at John. "Everybody out. I thought I made it clear only family. Out!"

Everyone emptied into the emergency room hallway. Maryanne circled Madeline but Madeline paid no notice, which seemed to infuriate her even more.

I looked back and forth between them. Was Madeline helping or making matters worse? I wasn't sure.

Madeline rubbed her ear. "Staci, dear, who exactly is that rude woman? And why is she here?"

Maryanne's face flushed scarlet. Just then the doctor came into the hallway from John's room, giving her an opening to repeat: "I'm telling you, that woman has no right to be here. She caused the accident." She again pointed at me.

Madeline stepped to his side. "Doctor, this lovely woman"—she touched my arm—"is John's girlfriend and from speaking with the EMTs who brought him here, I learned she saved his life." Her voice remained level, professional, a stark contrast to Maryanne's almost hysterical tones. "I think that loud, angry, so-called friend should not be allowed to see him until he's recovered. That kind of shrieking will only make him feel worse. Don't you think so?" She looked at the doctor, ignoring Maryanne.

Maryanne spat, edging toward Madeline, who held her ground with sublime indifference. "How dare you? We're his closest friends and have known him forever. We are his family!"

I stepped between them. "Enough, both of you." I hissed. "This isn't helping Natalie and Sophie." I turned toward the doctor. "How is he?"

"Better. His head injury was serious because he lost consciousness, but there's no internal swelling. He needs plenty of rest, but he'll be fine. Please go to the waiting room and for heaven's sake—stop fighting." He walked away.

Madeline wiped something away from her lapels as if insinuating Maryanne had splattered her jacket with her saliva.

Maryanne caught the gesture and swiveled around, furious, but Carl grabbed his wife and headed to the waiting room.

I pulled Madeline back before she entered the room and muttered: "Calm down, please. That nasty Maryanne isn't going anywhere. Don't give her any more excuses to hate me."

"Darling, I am calm. And she can't hate you any more than she already does. But we need to teach her she can't get away with her insinuations and accusations." She smiled at me.

That was Madeline. Always so convinced she was right. "How and when did you speak with the EMTs? How did you find John's doctor?"

She looped her arm in mine and we walked toward the cafeteria. "Let's get a cup of coffee."

When we sat down with our drinks, Madeline said, "You're a complete mess!" Have you seen yourself? I'm going to get my makeup bag from the car, and we are going to fix you up a bit."

"I washed my face at least." I took a deep breath. "Thank you for coming up here. I felt all alone in a hostile place." I blew on my coffee. "Maryanne hates me, and I don't know why."

"She's a bitch, that's for sure. But it was kind of fun. She loses control so easily." Madeline laughed. "Listen, my two cents: she's jealous. What else could it be?"

I shook my head. "Why jealous? Women always say that about other women. I don't think it's that. It's such a cliché."

"Well, I've only had one interaction with her, but that kind of anger usually stems from love." Madeline patted my hand. "I think she loves John, which I thought since you told me about the first time you met each other, when she cornered you in the bathroom."

"What? She's been happily married for a long time. Don't be ridiculous." I stood. "Let's go back to the waiting room."

Carl approached me when we entered. "John is awake. The girls are in with him."

I touched his arm. "Thank you."

*

Two days later John was released from the hospital. Natalie and Sophie were playing nurse and I was heading home with Madeline. We stopped by to say goodbye.

"Nice place!" Madeline said, pulling down his driveway. "This is a farm?"

"I know, I said the same thing." I giggled.

We walked into John's great room where he was sitting in a high back chair with his feet on an ottoman covered in a blanket. The lights were dim, per the doctor's orders.

"Hi, Staci." He started to stand up.

"No, sit. Your daughters will evict me if they see you standing." I walked quickly over to him and put my hand on his shoulder. "The girls are taking your recovery seriously."

He shrugged. "Tell me about it. They won't let me do anything." Then he smiled at Madeline. "Hey, Madeline. Thanks so much for coming up here and bringing Staci home. You're a good friend."

Madeline nodded, as if graciously acknowledging what she knew to be true.

"How do you feel?" I asked.

"Pretty much the same as yesterday. My neck is stiff and my head throbs."

I sat on the ottoman next to his legs. "I would have gladly stayed and nursed you back to health, but I think your daughters wouldn't . . ."

He shook his head. "There's no need for any of this. Really! I can take care of myself." He looked into my eyes. "I should have taken my other tractor and pulled the stuck one out of the mud. It was just stupid on my part."

I kissed him gently. I didn't want to leave. But watching how his daughters fussed over him, I thought it was the right thing to do. Madeline agreed. She thought that inserting myself into his household during his recovery would be too much too soon. John's daughters might grow to resent the intrusion and he clearly wanted to heal privately.

Natalie popped in full of energy, asking if we'd like lunch.

I stood. "No, thank you. We're heading back to Jersey." I placed a hand on John's shoulder. "Are you sure you don't need me to stay?"

John grasped my hand. "I'm so sorry our weekend turned out like this. Thank you for being there."

"I'm just happy you're recovering." I stood and bent down, giving him a long kiss, inhaling as much of him as I could.

"Do you want me to wait in the car?" Madeline teased.

"John . . . ." I wanted to tell him that I loved him. I knew he wanted to go slow, but I'd almost lost him.

The doorbell rang and in walked Maryanne and Carl.

I stepped back. Another time. It would have to wait. We needed to get out before Maryanne and Madeline got into another shouting match. They were both squaring their shoulders, looking ready to go at it.

On our way home, Madeline told me what she'd been going through. I couldn't believe it. We'd spent three days together and she'd never said a thing.

"I needed to not think or talk about it for a bit and give Stan a break. He had enough on his plate without me constantly asking him questions and giving him advice." Madeline set the cruise control to eight miles over the speed limit. "Although I wasn't able to block it out when I tried to sleep."

Even with this unbelievable turn of events, Madeline had maintained her dignity. No breakdowns, no rantings, no whining, not even a bad hair day. In fact, no one could have possibly realized how much stress she was under. She'd become a pro at bottling up her feelings except for those knife-edged barbs she threw at people. I'd gotten to know a different side of her these last few days. We'd laughed and cried together and ate our way through Burlington. Her normal caustic know-it-all attitude had all but disappeared. Except for when Maryanne was around.

"You have to teach me how you stayed so calm with Maryanne.

You're so quick-witted, too." I looked out the window. "I get so upset my words jumble and I sound like a fool."

"It's in the tone, dear. It conveys the message loud and clear without the emotions," Madeline said. "I knew it would piss her off."

I laughed. "Yes, you sure did that."

"I've had a lifetime of dealing with toxic people. It took time and practice not to overreact and remain cool," Madeline said.

My phone vibrated and I looked at the text. "Wow, I'm on a chain message with John, his daughters and Maryanne and Carl."

"What's it say?" Madeline asked.

Thank you all for helping me. I'm blessed to have you in my life.

"John is so thoughtful," I said. "Hey, Maryanne just answered him."

"That means you have her phone number now," Madeline stated.

"Yeah, so?" I said.

"Let's send her a text."

"No way." I shook my head.

"Yes. It's time you stand up to her." Madeline tapped her fingers on the steering wheel. "How about, 'Listen, Vermont Vixen, I don't know why you are continuously up John's butt. Seems like Carl should be concerned. Wrap your mind around this, bony bitch: John and I are perfect together in all ways—but most especially between the sheets—so get used to seeing me around! This Jersey girl isn't going anywhere.'"

"What? Have you lost your mind?" I cried.

As Madeline chatted on spewing forth numerous other insults, I knew she was right. I needed to address this situation but in my own way. Maryanne's like my ex bullying me into submission. The hell with that. I began to text.

**Hi, Maryanne—it's Staci. I realize the pain you feel over
losing someone close. I still grieve the loss of my father every
day. But that doesn't give you the right to hunt me down in
bathrooms and accost me. I care deeply for John and I'm not
going away because you want me to. The harassment has got
to stop. Maybe for John's sake we can salvage something civil
between us.**

I read the text to Madeline before I sent it.

"That's perfect. See, you're learning. Although, I still like the
bony bitch comment. Can you throw that in somewhere?"

I laughed. "I wish. But Maryanne is a long-standing friend of
John's and like it or not she's going to be around. But I'm done with
being treated like that."

Madeline slapped my arm. "That's my girl."

That weekend together had helped Madeline and me become
true friends, not just members of a book club. I'd gotten to know
the Madeline that Bri knew. I wondered if she'd revert back to her
less-than-charming self now that we were heading back to familiar
territory. But it wouldn't matter. I knew her now.

As we trekked down Route 22A, I thought back to how I'd left
Burlington brokenhearted last time. This time I had hope. Hope for
a future with John. I only wish I were more secure in the relationship. Instead, I still felt like a vulnerable teenager waiting by the
phone. *Will he call? Please call.*

"Is that the infamous racetrack where you first crossed paths
with John?" Madeline asked, pointing at the Devil's Bowl Speedway.

"Ah . . . yes." I sat straighter in my seat, barely catching sight
of it before we drove by. I turned and faced forward and rested my
head on the headrest. I knew I would miss John terribly, but today I
was happy to be going home.

Chapter 21

BRIANNA

BOOK CLUB HOLIDAY PARTY

THE DOORBELL RANG. I excused myself from talking to Staci and went to the front door. Tonight, my beloved friends and I would toast another year together.

"Ava. Merry Christmas." I smiled broadly, feeling the effects of the champagne.

"*¡Feliz Navidad!*" Ava beamed, entering the foyer. Neil stepped up behind her.

"Happy Hanukkah, Neil. Please come in." I ushered them both inside. "Give me your coats."

"*¡Guao! ¡Su casa se be bella!*" Ava pointed to the garland wrapped around the staircase and at my Christmas tree collection scattered through the rooms. "The decorations are beautiful. It's like a Christmas wonderland."

I hung their coats in the foyer closet. "Thanks."

Eric joined us at the bar. "Happy holidays." He shook hands with Neil and kissed Ava on the cheek.

I had hired a bartender and two servers to keep the party flowing. If my friends saw me working, they'd join in and only the men would enjoy the party. Not tonight. This was Novel Women's party and I wanted everyone to enjoy themselves, me included.

Ava and Neil ordered two dirty martinis that the bartender filled to the rim. Eric and I chatted with them at the bar as they sipped them down to a manageable level.

"I hear congratulations are in order." Ava said.

At first, I didn't know what she was talking about. Then I remembered. "Jesus, how did you even know about that? I didn't tell anyone. It happened so fast."

"Come on—small town."

"It was nothing." I shrugged. "Really. Just a lot of running around."

Ava sipped her drink. "Hey, you stepped in at the last minute and pulled together a wine and book party in a few hours for the library. I think that's something."

"Yeah, it went smoothly considering the frenzy before the event. I guess Nicole taught me how to work well in chaos." The head librarian had asked me to organize an event already scheduled for the next night. The person in charge had had a car accident the previous week and nothing had been done. They were going to cancel when I just happened to walk into the library to get a few books. She remembered me from an event I had just done two weeks earlier with Elevated Events.

"You always do a great job. You should start your own service," Ava said.

"I was fired, remember? I don't think being an event planner is the career for me."

Ava stepped close to me. "What? Nonsense. You're a talented person and an excellent event planner. Don't let that bitch Nicole take that away from you."

I looked down and inhaled, wanting to believe her. "Thanks. I guess I'm just discouraged, and. . . ."

Madeline interrupted us and said, "Always punctual, my dear," tapping Ava's watch before giving a peck on the cheek to both her and Neil.

Ava smirked. "¡*Feliz Navidad!* to you, too, Madeline."

Eric and I were thrilled that Madeline and Stan came tonight, and that both seemed to be in high spirits. It had been a tough few weeks for them.

"While I have the four of you together, I want to thank you for your support. It's meant a lot to us," Madeline said.

"Of course. I wish we could have done more," I said.

"No need. Stan got a call from his attorney late last night. No charges will be filed against him or his company." Madeline said.

"Wonderful!" I cheered, as the others echoed my congratulations.

Madeline spotted Staci and excused herself to go speak to her. She must have told her the good news because Staci squeaked and gave her a big hug and managed to spill her drink at the same time. Before the two had returned from Vermont, Madeline would have given Staci some lip about being so klutzy, but not anymore. Now Madeline just helped her clean it up.

Looking around, I noticed Hanna standing by our Christmas tree by herself. "How is Ashley?" I asked, walking up behind her.

"Much better." She grinned for a moment, then it faded. "At least for the time being. It's a waiting game." Collecting herself, she thanked me for letting her parents come to the party. "It's good for them to be around people who aren't dealing with a life-threatening illness." Hanna waved to her dad as he crossed by the door with two empty glasses.

I moved close so no one else could hear. "How has it been with your mom since the *talk*?"

Hanna grinned. "Good." She paused. "She struggles with it, but she's trying. Sometimes she reverts and begins to lecture me again. When she realizes it, she clamps her lips tight and leaves the room."

"That's progress." I hooked her arm. "Come on, let's get the women and do our Secret Santa."

Staci drifted over by us and said, "Hanna, I just talked to your parents. They're delightful. Bri told me you had a talk with your mom. It must have worked because she had only nice things to say about you." She blew out a deep breath. "I'm not sure a talk would ever work with my mother. She only sees my faults."

Hanna said in a light voice, "Just don't ask my mother anything about food."

They giggled together softly.

"Come on, gift time," I hollered, rounding up the members and ushering them into the living room.

Walking to the table I'd placed close to the Christmas tree, I said, "Everyone, sit. I'd like to raise a toast to another year together. And to say how grateful I am to have you in my life."

"And us you!" Ava shouted.

Shouts of "Yeah." And "To Bri," rippled through the room.

Putting my glass down, I said in a bubbly voice. "Okay, guys, settle down. Let's get to the gifts." As I picked up the first one, I heard Madeline's forceful voice behind me.

"Women just don't get it. It's about unity. Working together." Madeline raised both arms.

"I agree," Ava said. "Her coworker should have gone to bat for her instead of saying her husband made plenty of money, so the job really didn't matter to her."

Confused, I half turned. "Wait, who? What?"

Ava pivoted toward me. "We were talking about your pathetic coworker. You know. The one who chose silence instead of the truth."

Whoa . . . . "She's not pathetic. She did what she had to do."

"Bri, come on." Madeline's lips were a thin line. "That woman assumed you didn't need the job. She didn't care that you got fired for something you didn't do. All she saw was how it might affect her."

"I can't blame her. It's that horror Nicole." I cast my eyes to the floor. "And Jane really does need the job."

"Maybe she does." Madeline bellowed. "But we must stand up

for one another, especially when something like this happens. It's about holding that asshole accountable for his actions. She should have said something. And it doesn't matter if you need the money or not."

"Damn right, sister!" Ava clapped.

Wagging my finger, I said, "Easy to make that kind of moral statement talking at a party. But it's another thing in the real world when you need the job. You know that."

"Technically, you're right. It just frosts my ass." Madeline knocked back the last of her drink.

"Your ex-boss sounds like a bully," Charlotte said.

I nodded and turned back to Madeline. "Not everyone is as bold or righteous as you are."

Staci intervened. "Well, I'm glad Madeline's like that. She sure put Maryanne in her place in Vermont." She made a *V* sign with her fingers.

"Why, thank you, darling." Madeline beamed at Staci. "What Nicole did to you stemmed from nothing more than jealousy." She flipped her hand up. "That nasty boss of yours was just waiting for an opportune time to get rid of you."

My brows furrowed. "Jealous? Of what?" I didn't want to dwell on my firing all evening. But my concerned friends thought otherwise.

Madeline, of course, wouldn't let it go. "Haven't we all looked at ourselves and found some fault? Wishing we had her legs or her shape or her husband?" She glanced around the room. "Well, your ex-boss thought you had the perfect life. A life she longs for. She enjoyed making you struggle because she couldn't have what you do."

Astonished, mouth slightly open, I stared at her. "How do you know this?"

Crossing her legs as she sat down, Madeline said, "I guess I don't, not really. But I'm almost certain that's what happened. And it just makes her a fool as well as a bully. We all know that no one has a perfect life. No matter how good it looks from the outside."

"That's for damn sure." Charlotte nodded.

"I've always said that if women got rid of their petty jealousies, we'd rule the world." Madeline sat back on the couch, finally finished with her diatribe. She pulled her phone from her pocket and scowled at it.

Wanting to change the subject, I said, "Well, it's nice to see you all agreeing on something, even though it's my screwed-up situation." I turned toward the gifts.

Ava said, "Don't worry, I'm gonna have a talk with my friend Shelly, Nicole's boss. I'll get this straightened out."

"No!" I yelled. Clearing my throat, I turned toward her. "Sorry. That came out harsher than I meant. I have a meeting with the owner next week. Please, just let me take care of it."

"No problem." Ava said. "I'm happy to help even if it's to butt out."

Pushing a smile on my face, I returned to the gifts. I read the first tag, "Hanna."

She took her gift and opened it quickly expecting some gag gift, but it wasn't. "Thank you," she uttered softly.

Staci, not able to control herself, burst out, "I took that picture when your daughter was playing soccer. I was so happy it came out that well. Action shots aren't my forte."

Hanna, red cheeked, thanked Staci. "It's beautiful."

Something was wrong. I looked at the picture over Hanna's shoulder. It was a great shot of Katie kicking the ball during a game. At first, I didn't understand Hanna's reaction. Then I noticed that she was in the background with a man. Maybe the coach? Staci had managed to capture a warm gaze between them, a comfortable tenderness in that tiny moment, catching it for everyone to see their mutual affection. *Oh God!* Hanna never told me anything about the coach. Was I reading too much into the picture?

I reached for another gift. "Charlotte."

She eyed the gift. "A book?" She unwrapped it, roaring. "*Cougar*

Lovin', by Charlotte *Stiletto* Egan." Then she shrieked. "Wow! A picture of me in a provocative outfit and spike heels. How the hell did you do this?" She took a breath between giggles. "That may be my head, but that sure isn't my body. At least not anymore. Just brilliant! Thank you. I really needed a good laugh." She passed the gift around.

"Kudos to whoever thought of that." I searched the women's faces for a clue. Madeline looked smug.

By the time the rest of the women had opened their presents, hilarity was widespread enough to bring the men in to see what was so funny.

"Hey, there's one more gift, Bri," Ava yelled. "It's for you."

I unwrapped it. Holding back tears, I said, "Oh, it's lovely. Thank you." I held it up for everyone to see. "When was this picture taken?"

Staci answered, "Don't you remember last May at book club?"

I turned the picture around and reread the quote alongside a great shot of us in the kitchen.

Because of You
We Laugh a little Harder
Cry a little Less
And Smile a lot More

"This really means so much. Thanks." I placed it on the table. "But you know, I do have a sense of humor. You could have gotten me a gag gift, too!"

Madeline rose. "Nah! You do a lot getting this group together. We wanted you to know how much we appreciate you." She put her hand on my shoulder. "And I personally want you to know that I'm so glad that fate brought us together as class moms all those years ago. You are one of a kind."

Oh boy. Don't cry. I inhaled deeply and faced Madeline. "I don't know what to say. Thank you doesn't seem adequate." Every one of them came over and gave me a hug.

"Let's go have dinner." I stayed behind to pick up the discarded wrapping paper.

Madeline grabbed Ava's arm before they left the room. "Can I borrow that azabache charm you got tonight? It wards off evil spirits. Right?"

Ava laughed and handed her the charm. "I wonder who gave me this? It's part of my Hispanic culture."

Madeline waved her hand. "I'm just kidding." She picked up the book she got as a gift, *How to Make Friends and Influence People.* This has you written all over it."

Ava threw her head back laughing. "Guilty." After a minute, she said, "I'm really sorry for what you went through. Anything you need, please let us know."

Madeline took a deep breath. "We're probably going to down-size, and I could use your help."

"Yes, absolutely. Let's talk after the holiday," Ava said, grabbing Madeline's arm. "Let's eat."

Will you look at that? Ava and Madeline actually getting along. A true Christmas miracle.

On my way back to the dining room, I noticed Charlotte and Maxwell in the corner by the fireplace. Charlotte's face was flushed, and her hand gripped tight around his arm. Not wanting to stare, I walked away to get a plate of food.

Sitting next to Eric, I asked him if he was enjoying the party.

"Absolutely. It's great catching up with everyone." He shoveled down his dinner. "Food is delicious. I'm getting another helping."

Hanna was still in the living room talking with Mark. He was pointing at the Secret Santa picture she'd received from Staci and hissing under his breath. She shook her head and left the picture on the table. Grabbing his hand, she pulled him into the dining room to eat. I would have to find out what was going on—sometime later.

Ava brought a chair over and plopped down next to me. "Hey, nice party."

"Thanks. Is Neil having fun?" I asked.

"I guess. He wants to go to the City tonight. I don't. I wish he'd back down." Ava frowned.

She looked frustrated. I felt she wanted to say something else, so I prodded her. "How's that doctor friend you met in Puerto Rico?"

"He's great. He came to see his mother two weeks ago at my house before she and my mom returned to Puerto Rico." Ava brightened. "We all had a lot of fun. My mother loves him, but, of course, as her best friend's son he's high on her list."

"I think he's high on your list, too. Your face lights up whenever you talk about him."

She blushed. "Maybe he is."

Changing the subject, I pointed to Staci, who was sitting with Hanna's parents. "Look, she's wearing that medical alert necklace that someone gave her as a gift. Our klutzy friend is such a good sport." I put my plate on the table behind me. "It's too bad that John is still recovering from his accident."

"Yeah." Ava agreed. "She has . . . ."

Charlotte interrupted, plunking herself down in Eric's seat. "Shit, shit, shit!" She punched her hand into her lap.

Startled, I jumped. "What's wrong?"

Ava moved her chair closer.

Tears rimmed Charlotte's eyes. "His ex-wife is moving back here. He found out today." She choked up. "She relocated. She's really making a play for him after all this time." She tried to control her breathing.

Crap, what the hell do I say to that?

"I shouldn't have fallen for him. This is what happens." Charlotte moaned.

"Has he said he wants to try to work it out with his ex-wife?" I asked.

"No, but . . . ."

"Please, Charlotte, don't give up on him yet."

She looked away. "I can't go through this again."

Ava tapped her arm. "Hey, yes you can. You're not the same woman you were back then. Your lying ass ex-husband isn't cheating on you now. Maxwell was honest and told you what was happening."

"I was happy just keeping it light. But no, he kept pulling me closer and closer."

"How do you know it won't work out between you?" Ava asked. "Don't just let her waltz back in and take him. Hell, fight for him."

Nodding, I added, "I think he's fallen for you, too. Don't despair."

"I hope you're both right." Charlotte looked at Maxwell talking to Eric in the other room.

"We're all here for you." I draped my arm around her shoulder and squeezed tight. Time to change the subject. After all, this was supposed to be a party!

Madeline and Stan came over. "Dinner was delicious," she said.

"Did you make all this food?" Stan asked.

"Most of it." I was pleased by the compliment.

"You can cook for me anytime," he said.

"Again?" Madeline pulled her ringing phone from her pocket. "What the hell? A number I don't recognize keeps calling tonight. Some kind of robocall or a scammer on a Saturday night?"

"Here's an idea. Turn that thing off," Stan muttered.

"Block the number," I told her.

"It's a local exchange. If they call again and it's a scammer, I'm gonna give them hell." Madeline jammed her phone into her pocket.

I didn't envy whoever was on the other end of that line.

Staci bounded over, clearly tipsy. Her face flushed with excitement as she told us that she had talked to John for about an hour today. "I really want you guys to meet him. Madeline thought he was hot!" she boomed, louder than I think she intended.

Ava snickered and said, "I'm sure he is.

Staci wrapped both arms around herself. "Oh, I miss him." She closed her eyes and her euphoric demeanor calmed. When she opened them and peered into the dining room, she squealed, "Holy moly. Look at all those different desserts! I want one of everything." She scampered off. Madeline and Stan joined her.

Charlotte turned to Ava and me and said, "It's a good thing she's spending the night here.

"Madeline told me that one of John's friends was a real bitch to her," Charlotte confided. "She's gonna have to deal with that eventually."

Staci loaded a plate with cookies, an eclair, a slice of pie and a slice of cake. She waddled over to a chair trying to balance the huge plate of sweets on her lap.

"She's sure happy with John back in her life," I said.

"I've never seen her eat so much food. I'd keep a bucket by her bed tonight," Ava said.

Dessert wound down and music boomed from the family room. Had to be my hard-of-hearing husband. He thinks everyone's still in college and shares his love of blaring music. I got up to turn down Led Zeppelin, but someone else must have muscled Eric away from the controls.

A beautiful ballad came on. "Ocean" by Lady A. Charlotte took a deep breath and looked around.

Maxwell approached. "Charlie, would you like to dance?"

She stood and walked with him to the family room.

We watched as they snuggled into each other.

"Yeah, no love there on Maxwell's part." Ava declared. "Why's she so worried? They're going to be fine."

I looked on and hoped that my oldest friend had the strength to deal with whatever was coming. "There'll be some bumps for sure."

Eric extended his hand to me, "Dance?" My spirits soared as we swirled around to the music. He wrapped me in his arms when the song ended and kissed me.

What a damn tough year! But hell, we're all here. Together.

Acknowledgements

I want to thank my fellow writers and book club members for coming on this amazing journey with me. I'm forever indebted to my dear friends Fran and Jeanne. Thank you for being my pillar of support. I'm eternally grateful for your hard work, your wonderful ideas, your edits and for staying with me on this journey. It is so much better because of you.

I'd like to thank our editor, Lara Robbins, for her editorial skills and direction.

I also want to give a special thank you to my amazing Tuesday night workshop class for your patience and guidance. You are all such accomplished writers and you've helped and encouraged me all along the way.

A very special thank you to Michelle Cameron of The Writer's Circle for her dedicated work of *Novel Women 2* and *Novel Women*. Editor extraordinaire. Amazing how people come into your life and help you become more than you ever dreamed of.

Lastly, I'd like to thank my children who helped and encouraged me, my sister who read my drafts and urged me on, and to my wonderful husband who listened to me endlessly about every detail whether he wanted to or not. Thank you!

Kim Sullivan Harwanko

Thank you, Kim and Jeanne, for all you have done to bring this project to completion.

Kim's vision, drive and hard work are a testament to her passion for writing and the art of storytelling. Thank you for sharing your dream of writing a novel or two or three with us and taking us on this amazing journey. We have learned much, travelled some, have met some incredible people along the way while deepening our connection to each other.

Both of your friendships have been a steadfast source of love, strength, and inspiration. I'm grateful and feel truly blessed to have you both in my life. I hope that every single one of our reads have friends and sisters like you.

Thank you both for the warm, bright and beautiful light you shine on me.

Frances Furtado

Kim and Fran,

Never did I imagine, almost a decade ago, when Kim voiced her dream of "a book written by a book club for a book club", that today we would be preparing to launch our second novel. Thank you both for your friendship and for the unexpected journey. So many lessons, amazing people, and new experiences!

Our weekly multi-hour brainstorming and editing Zoom sessions are a source of stability and laughter. My family often wonders how so much can be accomplished amidst the chuckles.

Writing a book serendipitously set years before anyone ever heard of Covid-19 enabled us to immerse ourselves in the characters' unrestricted restaurant dining, active volunteering, in-office employment, out-of-state road and plane trips, mask-less exercising, and in-person book club meetings. This kept my eye excitedly on all that lies ahead as the world begins to reopen.

To my dear family, I'm grateful for your love, patience, good humor, and for generously sharing emotional and internet bandwidth as we worked together at home during this odd time.

Jeanne Ann

Made in the USA
Columbia, SC
25 September 2021

45399958R00153